Zinnia and The Original People

The Zinnia Series, Volume 1

Nicky Flinkfelt

Published by 7 Nations Publishing, 2021.

Copyright

ZINNIA AND THE ORIGINAL PEOPLE

First edition. August 8, 2021.
Copyright © 2021 Nicky Flinkfelt.
Written by Nicky Flinkfelt.
Book Cover Design by ebooklaunch.com
Edited by Lucky Jupiter Editing
NickyFlinkfelt.com

For April

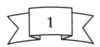

1

A breeze sent a chill through Zinnia's bedroom window. It wasn't like her to keep it open all night, but if she was going to get any sleep at all she needed to convince her mind she wasn't suffocating. Zinnia's stomach turned as she pulled herself out of bed. Standard government procedure required that all citizens move out of their parents' house and start their first job on their 30th birthday.

She never would have considered a job at New Life if it hadn't been for her sister. May had begun working there right before their father disappeared, and Zinnia never could wrap her head around her choosing to stay. But she didn't share Zinnia's skepticism, and it was her choice, after all.

At least Zinnia got to leave with a belly full of her mother's famous ration hash. Elise had a gift for turning government-issued food into delicious meals with limited supplies. Harvest was her only opportunity to work longer hours to earn extra credits. The farm was owned by the government and she, just like everyone else, made a small wage for half the hours she worked. The other half of her working hours were required to cover basic living expenses, such as housing, food, and medical. Elise was typically the master of finding ways to support her family, but since her husband's disappearance, she struggled more than ever to make ends meet. During harvest, she stocked up on spices, canned food, and soap. Whatever she bought had to last for the year. Sometimes she would sneak some of the wheat from the farm to make bread, but she kept it hidden in a small underground freezer. Having something besides cardboard protein bars made all the difference in the world.

After breakfast, Zinnia sat at the table with her mom for a while, taking in the last moments they had together. The dining room had already started to feel like a distant memory and she hadn't stepped outside of it yet. Elise took Zinnia's hands in hers and smiled warmly. "It's not forever," she said. Zinnia smiled back as a tear fell down her cheek.

When May finally arrived, she lowered her aircraft down in front of the small farmhouse. At New Life, they called them flybots. If Zinnia hadn't been so upset about leaving her mom, she would have been impressed that this particular one was made almost entirely out of glass—nothing like the tin box they had on the farm that nearly killed her every year.

"I'm gonna miss you," Zinnia said as she hugged her mom one last time.

"You'll do fine. I'm just a call away if you need me."

Zinnia nodded her head, let go of her, and wiped her face. It was time to be strong.

They lifted off, leaving a whirlwind of dust dancing around their mother. Her red hair always looked lovely against the golden wheat. May's hair color matched her mother's perfectly, but Elise's curls were so tight she kept them cut short to better manage them. Zinnia couldn't stand her tight blonde curls in her face so she always kept them tied back.

"Cheer up. You're gonna love it there. I promise," May said. Zinnia smiled back at her. It was all she could do to keep from breaking down.

It took a couple of hours to get to Seattle from Central Washington. The journey took them over the Cascade Mountains where Zinnia got to see the forest for the first time. She'd spent her whole life on the farm, so the lush greenery in front of a blue sky and billowy clouds was a nice change from the dust and tumbleweeds she was used to. She wasn't a stranger to blue skies though, as Yakima had nearly 300 days of sunshine every year. She wondered what life would be like with half of those days having rain instead.

Stepping into the New Life courtyard was like walking into a giant fishbowl with its glass ceiling and walls and everything rounded with no corners. It was beautiful with extravagant glass sculptures, but this place made her feel like she was drowning. The first thing that greeted her was a happy melody. "Welcome to New Life!" There were robots everywhere cleaning and delivering food. People were gliding through the courtyard to their jobs without a care, and to the clinics… The clinics…a place she never wanted to see. In her opinion, what that greeting should really have said was, "Welcome to your death."

Twelve stories above their heads was an enormous rotating clock that when upright read "NL" and when upside down read "7N," representing the 7 Nations of the world. There were glass sculptures of animals hanging from the ceiling, glistening in the sunlight. She found that ironic considering there hadn't been any animals living among humans for almost 200 years.

There were seven office buildings surrounding the courtyard. The first one to the right was the entrance to the Capitol Life-House. It was built in 2147 in celebration of the 100-year anniversary of the 7 Nations' union. With 250 stories it was crowned as the tallest building in the world. In three years, in celebration of the 200-year anniversary, they planned on building a second one right behind it. Apparently having the largest building in the world wasn't enough. They needed two. The other buildings were named after the other nations. Africa, South America, Asia, Europe, Russia, and Australia.

"People travel from all over the world to see this Life-House, since it is the largest one in North America," May said as they traveled through the courtyard.

Immediately to the left, there was an enormous glass bubble where people ate and met for their tours. Zinnia saw them crowding against the rounded walls, holding their personal electronic devices, or PEDs for short. She looked up at May confused.

"Tourists. They think they need to stand closer to the glass to keep them powered," May explained. Zinnia smiled and shook her head.

Thinking about her dad sent a stabbing reminder of his absence through her chest. He was one of the electricians who developed the technology to make glass generate electricity. "The secret is in the glass," he used to say. Since the technology originated in North America, they had a head start in transitioning to the glass system. The other six nations were still in the process of adopting it. Replacing everything with glass takes time. Despite her pain, she felt proud seeing his creation everywhere.

The clinics covered the entire basement floor below the courtyard and all of the buildings. Zinnia caught a glimpse of the waiting room when she got into the glass elevator. People were being called back by workers to a place she couldn't see. The sight of it put a lump in her throat, as if she wasn't nervous already.

The multidirectional elevator took them up to level five and over to Building Asia where they were greeted by a short and chubby man, although not too chubby given the mandatory fitness requirements put in place for all New Life employees. He had a honey complexion and coffee brown hair that pointed up in the front.

"Hello there! My name is Pacer!" The greeting burst out of his mouth as he grabbed Zinnia's hand and shook it excitedly. "I'm in HR and I will be showing you to your new job! May, thank you so much for bringing your little sister to me. I assure you she is in excellent care!" His smile didn't fade for a second. "You are welcome to make your way to your office. I'll message you if she needs anything." Pacer started pulling Zinnia down the hall by her hand.

"I'm on the 40th floor of the Capitol Building if you need me!" May yelled out to them as they left.

He took Zinnia to the 97th floor and led her into the library. The door slid open fast and startled her. They still had old fashioned doors on the farm. Everything in the library was glass too. To her left was a screen that covered the wall and displayed a slideshow of the 14 presidents of the world. Each nation required one male and one female. The large room was filled with people sitting at long rows of desks with no end in sight. She began to feel that lump in her throat again.

"This is your workstation. You can leave your stuff in this drawer..." He trailed off and paused for a moment when he saw the worried look on her face. "Zinnia, you are going to love it here. Don't be stressed. I'm your friendly HR Rep and you can come to me anytime you need help. Okay?"

She couldn't help but return his friendly smile. "I appreciate that. Really. I'll be fine. Thank you for showing me to the library," she said.

"That's my job, sweetheart," he responded kindly and then jumped back into instructing her on her duties. "This library comes equipped with the most technologically advanced computer cataloging systems. The only thing you will need to do is make sure our library patrons are able to find the files they need. Easy peasy! All of your actions will be logged in your PED and therefore in the New Life system."

He put his hand out in front of him, inviting her to grab it, and began leading her toward the front desk. "I'll tell you what, hun, take your time and familiarize yourself with your work area. I'll come back here before your shift ends to help you end your day. In the meantime, Shortelle here will help you get more acquainted with the library. Okay? Okay." Pacer motioned to an employee to come over to them.

"Hey," she said when she got there, raising her chin slightly in Zinnia's direction. "Shortelle."

Shortelle had long dark brown hair that hung over the left side of her face. Her nose had a tiny purple gem in it and she had a few tattoos on her arms. The tattoos seemed to be the only color she had amongst the all-black clothes covering her from head to toe.

The dress code was plain. Every person was required to wear any combination of black, gray, white, and tan clothing. All other colors were prohibited, "to preserve equality." The only thing not regulated was hair color and personal style. Zinnia was fine with the dress code. She preferred to go unnoticed anyway.

"Be sure to show her where the cafeteria is at lunch. Well, I'll leave you two to it!" Pacer's eyebrows raised and he tilted his head in Shortelle's direction as if telling her to behave.

She put her hands in the air and smirked. "Don't worry, Cupcake. I'll be nice."

"Ooh, cupcakes! I was trying to figure out what to make tonight! Thanks, darling!" Pacer exclaimed before leaving.

"I guess that makes him a Foodie?" Zinnia asked nervously.

"What, you didn't gather that from all the excess pudge he's packing around?"

Zinnia let out a nervous giggle. "What's your spur?" she asked.

"Gamer. You?"

Zinnia hesitated for a moment and grabbed onto the lightbulb charm necklace her father gave her for her tenth birthday. It became a comfort for her after he disappeared, and she turned to it for support. She answered quietly, "I'm a Learner."

"Huh, a Learner in a library. Go figure," Shortelle said, smirking as she looked Zinnia up and down.

Zinnia had been expecting that sort of reaction. Being a Learner was rare.

Living closer to 200 years had its downsides, like boredom. Shortly after the Fountain of Youth was discovered, categories were made and it was socially expected for a person to pick a spur by puberty. Not having one led to madness. Most people had the Thrill Seeker, Gamer, Foodie, and Lover spurs but there were also Leaders and Learners. There were a lot of Learners in the beginning but over time people started picking spurs that required little to no mental capacity.

Lunchtime came and Shortelle showed Zinnia to one of the cafeterias in the Asia Building. There were at least ten rows of buffet tables, each encased in glass with a robot inside serving food through a small door. Zinnia stopped when she saw them and tears began to form in her eyes. "I've never seen so much food before," she said.

May walked up behind her and put her arm on her shoulder. "See, I told you you were gonna love it here. And look who I found!"

Zinnia turned around and saw her best friend Lilly standing there with her arms stretched out for a hug. She leapt into them immediately. "I didn't know if I was gonna get to see you today!"

Lilly was about four inches taller than Zinnia. She had straight, dirty blonde hair that was always done up in strange and wild styles with fiber optic hair extensions that she set to different colors every day.

"How are you liking it so far?!" Lilly asked with a big smile.

"It's okay. It's a lot to take in, but it's okay," Zinnia answered. "How's your day been?"

"Great! Earlier today, one of my kids climbed up the tallest rock-climbing wall and didn't even break a sweat! I was so proud," Lilly exclaimed.

"I'm gonna go get some food. I'll bring you back to the library when you're done eating," Shortelle said before heading toward the buffet.

"I'm so glad you're finally here! Sure took ya long enough!"

"Lilly, you're three months older than me," Zinnia said, shaking her head and smiling.

They'd been best friends since they were 20, when Lilly first arrived at the orphanage nearby. Lilly went right up to Zinnia on the first day of school and said, "You look nice. Do you want to be my friend? Let's go to your house after school. The orphanage is boring." Lilly decided to go to New Life for her first job too, because she knew that's where Zinnia wanted to go to be with May when she turned 30.

"Felt longer. Anyway, later, after you're all settled into May's apartment, I'll come over and we can go do something fun since today is your birthday and all! Come on, let's get you some food!"

After Zinnia had stuffed herself full of everything she'd never had and never even heard of, Shortelle took her back up to the library. She started giving her instructions on the second half of the day's duties but stopped after a few minutes. "I have an idea. I'm gonna give you a tour of New Life. What have you seen so far?"

"Umm, just the courtyard, cafeteria, and here," she answered.

"Sweet. I'll show you the Spur Zones. They're my favorite part about working here."

When they got to the main floor, the door to the elevator opened in the back and they stepped out into a long and crowded corridor with hundreds of people pushing their way to a platform. Zinnia had never seen so many people packed into one place before. The sounds of chattering echoed off the glass tile walls and every few seconds there was a gust of wind. She didn't know where it was coming from until she got to the front of the line. There was an enormous tube filled with large glass spheres being shot out one by one with such force it practically blew the workers off the platform. When they got to the tube, Zinnia saw a sign above it that read, "Zero Gravity Station." She started to panic but Shortelle didn't give her a second to back out. The crowd wouldn't have allowed it even if she did.

They were shoved into a sphere and quickly fastened themselves in. As soon as the door closed, Zinnia immediately felt weightless and the sphere shot away from the platform at full speed. They started floating up before their harnesses stopped them and Zinnia looked over at Shortelle, completely frightened. Shortelle started laughing.

"What's going on?!" Zinnia yelled out over the sound of the traveling sphere.

"That's right! You guys don't have these out in the country! It's zero-gravity travel! It's so we can go really fast and not feel it!" Shortelle managed to shout out through her laughter.

"No, we only have the flybots!" Zinnia yelled back.

Just as quickly as it started, the vehicle came to a stop, their hair fell down to their shoulders, and they slowly lowered back down to their seats. Zinnia's heart was pounding and she felt dizzy. She didn't understand how Thrill Seekers did it. Adrenaline always made her feel sick.

"If that was too much for you then you really won't like this place," Shortelle said as she wiped tears from her eyes and began walking off.

Zinnia followed her and looked up as she saw a large sign that read, "Thrill Seeker's Zone."

"It'll take me way too long to show you each zone so we're just gonna do a quick pass through in a tour car."

The next sphere was in a half tube and painted along the bottom in big letters it read, "Take your time."

"Another sphere?" Zinnia asked, taking a deep breath, not looking forward to another surge of adrenaline.

"It's okay. This one goes a lot slower so you can see what's going on around you. It's not a ZGS," she reassured her.

Their car began taking them through the Thrill Seeker Zone. There was so much going on she didn't know where to look first. There were people jumping from flybots overhead, and some were sailing through the air on giant kites. Far off in the distance, people were climbing up a mountain, and some people were bungee jumping. In the other direction, she saw huge water slides that went on for miles. Down on the ground, there were crowds of people eating snacks, buying things at booths, and riding rides. She could see kids running around shooting lasers and paintballs and water balloons at each other.

Shortelle began telling her about the zone. "Over there," she said, pointing off to the left. "That is the Thrill Seeker water and theme park. Over here to your right is the carnival. Down that way you have rock climbing, cliff jumping, skydiving, obstacle courses, and almost every classic sport you can imagine, and my personal favorite, haunted houses." She paused to look at Zinnia and added with another smirk, "Well, I can tell that's probably not something you want to see… Moving on."

As the car continued, Zinnia spotted sports fields and arenas. There were flybots that had been decorated in bright colors and lights zipping around a racetrack. The crowds of people were absolutely endless and overwhelming. After a few minutes, she pulled her eyes away from the busyness outside and suddenly felt the need to defend herself. "I'm not a complete wimp, okay? I'm just sensitive to adrenaline. I choose to do more relaxing things in my spare time. Like reading, crossword puzzles—"

Shortelle cut her off, "Anything extremely boring you mean."

"It's not boring to me! Like I said, it's relaxing. Our brains are capable of so much. But…" she paused for a moment, "my dad did try to get me to do more exciting things. He said I needed to get out of my head more."

"Your dad was a smart man. Speaking of your dad… I kind of heard a little bit about all that but… what happened to him?"

"No one knows. He disappeared about three years ago…" Zinnia's words trailed off as their tour car entered into a tunnel.

"Woah. Where are we going now?"

There was loud music and game show noises as the whole tunnel around them turned into a large screen displaying pictures of video games and game systems with lasers and lights. A loud voice came over the speaker, "Welcome to Gamer's Stop! We have every game ever created! We have video making studios! Old fashioned arcades with every restored vintage gaming system you can imagine! Try our Virtual Reality games! Let them take you to a whole 'nother world! Battle dragons! Save a city from a zombie apocalypse! Or take a relaxing vacation on a tropical island! We have hundreds of gaming stations including ones you can spend the night in! Overnight packages include all the food and beverages you need to pull an all-nighter with your friends!

"You have to pay for all these places?" Zinnia asked.

"Not employees. It's all free for us. Perks of the biz. Like I said, it would take me days to show you everything. We're just gonna keep moving through," Shortelle continued. "We're coming up to the Learner's Point. It's not as big as the other Spur Zones, but it does come with all the classes you can think of, like old fashioned knitting, sewing, painting, and crafts. There are quiet reading rooms. They also have a library and education. In fact, they have some programs available for employees who want to continue their education. Which is cool, if you care about that kind of thing, I guess. Anyway, as you can see, this area isn't very popular. We don't see many Learners around here, let alone have them working here."

Zinnia felt a wave of heat spread through her body and her cheeks turned a rosy pink as she saw the empty walkways. There were a few people around, but it looked like they were mostly tourists.

"Next is Lover's Lane." Shortelle rolled her eyes as she said this. "This area makes me want to vomit. I mean– whatever, so all you care about is love, but why do the rest of us have to see it? Get a room. I mean a private room, like, at home."

"I totally share the sentiment. My sister is a Lover. It drives me crazy," Zinnia added as she thought about her sister's many date nights and gushing over guys.

"Anyway, as much as it pains me, I'll tell you what they have. There's private beaches, movie theaters, parks for…long walks in the park," Shortelle said, putting her clenched hands up to her cheek mockingly and batting her eyes. "There's a river for boat rides, hot tubs, picnics. Oh, and get this, there is even a DNA matchmaker machine and a virtual reality matchmaker game." She scoffed and rolled her eyes again.

"Okay, last but not least, Foodie Court." The car pulled up to a large billboard with a picture of slightly rounded people in all-white uniforms holding delicious looking desserts.

"There are thousands of restaurants, cooking classes, candy and ice cream shops, bakeries, fresh markets, whole food stores, and DNA-based perfect dessert machines. Thank goodness we have Foodies, right?"

"Yeah... Hey, can we try that machine out? The DNA dessert machine?" Zinnia asked.

"Sure! It's always a good time for dessert." Shortelle pushed the button to stop the car and it pulled into a parking spot away from the tube track. This platform was crowded too, and they had to stand in a line. "There's always one of those machines right by the tour cars because they know we can't resist."

When they got to the box, Shortelle put Zinnia's hand under a blue light and had her put her PED up to the scanner on the machine. "It's just a simple box. You probably wouldn't see it if you didn't know what it was. Everything around here is super simple. There's a theory going around that Foodies just don't want to take any more time away from their cooking than necessary. I heard Pacer say that the food itself is advertisement enough."

A bell dinged after a couple of seconds and the front of the machine opened up. There was a tiny plate with a chocolate chip cookie on it. Zinnia looked at Shortelle and raised an eyebrow.

Shortelle shrugged her shoulders. "It goes off your DNA and mood. It's never wrong."

"Okay," Zinnia said as she reached for the cookie and took a bite. She immediately closed her eyes and exhaled. "Wow, this is am-mazing…"

"Man, you'd think you never had a chocolate chip cookie before," Shortelle said. Zinnia looked up at her with a straight expression. "Are you telling me you've never had a chocolate chip cookie?! How is that possible?! They've been around for hundreds of years!"

"Well chocolate chip cookies may have been around for hundreds of years but I've only been around for 30, and I spent all 30 of those years on a government farm eating government rations," Zinnia responded, clearly starting to get irritated.

"Well, that's why it knew you didn't need anything fancy," Shortelle teased. "Anyway, my turn." She put her hand under the blue light and scanned her PED. "The dessert is different every time, but it's always delicious." The bell dinged and out popped a cupcake with frosting in the shape of a cactus. She stared at it for a moment before picking it up.

Zinnia started to laugh at the look on Shortelle's face.

"Hey, what's this thing trying to say?" Shortelle shrugged her shoulders and took a big bite. "I get it. Payback for calling Pacer 'Cupcake.' Whatever, it's still good," she said as she shoved another bite in her mouth. She began walking toward the tour car and announced, "This concludes our tour. Time to head back."

"What about Leaders? They don't have a zone?" Zinnia asked.

"No. They don't. There aren't many of them anymore either. Besides the presidents there's pretty much just the Life-House Leaders and the guards. But I don't think you could consider the guards Leaders since they just do what they're told."

They made their way back to the elevators and were just about to go up to the next floor when Shortelle stopped suddenly and blurted out, "Oh shoot! I forgot to show you the clinics."

"But I already know what the clinics are for," Zinnia protested. The mere thought of stepping foot near that place made her feel nauseous.

"Part of your job is to help direct people around and not just through the library catalogs. New Life too. People will ask you about the clinics. I've been asked at least a hundred times since I've been here. Come on. You gotta be able to show people where to transfer onto their next life." Shortelle motioned to her to follow.

Zinnia couldn't believe how easy it was for her to talk about it. She knew it was an acceptable practice that people had been doing for years, but it still never settled right with her. Any problems with your life, no money, don't like your family, lose a loved one, go get a New Life transfer and you're sent on to your next life. That's what they say anyway. She always found it strange that people followed this blindly. The only proof of this "new life" was so complicated, not a single person could explain it anymore. Scientists and the 7 Nations said that the people who made the discovery died and buried the secrets with them.

They both got onto the elevator and Shortelle pushed the button to go down to the basement floor. Zinnia was starting to get tunnel vision. She could feel the sweat forming along her hairline as her heart started pounding.

"Here we are," Shortelle said as she stepped off the elevator and turned to wait for her.

Zinnia looked straight ahead and followed in a daze. There were four counters, each with a long line of people. The different counters read: *Pre-Life Program, Little Angels Program, Private Pay Program,* and *Public Assistance Program.* She couldn't believe how busy this place was, but what caught her attention the most was the people standing in the Little Angels line holding babies and toddler's hands. One person was standing there with what looked to be a seven or eight-year-old in a wheelchair. The looks on all of the people's faces were happy. Not a single tear. Not a single worry as she watched them walk off to their deaths.

She took a few deep breaths in and tried to keep herself calm but it didn't work. She couldn't breathe. She felt like she was suffocating, and now she couldn't see because the room was getting blurry. She was shaking and just barely managed to get out, "I need to sit down. I don't feel good." She covered her head with her arms, fumbled her way onto a chair, and began counting through each breath.

"Dude, are you okay?" Shortelle asked.

After a few moments Zinnia slowly looked up and noticed that there were people standing around her, watching, so she stood back up even though she was still shaking. Shortelle grabbed her arm as she wobbled. "I'm sorry." Zinnia rubbed her head and looked around completely embarrassed.

"Alright, clear out people. Nothing to see here!" Shortelle commanded as she waved her hands at the people standing around. "Let's get you to the medical office. I think you've had enough of a tour for one day."

"I told you I didn't want to see the clinics."

"Yeah, but I didn't know you were gonna have a panic attack on me. Just hold onto me. I'll take you upstairs." Shortelle rolled her eyes as she helped Zinnia back into the elevator. The moment they got in; Zinnia felt like she could breathe again.

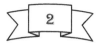

Zinnia had originally anticipated a sad and gloomy arrival at May's apartment. But after the day she had she couldn't wait to get there. Her bedroom pod slid out from the wall and had just enough space for a small bed and dresser. May could see the look of disappointment on her face.

"Are you okay, Z? I know apartment life is a little more cramped than we were used to out on the farm."

"I'll get used to it, I guess," she answered.

"Here, this will cheer you up." May tapped on her PED and the walls in her apartment turned from white to pink, then clouds, and ended on glowing stars. "We're in the high-tech world now, Z. You can download any background or wallpaper you can imagine. Personally, I like the photo slideshow." She pushed another button and thousands of their family pictures and videos popped up all around the apartment. Pictures of every vacation, every stage of life, every birthday. Pictures of their dad.

For the first time since leaving the farm, Zinnia finally felt a bit of comfort. "This is amazing," she said, holding back tears.

"I have a date tonight. I figured you'd want to hang out with Lilly, so I didn't think you would mind," May said as she took out her makeup and sat at the table.

"No, I don't mind," Zinnia replied. She sat across from her sister, still focused on the pictures on the walls. "I was reading on my PED about our history. Did you know that in America it used to be legal for people to move out when they were 18?"

"Really? I don't remember learning about that in school."

"That's because they didn't teach it in school. They also didn't teach us that we used to mature faster. People were considered *adults* at 18." Zinnia pulled out her PED and started reading. "Listen to this, 'In 2050 the legal adult age was changed to 20 in an attempt to rectify the damage the previous government had done. There were 15 million homeless people in North America before all housing and basic needs were provided by the government. Their hope was that requiring young adults to take two extra years of "Life Training" would teach them everything they needed to know to properly take care of themselves once they were out on their own.'"

"Well, 20 isn't much better. When did they raise it to 30?"

Zinnia scanned and tapped her PED a couple of times. "The year 2077. 'In 2077, scientists and researchers discovered that humans were developing at a slower rate. Legal adults began crumbling under the expectations of society. They acted out violently and attacked government employees. By scientists' calculations, 20-year-olds were mentally between the ages of 10 and 13.' So, I'm like 15 to 18 years old and you're like 18 to 21."

"That's interesting. How do you always find this information?" May asked as she got up from her chair.

"I don't know. I'm curious so I just start reading. Besides, it keeps my mind busy," Zinnia answered as she looked down at her lightbulb necklace and put her thumb through the chain. "When are you coming back?"

Suddenly, May's walls lit up and the North American Presidents, Sophia Smith and Liam Trembley, appeared, standing at a podium in their office.

"What's this?" Zinnia asked.

"Shh. It's an announcement," May answered.

Sophia Smith began, "Hello, good people of New Life. We are pleased to announce that researchers have discovered another link to the afterlife." Sophia was tall, thin, and had tan skin with dark brown hair pulled back into a tight bun. Liam had blonde hair hanging just below his temples, blue eyes, and olive skin.

"Transferring your child before the age of five guarantees them a fruitful life to follow. Scientists have discovered a pattern in the reincarnation letters. Every person in successful positions exited the previous life before the age of five. Many thanks to the citizens who shared their information. We couldn't have done it without you. With that, we have a great opportunity to ensure success for generations to come. Let us take this good news and do our part for our society. And as always..." Sophia and Liam both raised their right hands, brought their ring fingers to their thumbs, and said in unison, "Seven for life, seven for equality, seven for us."

Zinnia sat frozen feeling nauseous.

"Well anyway, I shouldn't be too late. Unless it goes well, then maybe not until tomorrow." May smiled as she headed to the other room to change her outfit.

Zinnia rolled her eyes and decided to go to her new bedroom pod to put her things away. After her bag was empty, she looked for a place to store it and saw a small shelf just below the ceiling. She shoved it up there but it fell right back down. She tried again but when it came down once more, she realized it wasn't going to stay. The shelf looked big enough so it didn't make sense. She stood up on her bed to see what might be blocking it and discovered a small box.

On the front of the box was a bird with its wings spread out in a perfect "T." Curious, she reached inside and felt something cool and smooth, with soft rounded edges. The tiny depressions across its surface reminded her of her mother's purse, her father's tool case maybe, or perhaps his work boots. She pulled the item out and her heart began pounding as she realized what the object might be. She was afraid to hold it in fear of damaging it.

"It's a book," she said out loud in disbelief.

Zinnia stepped out of the bedroom pod as May came out of the bathroom. "How do I look? May asked before noticing the book in Zinnia's hand. "What is that?" she added.

"It's a book," Zinnia answered, still unsure of what she found.

"Well, I know it's a book Z, but where did you get it?"

"Oh, um…up there," she answered and pointed to the shelf below the ceiling. "May, when was the last time you saw a book?"

"On a field trip to a museum, in like, grade 20," she answered as she put on her jacket. "My date is going to be here any minute. Throw it away."

"I'm not just going to throw a book away, May. This could be history!" Zinnia objected. She couldn't believe how stupid May was sometimes.

"You need to stay away from this, do you hear me? You just got here. I'd hate for anything to happen to you. Our neighbors just went missing." There was a buzz at the door. "I mean it. Get rid of it. Okay? Turn on your locator so I know where you are. I gotta go. I'll see you later," May said, and she grabbed her bag and left.

As soon as the door closed, Zinnia's PED rang, and Lilly was on the other line. "Hey, friend! I told you, we're gonna have some fun tonight! It's you and me! Put on your fun hat!"

Zinnia looked at the book in her hand. She didn't want to put it down. She didn't want to go anywhere. She wanted to stay right there and read every ink-printed word on every flimsy, delicate page. But Lilly had been looking forward to taking her out, so she decided she better put it away and look at it the next day.

Lilly took Zinnia to the Thrill Seeker Zone. "Look, I know you don't like crazy stuff, so I thought we could just go to the water park. It's open all night. The whole place is lit up with bright lights! You know how I like lights."

"That's cool. A water park that stays open at night. Sounds good to me," Zinnia responded with a smile. "A girl at work showed me a little bit today before I…"

"Before you what?" Lilly cut her off and gave Zinnia a motherly look. Lilly was well aware of Zinnia's panic attacks and wasn't surprised that she would have one on her first day of work. "I knew I should have stayed with you. I shouldn't have let that crazy lady watch over you," Lilly said, shaking her head.

"It's okay, Lilly. She was nice about it. I'm just embarrassed." Zinnia clutched her lightbulb necklace.

"Well, maybe this will cheer you up!" Lilly exclaimed as she dragged Zinnia up to the water park entrance.

It was way bigger close up than what she had seen from the tour car. There were water slides, wave pools, water obstacle courses, and water games. She liked the idea of the water games. It seemed mild enough.

"There are water roller coasters too! I know you don't like roller coasters, though, so I'll ride a couple of those later by myself if you don't mind!" Lilly said excitedly.

"Of course," Zinnia responded. She loved seeing her friend happy. She was always happy, but it was a nice change from her own constant unreasonable worry.

They got their passes and went to the changing room to get into their swimsuits and they put their belongings in the lockers. Their PEDs were waterproof and had to always remain on them. It held the details of their entire lives. You couldn't even get into restrooms without them.

As soon as they got to the nearest wave pool, Lilly spotted her friend. "Oh, hey! Kevin!" she yelled as she bobbed around in the water. Lilly swam toward him with Zinnia following behind her.

"Hey, what's up, Lilly!?" he asked after doing a somersault in the water.

"This is Zinnia! She just got here today! You know what that means!"

"Happy Birthday!!!" Lilly, Kevin, and a few of his friends sang in unison while one of them blew an imaginary horn.

"Thanks," Zinnia said, blushing.

"No being a bashful Betty in these parts! Kevin, he's good people," Lilly insisted with a grin.

"Hey, Lilly! Gamer's Stop, midnight," Kevin told her after doing another somersault.

"Sounds good. We'll be there," she responded as she and Zinnia swam toward the shore.

After swimming, playing games, and scarfing down some nachos, Lilly reminded Zinnia that she wanted to finish the park visit with a roller coaster ride.

"That's fine. I just can't believe what I just ate. Who on earth had the idea? It's too bad my stomach isn't bigger or I would have eaten a whole plate by myself," Zinnia said, rubbing her belly.

"I know right? They're my favorite. Okay, I'm off!" Lilly hopped up excitedly.

While Zinnia waited for Lilly to finish her rollercoaster ride, May came walking toward her, looking upset and slightly wet.

"May? What's up? Why aren't you on your date anymore? What happened?"

"This guy! The audacity! Who does that?" May yelled, sitting down on the bench next to Zinnia and taking off her high heels.

"Are you going to tell me what happened?" Zinnia asked. She watched May throw the heels down after getting them off.

"So, we're almost done eating, and guess who shows up?"

"Who?"

"His wife!"

"Oh, no. I'm sorry," Zinnia said sympathetically, shaking her head.

"Yeah! After she was done throwing a cup of water over both of us, he tried to tell me that they aren't together anymore and that she has an appointment at the clinic to get a Pre-Life transfer."

"Well, it's good you're at a water park then," Zinnia said with a nervous laugh.

May looked at her like she was an alien.

"Because...you're all wet," Zinnia added slowly. "Never mind."

"Did you hear anything I just said? Another waste of time! I'm about to call it quits. I'm so tired of finding these jerks," May cried out in defeat.

"But what about your date tomorrow? Haven't you already talked? At least give it a chance. You sounded like you really liked him."

"I guess. But seriously, if that date goes bad, I'm done," May decided.

Zinnia's PED dinged. "It's Mom," she said before answering it. "Hi mom!"

"Happy, Happy, Happy Birthday!!!" Elise sang.

"Mom, you saw me this morning."

"I know, silly! But it's almost over and I wanted to see how your first day of work went!"

"It went great," she lied, not wanting to worry her. "I'll tell you more about it tomorrow. May is here." She turned her PED so she could see her.

"May, why are you all wet in a nice dress?"

"Bad date. I'll tell you about it tomorrow too," May answered and began putting her heels back on.

"I'm sorry, hunny," Elise said sympathetically.

"Thanks, Mom," May responded and then got up and started walking away. "I'll talk to you later. And I'll see you back at the apartment. I'm exhausted."

"Bye sweetie! Zinnia, don't stay up too late. I'm sure you have some unpacking to do tomorrow," her mom advised.

"Already done…and I'm going with Lilly to Gamer's Stop tonight."

"Okay, well be careful. You know your anxiety gets worse when you don't get enough sleep."

"I know, Mom. Thank you. Love you," Zinnia said before blowing her a kiss.

"Love you too, hunny. Muah! Kisses!"

Lilly walked up to the bench right as she hung up. "Hey, was that May I saw?"

"Yeah, bad date."

"Darn. Another one bites the dust. You ready to get your game on?" Lilly asked excitedly.

"I'm ready, "Zinnia responded, smiling.

The entrance to the zone was in the dark tunnel she had gone through earlier that day. The platform was covered in lights, and she felt like she was walking into a spaceship. As soon as she entered there were signs pointing in multiple directions that read: *VR Games, Vintage Video Games, Game Making, Overnight Stays.* They decided to get the overnight passes and spent the rest of the night playing games with Lilly's friends.

After sleeping nearly the entire next day, Zinnia remembered the book she found on the shelf in her bedroom pod. May had already left for her second date so she decided to get the book out. Her stomach was in knots again. The first page had only one line that read, "And so the devil disappeared into the night and took God with him."

She flipped to the next page and read, "The Lost Cultures and Religions of the World." Zinnia had never heard the word "Religion" before. There were symbols and names and diagrams. It almost seemed like it was in another language, but Zinnia knew that was impossible since there had only ever been one language. At the very end of the book, in very tiny letters it read, "Go to net Greenbunk5142032."

Zinnia quickly opened her PED and typed in the address. What greeted her was a series of questions only a Learner would have taken the time to answer.

"What year did Advanced Gerontological Enterprises (A.G.E.) discover the Fountain of Youth and rebrand themselves as New Life?"

"2042. Everyone knows that." Zinnia typed in the answer.

"What year did New Life take over and unify the government as the 7 Nations?"

"2047.

"When did they discover that we could transfer to our next lives through transfer pods?"

She entered "2089" and shivered.

After what seemed like hours she finally came to the last question.

"Multiple choice: What is your spur?

A) Learner.

B) Lover.

C) Leader.

D) Thrill Seeker.

E) Gamer.

F) Foodie."

Without hesitation, she chose "A." She had known what her spur was going to be all her life. That was pretty uncommon, since the majority didn't decide on their spur until they passed through puberty. There were no rules. You weren't assigned a category. One day, you simply woke up and knew exactly what you wanted to spend your life doing and no one ever fought it or questioned it.

Zinnia was different. Growing up, her mother would tell her stories about when she was young. At two years old, she had written the alphabet and all the numbers on her walls in order. By four, she could speak and spell all basic words correctly, and by six she was studying algebra. She didn't like it when her mother bragged about how smart she was. She didn't want to be separated from her friends, and because of that she never skipped grades. She knew that her spur was rare. Leaders are rare too, but then again, we couldn't have everyone trying to run the world, could we?

The next screen that popped up was a video of an older looking gentleman, around 120 maybe. His dark brown hair and beard were speckled with the tones of salt and pepper. His skin was pale, but not as pale as Zinnia's, and his hazel eyes added to his kind and happy face, giving Zinnia an instant feeling of warmth and safety. Maybe that was because he reminded her of her dad.

"Hello. My name is Seth Astrid and if you have come this far…" he paused and chuckled to himself. "Most people wouldn't have made it through all of those questions. Forgive me for the torture." He continued, still smiling. "It is not a mistake that you are here. As a Learner, you set out for answers. Answers to questions only you are asking." Seth lowered his chin.

"But why are you the only people asking these questions? All will be revealed. The moment you went to this site your PED's connection to the New Life system was disabled. To continue on the path of knowledge, touch the green button at the bottom of the screen. If you choose not to go forward, press the blue button and you will be connected once more and there will be no evidence of the time you have spent on this site. If you choose to continue on, I look forward to meeting you soon." Seth gave another warm smile before the video ended.

Zinnia hesitated. Maybe May was right and this was asking for trouble. Would she be able to turn back from this? She knew deep down that something wasn't right about her father's disappearance. He was just gone one day. Maybe all of this had something to do with that. There was absolutely nothing leading up to it. Did he transfer? Did he die? Did he go outside of the dome shield to work on it and got killed by an animal? The man in the video said, "I look forward to meeting you soon." Maybe he went to this guy.

She wanted answers, but was the desire for these answers worth the risk? Go forward with the possibility of no return...or stay there, as safe as she could control. It wasn't like her to take risks, but she knew she had to. She knew she wouldn't get this opportunity again, and she'd be stuck wondering for the rest of her life. She clutched her lightbulb charm necklace, took a deep breath, and pressed the green button.

Within seconds, the doorbell buzzed. Zinnia jumped and her heart started pounding. She sat there for a moment, frozen. When she had mustered up a bit of courage, she slowly made her way to the door. She stood off to the side and reached for the button. The door slid open quickly when she pressed it, making her jump again. She peaked around the corner and didn't see anyone, so she stuck her head out to look the other direction. Still no one. She looked down and saw a small box, similar to the box she found in her bedroom pod. She snatched it up and quickly pressed the button to close the door.

The same symbol that was on the box with the book was on this one too. A bird with its wings spread out in a perfect "T." Inside, she found a small chip. She recognized the shape of it. They were used for storage for their PEDs a long time ago. She wondered, *is there even a place to put this still?* She looked for the slot where chips used to go and to her surprise, the slot was still there. The manufacturers didn't take them out for some reason. She wondered why. Once the chip was inserted all the way, her PED lit up and there was a list of instructions. The first thing she read was, "Go to the Tower at Greenwrich."

She pulled up a map on her PED. She tapped on "Greenwrich" and began reading out loud. "Mount Rainier is the tallest mountain in the state of Washington. It has officially been established as a wildlife reserve and entrance to the forest is strictly prohibited." *The Tower at Greenwrich is at least a three-and-a-half-day hike. Maybe four,* she thought. We won't be walking, though, according to these instructions.

Zinnia sat there for a few minutes. Anxiety surged through her body and she couldn't put another thought together. She was overwhelmed. *One step at a time*, she thought to herself. She took a few deep breaths with her eyes closed, and when she started to feel better, she got up, grabbed her bag, and began packing. She wasn't really into fashion so she hardly brought anything with her to May's apartment. All she needed were some jeans and sweatshirts. She put those in her bag and headed to the kitchen. She needed food and water, and maybe a cup or something. The kitchen was tiny so there weren't many places to look for food. Rations were all she found. She stuffed those in her bag too. She headed for the bathroom, but the door buzzed before she could get there.

"Oh no, no, no. This is horrible timing!" she said as she threw her bag inside the bathroom. She quickly pulled herself together, taking another deep breath. As she pressed the button to open the door, Lilly barged through.

"Where have you been? I've been trying to reach you all evening. I can't get through on your PED and..." She paused and looked Zinnia up and down. Her eyes narrowed. "Okay Z, tell me what's going on. I promise I won't freak out."

Zinnia took a slow, deep breath and told Lilly about the book, Seth Astrid, the box with the chip, and everything else. Lilly's face changed multiple times throughout the conversation and Zinnia could tell she thought she was crazy. But as always, Lilly went along with it and didn't try to stop her.

"Well, you know I can't let you go on this trip by yourself, right?" Lilly asked, giving her that motherly look again. "I'll go get my stuff, and then I'll come back here and we'll plan it out!"

Zinnia felt relieved. She was glad she didn't have to do this on her own. "Thrill Seeker or not, you have too much energy for me sometimes," Zinnia responded weakly.

3

The rooftop restaurant overlooked the canal gondola rides, where Lovers kissed and snuggled under the light of small lanterns and the moon. Each passing of a striped gondolier carried with it the sweet fragrance of lavender and lilacs. Every fifth boat or so, a nervous young Lover could be seen getting on one knee and holding out a ring while a young woman cried, laughed, or sat frozen and bewildered. May watched longingly as her desire for romance overcame her. It had always seemed so far from her reach but it was all she'd ever wanted. To love someone. To be loved by someone.

The restaurant was busy, but quiet enough for May and her date Theo to hear each other. Theo's light skin was illuminated under the soft glow of the candlelight, and his deep green eyes stood out from his sandy brown hair.

"So that DNA matchmaker really does a good job of pairing you up with beautiful people," May said as her face flushed with embarrassment.

"Well, I can certainly say the same. You're gorgeous," Theo complimented as he gently tucked a strand of hair behind her ear, clearing his view of her face.

Feeling slightly uncomfortable, May changed the subject, "So, tell me more about yourself."

"I've worked at New Life forever. My parents have worked there forever, their parents worked there forever. Basically, my family line has been with New Life since the beginning," Theo paused to take a bite.

"That's amazing. My dad worked here on the Glass Project, but when he wasn't doing that, my parents worked together on the farm," May explained. "They both grew up in Central Washington and met each other in grade 19. My mom's family begged her to stay in the country and my dad agreed because he wanted her to be happy. Once they had us it wasn't an option to leave anymore. Dad wanted us to have a simple life as long as we could. It took a while to get used to the noise here, but it's also nice having access to so many amazing things. Like this," May said, lifting her fork of steamed broccoli.

"It's just broccoli," Theo pointed out, confused.

"We lived on government rations on the farm. All the wheat we grew went straight here," May said. "It's okay, I really didn't know what I was missing until I got here. Zinnia has yet to discover it all. My plan is to take her around to some of my favorite places tomorrow. Her friend Lilly kept her up all night, but I'm glad she got to have some fun on her birthday."

"I bet she's looking forward to seeing everything you have to show her," Theo said and changed back to the previous subject. "My upbringing was more interesting than my last. I've been lucky enough to be here. Anything I want at my disposal," he bragged.

"Wait, are you saying this isn't your first life?" May asked, intrigued. She hadn't met a multi-lifer before.

Theo smiled and continued bragging. "This is actually my tenth life. As you know, when you're deemed a legal adult, New Life releases your files. Before you transfer, they have you write a letter to yourself. A sort of biography so that you can learn from your past selves. That is, of course, only if you transferred and didn't die naturally. I got nine files from myself."

"How do they know who the letters belong to?" she asked.

"It's in your DNA," he answered, matter of fact. "After they gather your reincarnation letters, they call you in for a meeting and tell you you're a multi-lifer. You read your letters and then you drink a serum that makes you remember those lives. I remembered mine as clear as day."

"That's amazing! I never got any, so I guess this is my first run. Zinnia's too. She didn't get any files either. She did find a book in her room today, though. That was strange," May said, letting the words escape from her mouth.

"What do you mean she found a book? Books are only in museums. There was a book in your apartment? Did you open it? Did you read it?" Theo practically interrogated. "My father would want to hear about this."

"Why are you getting upset? They aren't outlawed or anything," May defended herself.

Theo quickly calmed himself down and cleared his throat, "I'm not upset. Just shocked is all. I'm sorry. I didn't mean to ruin our dinner. It's just incredibly odd that a book was in your apartment."

May's stomach started doing somersaults and she suddenly had an overwhelming feeling that she needed to check on Zinnia.

"Will you please excuse me? I need to use the restroom," she asked as she got up from her seat without waiting for an answer.

She rushed to the bathroom to call Zinnia. "Come on, Zinnia…" It went straight to her voicemail. "What the heck?" She tried again. Same thing. "Ugh…darn it. Oh, I know…maybe she's with Lilly again tonight."

She dialed Lilly, who immediately answered. "Hey, May," Lilly greeted her through the PED.

"Lilly, is Z with you? It's urgent," she asked quickly, sounding out of breath.

"Yeah, she's right here."

"Hey, May. I'm glad you called. There's more going on with this book that you need to know about," Zinnia said, sounding out of breath herself.

"That's why I'm calling you. I mentioned the book and my date got really upset and then he said his dad would want to know about this. I'm not sure who his dad is but he said his family line has been with New Life forever. I don't know, Z. I just got a really bad feeling."

"Well, I need you to make an excuse for me at work. I'm probably not gonna be there on Monday. Lilly and I are going into the forest. I think I can find something out about Dad. This book—"

May cut her off. "Oh no you don't! You are waiting for me! There is no way you're going into the…" May lowered her voice in case anyone could hear her. "…forest. Just wait for me! I'm not leaving you alone to deal with this!"

May went back to Theo and he stood up as soon as he saw her. "I'm really sorry if I upset you, May. It wasn't my intention. If you want, we can go take a walk in the park, or on the beach."

"I'd really love that, but I'm so tired. It's been a long day," she lied.

Theo gave May a sideways look, clearly not believing her. "May, what can I do to get you to stay?"

"I mean it, honestly. I really actually want to hear about your nine lives, and now the tenth. Another night, I promise," she said and grabbed her jacket and purse, leaving him at the table again.

When May got to her apartment, she darted through the door.

"Hey, you're pretty fast in those high heels!" Lilly teased.

"Hush, Lilly! I got here as fast as I could. Z, I need you to tell me what's going on."

"I found a website at the end of the book and I went to it. May, I think we might be able to find something out about Dad's disappearance. I don't know why, but I need to get to the tower at Greenwrich," Zinnia begged her sister to understand.

"The tower at Greenwrich?! What is that?" May asked, clearly starting to get upset.

"It's a tower in the Cascade Mountains. I don't know. It just says to go there," Zinnia answered.

"Oh, so you don't know? You're just going into the forbidden forest to a tower you know nothing about? Mom is going to kill me!"

"I don't know what's up there but I have to go!" Zinnia looked into May's eyes pleadingly.

May knew there was no convincing her. Zinnia was stubborn and when she set her mind on something, she saw it to the end and wouldn't let anyone stop her. May thought to herself for a few moments. Her eyes shifted from Zinnia's then to the ground and then back to Zinnia's again. "Okay, well you aren't going alo—"

"She's not! I'm going with her," Lilly interrupted.

"Oh great, so now two mothers are going to kill me." May rolled her eyes.

"Nope. I don't have any parents, remember?" Lilly happily reminded her.

May looked mortified that she could have forgotten such an important detail. "Yes. Lilly, I'm so sor—"

"Don't even worry about it, sis. It doesn't bother me. Besides, don't we have bigger fish to fry right now? Like… Greenwrich, and shouldn't you be packing? I sure hope you don't plan on bringing those high heels out there," Lilly laughed. May and Zinnia stared at her. "Oh, geez you two, lighten up!"

"Before we go any further with this, you both need to disconnect from the New Life system," Zinnia instructed.

"How do we do that?" May asked.

"When I went to the site I found at the end of the book, there was a video of a man named Seth Astrid. He said that the moment I went to that site, I was disconnected. You will both need to go to that site too."

May and Lilly took out their PEDs and went to the same site Zinnia had gone to and then they looked at each other with the uneasy realization that there was no turning back from this now.

"We need to plan this out. First of all, how are we going to get into the forest? The walls circle around the city, and don't forget about the force field, the dome shield," May stated as she watched Zinnia pace around the room.

Zinnia stopped pacing and looked at May. "No, we don't need to plan it. It's all been planned out already. I got this chip with detailed instructions on what we need to do to get out of the city," Zinnia said, pulling out her PED and handing it to May.

May began reading aloud. "At exactly 11:55 AM, you will take a ZGS underground tunnel starting at Interstate Station 75938 to Ellensburg, Washington. A ventilation system maintenance check is scheduled at 12 PM each day, and tomorrow it will be on Vent 87. When you enter the ZGS, you must move fast. Put this chip on the right side of the dash screen."

May paused to show Lilly and Zinnia a detailed picture of the side of the dash and continued reading. "This will set the destination and override the scheduled maintenance personnel. As soon as this is done, the New Life guards will receive a flag of the unauthorized change of staff, and they will send in the bots. So again, you must move fast. When the ZGS stops, grab the chip and exit the sphere. Use the chip again in the keypad on the hatch door. Once inside, you will see the first of two fans. You will need to bring something large enough to stop them so you can get through. Once you've made it outside, head west toward the tower. You will need to hike, so bring appropriate footwear. When you arrive, enter the tower, take the ladder down, and head west again. You will arrive at your destination when you reach a large steel door. Knock on the door twice, pause for three seconds, and then knock one more time. Good luck and we look forward to meeting you soon."

"Okay then! Let's get some sleep tonight and head out first thing tomorrow. This is exciting! Just the three of us on an epic adventure!" Lilly yelled out, almost too enthusiastically.

***

Zinnia could hardly sleep. Her anxiety ran through every possible horrible scenario that could unfold with their plan in her mind. She was dressed and ready to go as soon as the sun came up. It didn't take much to wake the other two, so she assumed they must have had the same sleepless night she had. They drank down their coffee and quickly stuffed their breakfast rations down their throats. Zinnia's stomach was in knots. Lilly was as pumped up and ready to go as ever. Zinnia felt a slight hint of jealousy as they left the apartment.

They departed and reached Interstate Station 75938 to Ellensburg, Washington at 11:50 AM. This station wasn't quite as busy as the station at New Life, but they'd still have to time it just right to get to the platform at exactly 11:55 AM. Just like the station at New Life, the crowd pushed each other down the long corridor with loud chattering echoing off the glass tiles and gusts of wind that turned Zinnia's stomach with each blow. Zinnia, May, and Lilly had to link arms to stay together as they steadily made their way down to the platform in what seemed like a never-ending sea of people.

May yelled out to them over the noise, "Z! Lilly and I will get in first. That way you're closer to the right side of the dash screen! Don't worry about your belt! I'll buckle you in while you put the chip in!"

Zinnia nodded her head rapidly, as her heart pounded out of her chest. Every surge of adrenaline felt unbearable for a person with anxiety. If it wasn't for her uncontrollable shaking, she would have noticed how bad her palms were sweating. She started wishing she hadn't had coffee. It just makes it worse. She clutched her necklace, still linking arms with May.

When Zinnia was younger, she was put on medication for her anxiety, but she didn't like the way it made her feel. She didn't feel much at all, actually. She didn't like not having her emotions guiding her... Keeping her away from trouble. She knew it sounded silly to everyone else, but she didn't feel safe hiding behind the medication. Besides, mental health in the world wasn't a priority since everyone was happy and stress-free, or they could just transfer if they weren't. She was convinced she had anxiety because she knew something wasn't right, and now she had the chance to prove her feelings were valid all along.

"We only have a short window of opportunity here," May yelled. "Everyone clear on what you need to do?"

"Yes!" Lilly yelled back.

"Z?" May asked, looking down at her.

Zinnia nodded her head rapidly again.

When they reached the platform, the attendant yelled out, "Step in! Mind your head! Buckle up! Exit quickly!"

The girls were shoved into the ZGS and as the door started closing, May and Lilly fastened themselves in. After May was done with her belt, she reached over to fasten Zinnia's while Zinnia went for the slot.

As soon as the door was closed, they started to feel weightless as the sphere was shot away from the platform. Zinnia fumbled with the chip and her shaking hands were making it impossible for her to get it into the dash. It suddenly slipped out of her fingers and started floating in front of their faces.

With time running out, Lilly quickly unbuckled herself, snatched it out of the air, reached around to the right side of the dash screen and shoved it into the slot. Within seconds, the ZGS was pulled off the track and into a parking spot in front of Vent Hatch 87. They quickly scrambled out, and the sphere sucked back out onto the track, disappearing in an instant.

They stood there for a second to catch their breath. "Come on. We gotta keep moving," May said frantically, as she approached the utility room door and started looking for the slot on the keypad.

Lilly smiled at Zinnia, who was wiping sweat off her forehead, and handed her the chip. "Oh, good," Zinnia said, relieved. "I'm glad you remembered to grab it. I'm sorry I couldn't hold onto it. I couldn't stop shaking. My hands were so sweaty."

"It's okay. I got you," Lilly said, resting a hand on Zinnia's shoulder.

May found the slot and pointed to it as Zinnia took a deep breath and inserted the chip. The door quickly slid open, exposing a small room with a chair and a glass computer screen.

Once inside Zinnia spotted the first fan just below the ceiling. She sighed heavily, rolled her eyes, and said, "We forgot to bring something to stop the fans."

After standing quietly for a moment, Lilly suddenly exclaimed, "I know!" She grabbed the chair sitting in front of the computer screen and set it just below the fan. She hopped up onto the chair and said, "Watch this!" as she took her belt off and tossed it up like a lasso. The belt whipped around one of the blades and she yanked on it so hard the whole fan came out in one piece.

"Good job, Lilly!" May cheered, impressed.

"Here, give me your hand, Z. I'll boost you up so you can crawl through," Lilly said as she motioned to Zinnia to get onto the chair. Zinnia stepped up and Lilly put her locked fingers out so she could use them as a stool. She lifted her up and Zinnia climbed into the vent. Lilly looked down at May and motioned for her to go next. May looked around the room for a second before stepping up onto the chair. After both May and Zinnia were safely inside, they reached their arms down and hoisted Lilly up into the vent beside them. It was only a short crawl before they got to the fan that would lead them outside. They could see right away that this fan was much larger than the first one. They stood up and looked at each other, completely at a loss of what to do.

Suddenly an ear-piercing siren erupted, echoing throughout the tunnels. They looked at each other with panic in their eyes.

"The bots are coming! Uh, Lilly, I don't suppose you have another belt anywhere, do you?" May asked nervously.

"I'm fresh out of belts, May!" Lilly yelled out over the siren.

"How are we going to get through this one? We don't have anything big enough!" May yelled back.

They thought for a few seconds and then Zinnia's face lit up as an idea came into her mind. "Hold on! I'll be right back! Lilly, come with me! I'm going to need your help!" They darted back the way they came from and when the ventilation tunnel narrowed, they got down and crawled as fast as they could. They made their way back to the small room and Zinnia yelled to Lilly, "Here, hold onto my feet! I'm going to reach down for the chair! Don't drop me!"

Lilly yelled back, "I got you! Don't you worry! I have Thrill Seeker arms!"

Zinnia reached down as far as she could as Lilly held her feet tight. She grabbed the chair and yelled to Lilly to pull her up. As she lifted the chair into the tunnel, she could just barely see the door to the small room open and hoped with all her might that they weren't seen. She knew they needed to move fast. They dragged the chair all the way back to the second ventilation fan, as quickly as possible, and rejoined May. "We're back! Here! We got this!" Zinnia lifted the chair up to show her.

May looked at them nervously. "That seems dangerous!"

"It's worth a shot!" Lilly yelled as she grabbed the chair from Zinnia and ran up to the large fan. She jammed it between the rotating blades and held on with all her strength as the fan started to pull her. May and Zinnia immediately ran over and grabbed Lilly to steady her while their weight slowed the fan down. Much to their disbelief, they got it to stop.

"Come on! We have to get through! We don't have time! They're going to be here any second!" Lilly yelled, as they struggled to hold onto the chair.

"Z, you go first! I'll stay here with Lilly and hold the fan!"

Zinnia looked her sister in the eyes and nodded. She didn't have time to be scared. She let go of the chair and slipped in between the fan blades and grabbed the chair from the other side as she let out a sigh of relief.

"You next, May!" Lilly insisted as she adjusted her hold on the chair. "You two hold the chair from that side!" she yelled.

"Okay!" May and Zinnia yelled together.

"Okay!" May slipped through the fan and joined Zinnia on the other side. After they had a good hold, Lilly let go of her grip and darted through the fan. As soon as she got through, Zinnia and May exhaled, let go of the chair, and watched as the fan started to spin again, shooting the chair back the direction they had just come from.

"Oh, man! That was crazy! I can't believe we just did that!" Lilly yelled out excitedly.

"We aren't out of the woods yet," Zinnia said.

"You mean, into them!" Lilly added with a smile and her typical cheesy grin.

Zinnia smiled as she realized how right she was. They took a few steps up a grassy hill and at the peak, they saw an endless, beautiful forest greeting them. They stopped for a moment to take it in. They had no idea what to expect from this mysterious journey ahead of them, but they knew one thing for certain—they couldn't turn back now. The only direction for them was straight forward into this magical green curtain of uncertainty.

4

Standing in front of them was a forest of Douglas fir and spruce trees. They could hear the strange, unfamiliar sounds of birds, frogs, and insects. It almost seemed as if they were playing a song together. The air was cool and crisp on their skin while the fragrance of wildflowers, spread out like a blanket across the forest floor, overwhelmed their senses. They stood quiet and still, absorbing their surroundings.

After a few minutes, May finally interrupted the silence. "What do we do from here?"

"We head this way," Zinnia answered as she took the first brave steps toward the unknown. "Let's hike as far as we can while there's still daylight and find a place we can sleep tonight. We can travel further tomorrow. We need to get as far away from this vent as possible."

Zinnia grabbed her pack and began rummaging through its contents. "The ZGS took us east of Mount Rainier. We need to head west." She brought out her PED's GPS. "These won't last us very long without glass. You should turn yours off and we'll use one at a time until we get there."

May and Lilly nodded, powered off their PEDs, and tucked them back into their bags.

"Okay. Let's go. My GPS shows this way," Zinnia instructed as she pointed in a direction with nothing but thick trees and weeds. Lilly ran forward excitedly as May looked over at Zinnia, worried. Zinnia returned her look and grabbed her sister's hand before following Lilly.

They forced their way through the thick weeds and bushes, panting as they swung their arms in front of them to knock down the brush. Branches smacked their arms and faces as they pushed through the trees. Every few feet felt like an obstacle course as they stepped around massive trunks just to meet another one, dead and lying on the ground, practically impossible to climb over.

After what felt like hours, May stopped and exhaled loudly. "This. Is. Not. Working!" She leaned up against a tree and rested her hands on her knees as she worked to catch her breath. "It will take us a week to get there at this rate. There has got to be a different way."

Zinnia pulled up her PED and zoomed out a bit to see a larger area on the map. Her eyes lit up. "Look, May." She turned her PED so she could see the screen. "Just up ahead there should be a clearing. And if you look just past that, it looks like there is some sort of a trail. I learned about this in my mapping class. They paved big trails years ago before the forest was cut off to humans. They used to drive these things on them called motor vehicles. They were kind of like the ZGSs, only they weren't in tubes and there was no antigravity."

"Oh, man. That would hurt." Lilly responded, shaking her head.

"They didn't go as fast as ZGSs," Zinnia replied. "Fastest they usually went was 80 miles per hour. At least that's what I read. I assume they went even slower off the interstate. Anyway, they called them 'roads,' I believe. May, once we get past this clearing, we'll hit that road, and then there shouldn't be so much vegetation." Zinnia encouraged as she stuck out her hand for her sister to grab. May took it reluctantly and they continued forward.

Lilly began mumbling to herself as she followed. "80 miles an hour? How in the heck did they get anywhere? It must have taken them a week just to get to the next state. Life must have been so boring back then."

Zinnia turned around to ask Lilly what she was mumbling about, but Lilly waved her hand in the air and said, "Nothing. I'm just thinking out loud. On we go."

Finally, after hours of fighting with the forest, they reached the clearing Zinnia had pointed to on her PED. The same wildflowers that laid below the forest's trees outside of the vent coated the meadow floor. The grass was tall but not overgrown and they could see a perfect spot to set up camp. "Okay, we need wood for a fire, according to this survival site. It also says something about tents—"

"Oh, yes!" Lilly cut Zinnia off. "I got mine right here!" She threw her pack down to the ground and pulled out a little box. May and Zinnia looked at Lilly curiously. "What? You guys didn't bring your tents?"

"No. We didn't think… We don't even have—" May said before Lilly cut her off again.

"Well camping is what we do in the Thrill Seeker Zone when we spend the whole day rock climbing and white river rafting, and sometimes right on top of the mountains! You don't have camping in your zones?" Lilly asked, puzzled.

"We sleep in cabanas in Lover's Lane sometimes. That's like camping, isn't it?" May asked.

"Uh… I don't think so," Lilly pondered.

"Whatever you guys! I don't care what it's called. You are obviously the only one who brought a tent so we're all going to have to snuggle up tonight," Zinnia stated, putting her hand in the air as if to stop any possible protest.

Lilly smiled. "Well shoot, Z, you know I don't mind snuggling up. Besides, we'll be nice and toasty all night!" Lilly set her little box on the ground and told them, "Alright, back up now."

She pushed the button on the top of the box and in an instant, out popped a perfectly rectangular structure as tall and as long as May. "It has auto-sensing so it knows who the tallest person is standing by and it expands to that size. Pretty cool, huh?" Lilly said with a grin.

"Wow! That's amazing," Zinnia replied.

"Glad I could finally impress you, my little genius friend," Lilly said, still beaming.

"I'm not a genius. You know how I feel about being called that. I'm not any smarter than anyone else," Zinnia responded.

Lilly put her hand up to her mouth and leaned toward May. "She's humble too."

May giggled as Zinnia rolled her eyes at both of them.

"Okay, the sun is going down," Zinnia pointed out. "We need to make a fire for heat. According to this site, we need pieces of the trees that have already died. They should be lying around on the ground somewhere."

Just as she finished her sentence, a creature broke through the bushes on the far side of the meadow. Its sleek, deep brown fur blended in with the trees so perfectly, had it not been for the meadow, they may not have seen it. Its strong, muscular body stood sturdy and unwavering and yet it seemed graceful, elegant, and peaceful. Its majestic beauty captivated them.

"What...is...that?" May asked, keeping her eyes fixed on the creature.

Zinnia pulled up her PED to take a picture of it, and the name of the creature popped up with some facts. "It's a deer. They are herbivores and only eat plants, grass, shrubs, nuts, and acorns. They have four stomachs," Zinnia said, skimming over the facts. "Those spikes on the top of its head are called antlers."

They watched the deer walk through the meadow and disappear on the other side. They looked at each other bewildered. May knew there was a chance they would encounter animals but she had no idea they would be so amazing. She learned about them in her favorite class and always dreamed of seeing them. She just hoped she'd get to see more.

"Okay, let's finish setting up camp," Zinnia said, breaking the silence.

***

As Theo ate his lunch alone in his apartment, he couldn't help but think how his date with May had been nothing short of strange. They hadn't gotten more than two subjects in before she began acting strange. He kept replaying the date over and over again in his head. *What did I say that caused her to run so fast? Was it the nine lives? No, she didn't seem weirded out by that. It was the book. That stupid book! Ah, and then I brought up my father! On the first date?! Good job, Theo! If I'm ever going to be seen as anything other than the son of the President's personal guard, I'm going to have to stop bringing him up!*

Just as Theo stood up to put his dishes away, he heard an alarm go off by his front door. Startled, he ran over and pushed the button to read the alert. "An unauthorized personnel override for vent maintenance was activated at 11:55 this morning. Three females have been identified as May Waters, Zinnia Waters, and Lilly 573922. They were reported heading east on the ZGS Interstate Station 75938 and exiting at Vent 87. Any information in connection with this infraction will help lead to their capture. Please report on your PEDs and you will be rewarded with credits."

Theo, in utter disbelief, didn't hesitate for a second. He hopped on the elevator and headed straight up to his father's apartment.

Colton Armstrong opened the door with an intense, angry look on his face. His square hairline was wet from the sweat beading on his forehead. "What do you want?!" he yelled at Theo and then walked back to his desk, not giving him a chance to answer. "No! I did not authorize it! My lead maintenance officer didn't have anything in his box! I'm on it! I'll keep you posted, Mr. President. This will not slip past me! I'll call you back as soon as I have a lead." He hung up his video chat with the President and turned to Theo. "I asked you what you want?!"

"I saw the alert and I have some information to report," he answered, suddenly feeling ill.

"Well, what is it?!"

"Last night, I went on a date with May Waters, and she mentioned her sister finding a book in her apartment. Then she left quickly after I told her that you would want to hear about it."

"And why are you just now telling me this?!" The anger rose in his voice again and his face turned a deep shade of red.

"I just thought—"

His dad suddenly grabbed his shoulder, dug his fingers into his collar bone, and brought Theo to his knees. "Just thought what?! Had you come to me right away, we could have avoided this whole mess!" He shouted as spit flew into his face. Theo lowered his head in shame.

"Lift your chin, son!" Colton said, grabbing and pulling it up hard. "You're an Armstrong! It's time you start acting like one! You Lovers are useless! Always thinking with your damn heart and not your head!"

Colton dialed the president again. "Mr. President, I've got a lead. Theo had a date with Miss Waters last night."

"Both of you, come up to my office now," Liam said before hanging up his PED.

"Get up!" Colton commanded as he grabbed the back of Theo's neck and pushed him toward the door. "Tell him everything! Leave nothing out!"

Theo stood in front of President Liam, nervously flicking his fingernails, after telling him about his date with May.

"What was your involvement in all of this?" Liam questioned.

"Nothing! I just went on a date with her. Then she left. That was it. I swear!" He had dealt with these presidential encounters his whole life and still couldn't get used to them. President Liam wasn't anywhere near as scary as his father, but he was just thankful it wasn't President Sophia standing in front of him. He'd take his father over her any day. She transferred people left and right. You couldn't even look at her wrong without risking being sent off to the transfer pods. He wasn't afraid of the pod; he just wasn't ready to move on to his 11th life yet.

Escaping into his thoughts, all he could think about was May; about how beautiful she looked in that long red dress, with her red, wavy hair beautifully shaping her face. His heart sank for a moment as his thoughts were brutally interrupted.

"Do you think you could call her?" President Liam questioned.

"No, I totally blew it with her last night. There's no way she'd answer. I'm sure of it." Theo's thoughts began to trail off again. This time he thought about his mother and how much he would give to have her there right then. She was soft, kind, and loving, unlike his father. He often wondered how she could stand him as long as she did, but he wished she would have stuck it out just a little longer. "I wish Mom…" The words escaped his lips against his better judgment. He immediately regretted opening his mouth as his father tore into him.

"What have I told you about wasting your time thinking about her?! She's gone! She left us to go on to her next life! She didn't want you anymore! Now stop whining like a baby! We have work to do!"

President Liam turned to Colton and said, "I want you to put all of your best guards on this. Report back to me." He pointed his finger toward the door, instructing them to leave his office.

Colton turned to his guards. "Search their apartment! I want someone sent out to the farm to question their mother! Check the vent again! Look for any clues they may have left behind. Check all PED activities for the last 48 hours! Out! Go!" Colton commanded as he rushed them out of the office.

***

The girls built their fire with the instructions from the survival site. It took them a few times to get it started, but once they figured it out, they were able to warm up before eating their dinner rations and tucking themselves into bed. It was all so overwhelming for them. Lilly, however, was already snoring heavily while May and Zinnia tried to fall asleep.

May rolled over and sighed. "Strange that nothing fazes her. I wish I were a Thrill Seeker sometimes."

"You and me both," Zinnia agreed, shaking her head. "I struggle just to make it through a normal day without having a panic attack. I wish I had her strength." She paused for a moment. "Hey May, I was wondering, why were you so willing to risk your job to help me?"

"Because, Z, I want to know what happened to dad too and I knew you weren't going to stop until you got your answers. I had two options. I could have stayed back and left my little sister alone or I could go with you and maybe get some answers myself. Either way, no matter what happens, our family means more to me than a job. I already lost one person. I'm not going to lose another." May adjusted her body to get comfortable. "Try to get some sleep. We have a busy hike tomorrow. Love you."

"I love you too." Zinnia rolled over, pulling the blanket over her head in an effort to drown out the strange forest sounds.

The girls awoke to the harmonious sound of birds whistling in unison. They had learned about birds in school, but none of them had ever seen one before entering the forest, let alone heard their beautiful music. They sat up one at a time and listened quietly.

"I've never heard anything so beautiful," Zinnia said as she stood up and opened the tent door. They stepped outside to see the birds and their mouths dropped open at the sight. Hundreds of them, with very sharp, pointed beaks and sleek feathers, lining the branches of the trees surrounding the meadow. Some were a deep dark purple, some deep navy blue, and some were deep forest green. The colors were richer than any of them had ever seen.

Just when they thought they couldn't be more impressed, the birds darted off their branches and hovered right above them forming a perfect square in the sky. Under their wings were bright glowing fuchsia, turquoise, and emerald feathers. Then they spread out into the shape of a diamond, and then a triangle, doing a flip and then a dance from left to right, as if they were putting on a show for them. Their music continued as they formed more shapes and danced. Then just like that, they all flew off, leaving the girls speechless.

"Well, wasn't that something?" Lilly asked, breaking the silence.

Just as she finished her sentence, they heard the sound of crunching leaves and a loud, horrible screeching behind them. They immediately turned to see where it was coming from and gasped in terror, as a large group of feral cats started charging towards them. May let out a blood-curdling scream and ran for the tent as Zinnia ducked to avoid one flying at her face.

Each cat was a different color with stripes or markings of some kind. All of them had extremely long claws that extended out as long as human fingers. Their feet were huge, way bigger than they remembered seeing in the pictures at school.

Lilly immediately started kicking them with her heel as they launched themselves at her. She fought them off as quickly as she could, as they sliced at her legs and arms. Zinnia ran to Lilly and followed her example and then a cat grabbed hold of her leg and pierced it. She grabbed it by its tail and ripped it off, tearing flesh from her calf in the process. The cats began to surround them, crouching low to the ground with their behinds wiggling. The girls stood with their backs to each other waiting for them to strike all at once.

Zinnia reached behind her and grabbed Lilly's hand. "Lilly, what do we do?"

"I-I don't know!"

Just when all hope seemed lost, a large pack of dogs, both big and small, jumped over the bushes and charged towards them. They barked and snarled as the cats fought to escape. They tossed them into the air and trampled on them as they grabbed hold of their necks and cracked them between their tight jaws. The ones who didn't get caught bolted away as some of the dogs chased after them. May burst out of the tent and ran to Lilly and Zinnia. They stood there panting as their hearts beat wildly out of control.

Following closely behind the dogs was a tall, muscular man with brown skin and pearly white teeth that stretched out across an enormous smile. His hair was in perfect tight braids in lines across the top of his head and his chest was bare. May felt her cheeks flush as she stared at him. She thought about the deer they had seen the night before. He matched it perfectly. His strong, muscular body stood sturdy and unwavering, and yet he seemed graceful, elegant, and peaceful. His beauty captivated her.

"Hi. I'm May." She didn't lose eye contact for a second. "Thank you for saving us."

Lilly and Zinnia thanked him too.

"Hi, May. My name is Horizon, but I go by Zon," he said, offering his hand.

May shook it nervously, still in awe at the sight of him. She couldn't feel her feet anymore, only the beating in her chest. His hand was calloused, but soft. Her head felt light and warm, and she felt strangely safe, protected, and then all of a sudden completely embarrassed.

Zon smiled, then pulled a whistle up to his lips and blew. After a couple of minutes all the dogs were right back by his side. Some of them were licking blood from their paws.

Zinnia began to speak. "We're on our way to the Tower at Greenwrich. We have instructions from a man named Seth. I saw his video."

"Z, tell him what you are." May insisted, poking her with her elbow.

"Uh. I'm a Learner," Zinnia said hesitantly.

"Yes, I assumed you were given instructions to go to the tower. Only those sought out by Seth are found wandering around this area. I'll lead you the rest of the way. It's less than half a day's hike. It's a good thing I was close by when those cats attacked. They would have torn you to shreds and feasted on your bodies." He laughed as he started walking.

The girls looked at each other nervously as they grabbed their stuff and ran to catch up with him. "Hey, back there, before the cats attacked us, there were birds making geometric shapes in the sky. Do you know what that was all about?" Zinnia asked.

"They were warning you about the cats. The birds are the watchers of the forest. Our friends. And the dogs are the guardians." They continued walking as Zon told the story. "Over time, after all of the pets had been banished to the forest, the cats grew feral, with larger claws and the ability to jump to impeccable heights. More and more, they hunted and killed the birds. But the birds evolved too. They learned that warning other creatures would ultimately help them, because the creatures of the forest began defending the birds. The birds warned the creatures, and the creatures defended the birds. They developed a symbiotic relationship."

"But the warning didn't help us," May interjected.

Zon threw his head back, erupting into a bellowing laughter. May's cheeks got warm with embarrassment.

"That's because you are not a forest creature. They did not know you would have such limited understanding," he said as he continued walking and laughing to himself.

He led them up a road covered in weeds and wildflowers. Tree roots pushed up from the ground, creating cracks in the concrete. The road zigzagged as they hiked tirelessly uphill. Lilly wasn't fazed at all. She was having no trouble keeping up with Zon. Zinnia and May, however, kept falling behind and had to take frequent breaks. Zinnia, overwhelmed with curiosity during one of their breaks, decided to ask Zon about the dogs.

"How is it that these dogs follow you? It seems like they'd do anything you tell them to do," she said.

"Dogs are pack animals. They have long been loyal creatures to man," he answered.

"What are pack animals?" Zinnia asked, even more curious now.

"They stay in large groups. They are social animals and cannot survive alone. Humans are also social creatures but have forced themselves unnaturally to live divided. You live in your separate houses, sleep separate, eat separate," he went on.

"We don't live separated. There are billions of people everywhere," Zinnia argued.

"There are many of you but you are still very much alone," Zon stated blankly. He continued walking forward, leaving Zinnia lost in thought.

She ran to catch up with him. "Hey, what is that pack you have on your back?"

"It is full of medical supplies and organ bots for our people."

Zinnia was taken back by his words "our people." She thought about this for a moment and realized that where they were going must be so much bigger than she had imagined. She felt a bubble of excitement, as well as nervousness, building up inside of her.

"How do you get these medical supplies and organ bots?" She asked.

"I'm a Runner. I work closely with intelligence inside the city. They supply what they can from the clinics and send them via bots," Zon explained.

"How come we couldn't get into the forest the same way the bots do?"

"The bots travel through a small tunnel that goes far below the wall, too small for people to pass through comfortably. We considered making the tunnel bigger but decided it wasn't worth the risk of jeopardizing a crucial lifeline. Our people depend on these supplies, most of the time with their lives. Our agents fill the bots' containers and send them back." Zon adjusted the bag on his back and continued, "Anyway, that is enough questions. Seth will catch you up when we get there."

***

Waiting in the Capitol Office for Colton to bring news of the escapees, President Sophia Smith tried to discuss business while Liam paced around the room impatiently.

"Can we get on with this? It's late and I should be home with my family," Liam complained. He had little patience for Sophia at times. She didn't seem to value family, or time, or his time with his family. He knew it was because she was alone and had been for a very long time, so she didn't understand the importance of it. He tried from time to time to include her in things, but she never seemed interested.

"We have surpassed our transfer quota by 20% the last six months in a row. I think it may be time to increase the quota. What do you think?" Sophia asked.

"Agreed. What's next?"

"Liam, I need you to be present. I cannot do this without you. We must maintain the balance of equality. Your family will understand you taking care of business for one hour."

Liam exhaled and plopped down in the chair across the desk from her. "Fine. Alright. How many Little Angels did we acquire this week?"

"Each state's Life-House recruited close to 7,000 little guard trainees and more than twice that number were transferred, which means, that many more mothers have lost their children," Sophia stated with a smile on her face.

Liam rolled his eyes. "I still don't get what you have against mothers."

"Population control, Liam. They keep populating. Anyway, we were also below our Basic Living Budget thanks to the increase in transfers."

Just then, there was a quick knock on the door and Colton entered the office. "Presidents," he said as he nodded respectfully.

"What have you found out?" Sophia asked.

"The mother knows nothing. There was a phone call between May Waters and Lilly 573922 close to 1700 hours. A few hours before that Zinnia Waters' PED was disconnected from the New Life system for a split second. About an hour after the phone call, both Lilly 573922 and May Waters' PEDs also disconnected for that split second. We have reason to believe that the book was planted in the apartment for them to find. We found a strange box in one of the bedroom pods."

"What do you mean they were disconnected from our system for a split second? Did your men not see this? They were supposed to be watching them!" Sophia yelled.

"It was a flicker, a hiccup. We see it all the time. No one thought anything of it," Colton answered, his anger starting to build inside. One of his guards entered the room to report. Colton turned around, pulled his gun out and shot him in the face, making everyone in the room jump. Blood splattered on the walls behind him as his body fell to the ground, spasming.

"Clean that up, Colton," Sophia said flatly, glaring at him.

He took a deep breath, pulled up his PED to call for a cleaning bot, and then apologized for the mess. Sophia kept her eyes on him without saying anything.

She raised from her chair after a few moments and said, "Well, it looks like they got to her. Colton, get your men to find every mole in this place. Do I need to tell you what will happen if you don't?" She gave him a serious look and he nodded once and left the room.

5

After hours of hiking up steep terrain, the girls were all exhausted, panting, and sweating from the long journey. Even Lilly was starting to fade. Zon rambled on about Greenwrich being an old communication tower back during the government takeover. He explained, "None of your people know this, but the towers are also entryways to what we call The Underground."

They arrived at the base of the old, rusty tower that you could hardly tell used to be green. The door was made of heavy steel, and Zon had to use all of his strength to open it. He blew into his whistle and the dogs immediately surrounded the tower to stand guard. Once inside he strained to close the door and pulled down a large metal latch that screeched so loud the girls had to cover their ears. The tower wasn't very wide, just barely big enough to hold them all. There was a winding staircase that led up to the top of the tower and another metal door on the ground below their feet. Zon motioned to the girls to get onto the bottom of the stairs. After they got out of the way, he opened the door, revealing a ladder that led down a dark tunnel. The girls exchanged worried looks and Zinnia's heart began to race. Zon put his hand out in front of him, instructing them to go down. Zinnia and May leaned slightly over to look down to the bottom, both of them reluctant to take the first step.

"Oh, here, ya big sissies! Let me go," Lilly burst out as she stepped down onto the ladder. "No monsters are grabbing me yet," she announced as she made her way down.

Zinnia followed, then May, and then Zon. The journey to the bottom of the tunnel felt like it went on for miles. Once they reached the ground, they saw four tunnels leading in different directions. Tiny lights lined the sides, barely illuminating the darkness. It smelled musty, with a hint of mold, and they could feel the damp air on their skin.

Zon pointed to the tunnel behind the ladder. "That one will take you to California. That one, over there, takes you to the Pacific Ocean. That one takes you to Canada, and the one over here will take you to Idaho. We go this way," he said as he pointed to the tunnel leading to the ocean. "This is west."

He wasted no time as he marched ahead. The girls quickly followed, and after what again felt like miles, they reached another tunnel that split off. Zon pulled a light out of his pocket and shined it ahead as they reached another large, steel door.

Posted on the outside of the door were two flags. The flag on the bottom had 10 of the colorful birds they had seen in the woods. They were arranged in the shape of a triangle with trees in the top corners and the words "TOP of Washington" displayed across the bottom. The flag above had the word "TOP" in large letters with a sun on the bottom and upside-down trees across the top.

Zon banged his walking stick against the door two times, paused for three seconds, and then banged one more time. The door screeched loudly as it slowly swung open. Standing right inside the door were two tall men holding some sort of metal contraption in their hands. They stepped aside as the girls and Zon entered, and they closed the door behind them. The girls looked ahead and stared at the jaw-dropping vastness that laid in front of them. They walked forward and grabbed hold of the railing, which was the only thing separating them from the massive drop to what seemed like a never-ending black hole.

"How far down does this go?" May asked in disbelief.

"There are more than 2000 levels, and we are almost filled to capacity. Every level houses many families, and every level has a common eating and gathering area. You will get a tour after you talk with Seth," Zon informed them as he walked off to the right. "Follow me."

About five steel doors down they entered a room where Seth sat in a chair behind a desk. He peaked above his computer as they entered and immediately jumped to his feet. He stuck out his hand and shook each of the girls' firmly. Zinnia remembered him from the video.

"It is so good to finally meet you girls. My name is Seth Astrid. Please, have a seat." He led them to a few chairs sitting across from his desk. "I knew your father for many years before coming here to the Underground. When I heard that you had reached adulthood, Zinnia, I knew you would be moving in with May right away. We made sure you would find that book, per your father's request. With his curiosity and smarts, there was no way you wouldn't be driven to find answers. I'm just so happy you both came along, and also with—" He looked in Lilly's direction and asked politely, "What's your name, dear?"

Lilly answered, matter of fact, "I'm Lilly! This is my best friend!" She put her hand on Zinnia's shoulder and flashed a cheesy grin in her direction.

"Excellent! Well, welcome to TOP – The Underground." He stretched his hands out in front of him, palms up, before moving them out to the side.

"We saw that on the flags outside. What is TOP?" Lilly asked.

"T.O.P. It means, 'The Original People.'"

The girls exchanged curious looks. "TOP… The Original People? What does that mean?" Zinnia asked.

"It means that the people in this underground have been here for a very long time, since the government took over. Those who fought against the government had to flee. There was no way for them to beat New Life after they formed the 7 Nations. The Original People discovered the Underground, expanded it further, and built a life for themselves, free from the constraints of forced commonality, free from conformity. TOP has grown and flourished since then, and we believe it's time to take back our home," Seth said with a smile stretching from ear to ear.

Chills spread down Zinnia's spine, but she wasted no time. "What happened to my dad?"

"Yes! Of course. That is, after all, why I know you made the journey here. Your father discovered TOP when he was working closely in the offices of New Life on the Glass project. He found the same files that have led many of us here, so naturally, being a Learner, he dug deeper. He found the files and data sheets that were so cunning, so disturbing, there was no way he could look back. There were quotas for transfers, transfer goals, budgets based on how many transfers they could push, Little Angels recruitment program. Those are the children they decide to keep and train as their guards, instead of transferring. He read all about the underground, and worst of all, he found out the truth about transfers."

The girls were on the edge of their seats now. Zinnia was clutching her lightbulb necklace as tightly as she could. This was it. This was the moment she had been waiting for. Answers. They leaned in and waited for Seth to finish his story.

"He discovered that the claim you go on to your next life through transfer pods was completely fabricated. It was made up to convince the people to kill themselves. Once they discovered how to prolong our lives, the population increased to unimaginable numbers. Given that all basic living necessities were provided for the population, they feared resources would be depleted within a hundred years. They came up with the transfer story, controlled the population, and provided for the remaining citizens. It's a long-standing philosophical question. Do we sacrifice the few to save the many? They decided it was necessary. Thus, it begs the question—are they wrong?"

"Of course, they're wrong!" Zinnia cried as she stood up. "We should be able to decide for ourselves! They lied!" She was beginning to feel dizzy as her heart beat faster again. Sweat was forming along her already damp forehead. She didn't feel like she could handle any more, and he still hadn't answered her question! She took a deep breath and tried to calm herself down before she had a panic attack.

"What happened to my dad?" she asked again, sitting back down.

"They saw his activities, of course. They see everything. You know that. He was eventually transferred," Seth said softly. "Your dad was a smart, passionate, honest person. I was very sad to hear of his passing."

"Why didn't they just tell us that he transferred? Why the mystery? Why let us believe he disappeared like the others?" Zinnia continued to probe.

"They knew you wouldn't believe that. Do you think in a million years your dad would ever leave you two girls behind?" Seth reasoned with warmth and compassion, bringing them a small amount of comfort.

Both Zinnia and May had fully begun crying. "No. You're right. He would never have left us," May said as she put her arm around Zinnia's shoulder and gave her a gentle hug.

"If you thought he disappeared, it's more likely you'd be hoping for his return and any attempts to find him would have been confined to the city. You'd never think to look outside those walls. Accidents happen. People have gone missing, and they find them a week later in the Thrill Seeker Zone rock climbing mountains," Seth said. "I'm sure you girls have run through every possible scenario in your heads. Thinking he transferred would have caused you to question, and they knew that."

After a few uncomfortable moments of quiet, Lilly broke the silence. "Well, we can't 'TOP' that story!" She heard a small chuckle behind her and whipped her head around to see who it was, wearing a cheesy grin on her face.

"Hey. I'm Cypher. I'm here to show you around. This is Florian." He introduced them as he shook their hands.

Cypher was extraordinarily tall and skinny with light, sandy brown hair and olive skin. He had slightly sunken, tired-looking eyes. Florian was a bit shorter than Cypher with a tan complexion, dark brown hair, and an arrogant look on his face.

"Zinnia, May, Lilly, this is my son, Florian, and our lead computer tech, Cypher. I've asked them to show you around. We have a room for you all set up. That is, if you've decided to stay with us, of course. We'll be having dinner soon," Seth said as he motioned them to the door.

Up until then, they didn't know where this adventure was going to take them, but they knew they couldn't go back. They *wouldn't* go back.

"Nice to meet you, Zinnia," Florian said as he lifted her hand and kissed the back of it slowly.

Confused and slightly repulsed, Zinnia pulled her hand away, "Uh, nice to meet you, too."

"Awkward!" Lilly blurted out, laughing loudly, and embarrassing her friend. She jumped to her feet and was the first one to leave the room. "Let's go! I want to see this place!"

Seth rolled his eyes at his son, as Florian left the room with the others. May looked at Zinnia with concern and put her arm around her shoulders again as they walked out of the office. She leaned in close to Zinnia and whispered in her ear, "I'm guessing he's a Lover. Don't worry about it. Just ignore him."

Cypher and Florian were walking ahead when Cypher turned around and said, "You're right. He is a Lover…and a Learner, and a Gamer, and a Thrill Seeker, and a Grower, and an Animal Lover, and a Musician. He has all of them, and so does everyone else down here." May's face became flushed, caught off guard that she was heard.

"What do you mean you have all of the spurs? No one has all of the spurs. Everyone has just one. It's been that way forever," Zinnia insisted, confused by the other things he listed.

The boys had slowed down so the girls could catch up to them. "Maybe for you city folk up there. Down here, we don't put people into categories," Florian responded, matter of fact, skipping backward so he could see them as he talked.

"They made up all that crap to keep you distracted and busy. Anyway, we'll take you to your room, and then after you settle in, we'll head over to the kitchen to help with dinner," Cypher added.

May asked curiously, "So is your dad in charge here?"

Florian shook his head and answered, "No one is in charge down here. We all work together. Everyone decides everything together. The teachers and preachers are the speakers. My dad addresses the Underground regarding the upcoming events. And he's Head of Recruiting, but not the leader."

After taking a few elevators they reached an area with long hallways branching off in many directions. The girls were utterly astonished at every turn. "How do you not get lost down here?" May asked as they entered a large room with couches, TVs, and bookshelves.

"Bookshelves…" Zinnia said when she saw them and her mouth dropped open. Not only had they only ever seen books in museums, but now there were bookshelves with people all around them, reading them…touching them.

"Here we are," Florian announced as he stretched his arms out. "Everyone, this is Zinnia, May, and Lilly. Zinnia, May, Lilly, this is everyone. This is the recreation room. You can watch TV, movies, read books, study, hang out, take a nap, whatever the hell you wanna do."

"What's 'the hell?'" May inquired curiously.

Florian smirked. "You'll learn all of that in your classes. They start tomorrow."

Zinnia got an excited look on her face. He continued, "There's plenty of free time, but we do have a pretty strict schedule. I sent the schedule to your PEDs. Speaking of PEDs…there are charge ports in your room. We do it the old-fashioned way down here. Fresh out of windows."

"Speaking of PEDs..." Zinnia began. "How was it, exactly, that the link we went to was able to kick us off the New Life system? I didn't even think that was possible."

Cypher answered, "The link uploaded an algorithm that simulates your daily routine. It creates a ghost. As far as they can see, you're still on your PEDs, living your lives."

Continuing on, the girls were directed to a room that took their breaths away. It didn't have fancy electronic walls and bright lights. It was a simple room with four beds, dressers, and plants. Plants everywhere.

"Plants inside? Plants inside!" Lilly blurted out excitedly as she ran into the room.

Above every plant was a small battery-operated pink light. Zinnia rushed over to one of them. "I've heard of these! These are sun-lights!" She exclaimed. "They never became a thing at home. Anything can grow under these lights. Absolutely anything. Mom and Dad actually wanted to get some of these when the crops struggled that one year. Remember, May?" May nodded. "Only problem is no one could afford them, not farmers anyway. Which is sad because farmers were really the only ones who actually needed them. In the end, it made them obsolete. Such a waste of a good invention," she said as she inspected the light intently.

"Well, Cypher here can pretty much figure out how anything works technology-wise," Florian bragged, patting the top of Cypher's shoulder. Cypher turned red in the face. "Zon brought one of these bad boys home, and Cypher pulled it apart and made replicas in less than a week. Now we have them on all of the crop levels. It was a struggle feeding everyone down here for years."

"It was a team effort," Cypher said unenthusiastically. "I keep the lights on, but you feed the kids."

"This is true," Florian polished his fingernails on his shoulder, obviously pleased with himself.

Zinnia rolled her eyes. "Yeah? And what exactly is it that you do around here?"

"I…plant, grow, nurture, and I feed our people," Florian replied as he stood tall.

"Well, you better tell that head of yours to stop growing there!" Lilly blurted out, making the whole room go into a fit of laughter.

Florian rolled his eyes and headed for the door. "Get cleaned up and meet us in the kitchen. This is August, by the way. She's your roommate. She'll show you the way when you're ready."

"Wah! I don't get a room to myself anymore," said a short, simple looking girl with a pouty face. "I'm just kidding! I'm August. Nice to meet you." She had straight, black, shoulder-length hair, and was wearing jeans and a button-up shirt with little flowers on the collar.

"Hey! Two months and two flowers all in the same room. That's cool," Lilly said as she shook August's hand. Just then, an orange striped cat came into the room and let out a tiny meow. It rubbed up against Zinnia's leg and she immediately jumped back as all three girls let out a loud gasp.

"Don't worry! This is Cinnamon! She doesn't hurt anyone. We have lots of cats down here. They aren't like the feral cats outside. These ones are friends," August said kindly as she picked up Cinnamon and started kissing and hugging her tightly. Cinnamon let out a long purr.

"Well, this place sure keeps getting weirder and weirder," Lilly said as she reached out to pet Cinnamon, who happily rubbed her face on Lilly's hand.

"I agree," May added, raising her eyebrows.

"The bathroom is right through there. You can take showers if you want. The towels are in the wicker basket." August pointed to the far wall. "Here are some fresh clothes. I'll take you to the kitchen when you're done getting cleaned up."

After the girls freshened up, August took them back through the many winding tunnels. They tried to memorize each turn but it seemed impossible. August could see the worried looks on their faces. "Don't worry. You'll figure out these tunnels eventually. They actually go in a pattern. I'll draw it for you later."

The group finally arrived at the kitchen where Florian and Cypher were waiting for them. The kitchen was much bigger than they had imagined. It seemed like there were hundreds of people running around. Some were cooking, some were cleaning, some were setting up huge pans of food, and some were doing dishes.

Florian tossed aprons at them and said, "You can help take the garbage to the shoot."

"We all have jobs. You'll get your job assignment tomorrow," Cypher added and handed the girls some garbage bags.

"I'm always in the kitchen. I'll show you where the shoot is," August said as she directed them through the crowd of people.

After about an hour, a bell rang and all the pans of food were brought out to a large room with many tables. Everyone took their seats, including the girls, who were feeling a bit unsure of themselves. They looked at each other nervously, wondering what was supposed to happen. After a few seconds, the back wall lit up and a very large screen appeared. There was a plump, kind looking woman with dark skin on the screen holding a sound bot up to her mouth. She smiled, then closed her eyes and began speaking. The girls looked around and noticed that everyone else had their eyes closed too. Some had their heads turned up and some had them turned down. They quickly turned their heads down but kept their eyes open, looking around the room.

"Let us be thankful for the nourishment we are about to receive," the woman began. "To the people of the Underground who work tirelessly every day to put meals on our tables. To the gardeners who grow the crops, the techs who provide the light, the treatment plant operators who provide the water, the kitchen staff who cook the food, and all the others who help keep this Underground going. Let us be thankful for each other, for our family and friends, our freedom, and our love. Please, enjoy your meals."

Zinnia saw some people touching their foreheads and chest and some people still had their eyes closed, speaking quietly to themselves. She caught a word here and there that she remembered seeing in the book. "What are they doing?" she asked in a low voice.

"They're praying," August whispered. "Everyone has their own beliefs as far as who they believe created the world and everything. Everyone prays in their own way before dinner. None of us got taught about religion up there. But it's nice to believe in something. Gives you hope, and peace, and all that stuff." She shrugged as she started dishing servings onto their plates. "Everyone also has their own belief as to how their God manifests him or herself, and they all have different names, but most people use 'God' when they pray before meals. Some people don't believe in a God at all and that's totally fine. They believe in TOP and that's spirit enough!"

"Everyone keeps throwing around words we don't know. It's confusing," May interrupted.

"You'll learn about all of this in your classes. Funny thing is, we ended up with no religion and only one language up there. Kinda boring if you ask me," August added.

"Wait, are you saying there's more than one language down here?" Zinnia asked, completely intrigued.

"Oh yeah! Loads! They really did their best to preserve traditions, religions, languages, everything from the original people. Speaking of traditions, we also have holidays! You should see this place around Christmas time. It is lit up!"

Lilly's face grew excited.

"It's my favorite time of year. Then you have New Year's Eve, Valentine's Day, Easter," August said, as she shoved a bite into her mouth. "Independence Day... That's the same day you celebrate the take-over, only TOP celebrates their escape *from* them. And that's just the American holidays!"

"The. Original. People." Lilly went into a zone as her mind absorbed all of the information. August giggled.

"Dang, there are some really cute guys down here," May said, looking around the room. Zinnia rolled her eyes and then exchanged a look with Lilly who smiled and laughed.

They all dug into the most delicious home cooked, not from a package, not rationed food. There was pasta, garlic bread...pizza. They ate as if they had never eaten before. They certainly hadn't eaten this kind of food. Even the food at New Life couldn't compare. They felt comfortable, warm, happy, and now completely...and...utterly exhausted.

They returned to their room and went straight to bed while everyone else lounged around in the recreation room. It had been a long day, but living life in a lie was longer. They slept soundly as they waited to start their new life...for the past to fall away and a future of truth, and choice, and true freedom to begin.

6

The lights came on bright and early the next day. Everyone showered like any other morning. May put on her makeup. Lilly put in her fiber optic hair extensions and decided on pink for the day. Zinnia pulled up the notepad on her PED, ready to learn. She was more excited than anyone, she could hardly contain it. Learning was what she loved most. After breakfast, August took them to a classroom where there were many long tables, just like the room they had eaten in.

August pointed to the table near the front for girls to sit at. "I'm heading to the kitchen. I'll come back for you before lunch. There are always new people in here, so he's just gonna jump into it. He'll ask your names and where you came from in a bit. See ya later," she said, waving happily as she left the room.

"Welcome to our 'Newcomers Course.' My name is Atticus Barrington," the teacher said, wearing sophisticated-looking glasses with hair that almost matched Seth's perfectly. "You'll be here for a few weeks. Seth Astrid, is in charge of recruitment, in case you didn't know, and has decided on your job assignments based on where he thinks you and the Underground will benefit most." He pressed a few buttons on his PED. "Here you go. I have just sent you each a video from Seth explaining the job he chose and why he chose it for you. You can always change your job later. We want you to be happy here. And please don't feel stressed about this class. There are no tests or anything like that. We just want you to learn our history and our future goals. We are very close to sprouting and you all get to be a part of this revolution," Atticus stated joyfully. "Take a few minutes to watch your videos and then we'll jump into the history of TOP."

The girls took out their PEDs and each of them took turns watching their videos. Zinnia played hers first. Seth popped up on the screen and began, "Welcome Zinnia. I have assigned you to the grow rooms. Florian will be training you."

"Great," she grumbled.

"He said you can change your job later. Don't worry about it, Z. You got this," May encouraged.

"I have chosen this job for you because we can all agree that you have what it takes up here." He tapped on his temple. "But down here you're going to have to be able to work with your hands too. I want you to stay in the grow rooms for at least a couple of months. If you decide you want to change jobs that will be completely up to you. Welcome to TOP."

Lilly pulled up her video next. "Welcome, Lilly. For you, I have chosen the tech level with Cypher."

"Yes!" Lilly exclaimed. "I like him! He laughs at my jokes!"

"I have chosen this job for you because it is very fast-paced and you have just the right amount of energy needed to do the job. Plus, they could use some sunshine around there. It's been a little depressing lately," Seth winked. "Welcome to TOP, Lilly." He nodded and smiled graciously. Lilly slowly turned her head toward Zinnia and May with her mouth half open, as the corners began curling up into a smile. "He said I'm sunshine. Did you hear that? Whelp, I am officially in love with this place," she announced as she nodded.

"Alright, my turn," May said.

"Welcome, May. I have decided to have you running with Zon. We have some people running between cities in the tunnels and just a few going above ground. We try to limit the amount of people going up, as it is incredibly dangerous." A worried look spread across May's face. Zinnia put her hand on her shoulder and May put her hand on top of Zinnia's, welcoming the support.

"You bravely made the journey here, but I'd like to expand on that a little further. It isn't easy living here and certainly won't be easy when we eventually take back our cities. Zon will help you gain a little courage. He's our strongest and bravest Runner, and he will be the best teacher for you. Good luck, and welcome to TOP."

May looked at Zinnia and Lilly and smiled slightly. "Well, at least he's beefy and super sexy."

Exasperated, Zinnia rolled her eyes and let go of May.

"What? Come on, you've known me your whole life. A Lover never gives up on love," she stated confidently.

"That's funny, considering you were about to give up on it before we left the city," Zinnia reminded her and laughed.

May returned the laugh mockingly. She had gone through many relationships in search of the right one. Every attempt had failed. She put her whole heart into it, just to get thrown away, abandoned, forgotten about, or cheated on. It often left a gaping hole in her chest that always took a long time to sew back together. With a big heart comes big pain. Some holes never were stitched, but she never gave up. Theo seemed like the perfect guy for her. He was tall, handsome, had a great job at New Life just like her, and was genuinely just a sweet guy. They spent quite a lot of time talking through their PEDs before meeting. She was more than excited to have that first date. A part of her wished it hadn't been interrupted but she was glad it was. She was glad to be there in the Underground. Maybe she could get him into the Underground eventually. That is, of course, if things didn't work out with Zon.

May and Lilly were beaming.

"Well, I'm glad you two are happy. I get stuck with arrogant Astrid," Zinnia complained.

May gave Zinnia a sad face and said, "Sorry, hun."

"Whatever. I'll definitely be changing my job as soon as I can."

"Now if I can direct your attention this way, I'll begin with the history of TOP. You are all aware of what you were taught at New Life. Well, I'm here to tell you that was not an accurate depiction of what actually happened 200 years ago. "In 2042, scientists discovered The Fountain of Youth, the expansion of life. New Life took over and unified the world as the 7 Nations in 2047. How did they do it?" he asked rhetorically, as he turned the wall screen on, displaying a timeline of events. "They had something the world wanted. Longer lives. As you have learned since joining us here in the Underground, many people fled, never to return again. New Life built the walls and force field dome as their first order of business. They banished all the pets and animals and claimed it was to preserve wildlife, but it was actually to keep the resistance out.

Just over 30 years later in 2089, New Life claimed to have scientifically discovered the answer to life and what happens after we die. They built transfer pods, produced letters, and gave them out to people on their 30th birthdays. If you got a letter, that meant you were not in your first life. Some of you got multiple letters. Following this was the eradication of all religions, although it took some time. They began brainwashing the youth, and soon enough transferring became the only religion the people needed. They were fed lies and they believed them. You all…believed them," he said, putting his hands out in front of him, pointing to the people in the room.

Everyone listened to the story intently with a look of shock on their faces.

"Now it is the year 2244. 197 years after New Life took over, and TOP has flourished, prepared, and is now ready to fight to take back our home. We will deliver the truth and take down the New Life government."

One of the kids in the class raised her hand and asked Atticus who the lady on the screen was the previous night and that morning before breakfast.

"Ah, yes. That is Roberta Blake. She is one of the preachers here in the Underground," he answered. "There are many preachers, churches, and gatherings within each religion, but you will learn more about that during our week of religion studies. Please know that it is absolutely your choice as to whether you join a religion or not. It will not be forced upon you and will never be a requirement for you to be here."

Atticus continued teaching the history of New Life and TOP. He went into the war, what it meant, and what used to happen during war. Zinnia's stomach turned. She was driven by her father's death, but fighting was not something she ever thought she'd do in her whole life. They lived in peace at New Life. They knew nothing about war. She wondered what this would mean for the people. She wondered how they were going to take over without uprooting the people's entire lives. Would they look at this as a rescue, or would they hate them for changing the way things have always been? No one ever likes change, but then she thought to herself, *People deserve the truth and the option to choose their own beliefs. It might be uncomfortable, but there's no way I could know the truth and not try to bring it to the people of New Life. You have to stand up for the truth.*

"Uh, whatcha thinkin about over there, space cadet?" Lilly asked, interrupting Zinnia's thoughts.

Zinnia snapped out of her daze to find Lilly, May, and August standing there staring at her. "Ah. Geez, I don't know. Lunch time?" she asked as she stood up and rubbed her eyes.

After lunch, they learned about the Underground politics. Atticus explained in great detail their process for handling decisions.

"Our people bring ideas, complaints, or requests to the Solutions Office and they see to it that it's brought up at dinner. Everyone has a couple of days to add their opinions on their level, and each level designates someone to bring their thoughts on the matter to the Underground. We consolidate the options and present them. Most of the time we come to the same few conclusions. After that we vote individually, not per level. If there are sub decisions that need to be made within the original issue, we address those first and then move on to the larger issue. We don't usually have anything too big to decide on together.

"As you know, things such as hunger don't exist. We all have jobs. Every so often we end up with a few bad apples or people who just can't seem to keep out of trouble. If the crime is big enough, they get sent to a separate underground colony that has no outside access. The only way you can get in or out is through a tunnel that connects between our Underground and Montana's. It falls right below the tip of Idaho."

Zinnia raised her hand.

"Yes, Zinnia. What is your question?" Atticus asked, pointing in her direction.

"How do you decide if someone has to go to that Underground?" she asked seriously.

"Well, we have trials. We all decide together as a whole. This is, of course, after we've tried everything we possibly could to help redirect their behavior. At New Life, they don't have trials. They figured that if New Life was wrong about the crime or who had committed it, the accused just went on to their new life anyway. No big deal. And they didn't really look at it like a punishment. It was more like a clean slate, a second chance to get it right. When they turn 30 in the next life, New Life wouldn't release their past life letters. They were just told that they had a forced transfer before, and this is their clean slate. You usually see those people being the most upstanding citizens who are trying to make up for their past life mistakes, even though they don't know what they were."

Zinnia zoned out, processing what Atticus was saying as his voice faded out. Her brain hurt. She couldn't believe how unjust New Life was. If they didn't know whether they were actually going on to their next lives, then they were just plain being murdered for something they may not have even done. No trial, no voice, no way to prove their innocence. *It's so wrong. It's all so wrong,* she thought to herself.

The girls had some free time before dinner and decided to do their own thing. Of course, Zinnia dove straight into the history books and lessons on her PED. She wanted to know everything there was to know and decided she was going to spend every free minute she had studying. Lilly invited herself to a game of pool in the rec room. She had no idea how to play but insisted the other kids teach her. Zinnia could hear her cheering every time she made a ball into the pockets. May found a fashion magazine full of the most peculiar looking outfits. She flipped through a few pages and found an article giving relationship advice.

"Oh, yes. This is what I'm talking about." She turned over onto her stomach and started reading aloud.

"May, please. I'm trying to study." Zinnia shot May an annoyed look.

"Oh, don't be a brat," May retorted. "You'll have plenty of time to learn this stuff."

"No, May. I won't. Exactly when do you think they plan on starting this revolution? Huh?"

"I don't know. They didn't say."

"Exactly! And judging by the smiles on everyone's faces around here, I have a feeling it's happening sooner than we realize," Zinnia expressed gravely.

"Maybe the people down here are just happy. Anyway, I doubt they're going to expect us to do anything too crazy. We're new," May insisted. Zinnia scoffed and rolled her eyes. "Fine, party pooper, I'll go take this quiz on 'The Perfect Date' with Lilly. She's funner than you anyway."

May got up and left to join Lilly in the rec room. Lilly showed her how to play pool, and they read through the magazine together. They met the people in the rec room, taking time to introduce themselves and having lengthy conversations about life at New Life. Some of the people had lived their whole lives underground. They knew nothing about life above.

After a while, a couple of boys entered the room. "'Sup girls, who might you be?" The taller boy with a large nose asked with a crooked smile. May raised her eyebrows and smiled. The smaller boy looked up at the taller boy nervously and then back at May and Lilly.

"I'm Luke and this is Toby. He's shy. We all call him Fireball, though, because he works in Hell." A few of the people in the room let out a small giggle. "If you don't know yet, that's the heat room on the bottom level, and…if you hadn't noticed, the flaming red hair on his head." He put his hand on Toby's head and ruffled his hair, clearly annoying him.

"What's the heat room do?" Lilly asked.

"Uh… gives us heat," Luke answered with a sneer.

May rolled her eyes, "Hmm… I wonder if you're related to Florian."

"Yep. He's my cousin!" Luke responded proudly.

"Surprise, surprise," Lilly laughed.

Toby flashed an apologetic look in their direction and then looked down at the ground as soon as he saw Luke's eyes on him.

"How is it that you two are nothing like Seth?" May asked, smiling and shaking her head.

"Seth is my uncle by marriage," Luke answered.

"Ah, so the arrogance runs on Florian's mom's side. Got it," May concluded. "Where is his mom, anyway?"

"She's still at New Life. Her sister, my mom, is still there too. And don't talk crap about our moms! You don't know anything," Luke barked back at them.

"Alright, I'm sorry," May said sincerely. "Our mom is still there too. It sucks. I wish she was here with us. We left in a sort of a rush though."

"Yeah, us too. I think that's how everyone ends up here. Go fast or die, unless you're born here…or got here as a baby like Florian," Luke added in a much calmer tone. "I actually never met Florian's mom. My mom told me I had an aunt but she didn't like to talk about her. I found out from Seth that he's my cousin when I got here."

"Well, nice to meet you two. I look forward to seeing you around," May said before she and Lilly headed back to their room.

Same routine as the night before, a prayer was said over the food, they ate a delicious dinner, and snuggled up in their beds. They weren't as tired as the night before. That trek to the tower really took it out of them.

They lay in their beds and exchanged stories with August. She was fairly new there too and her story was crazier than theirs. Her escape involved a flybot and a parachute. The girls listened intently, all the while laughing at Lilly's jokes, petting Cinnamon, and eating caramel candies that August had made in the kitchen. Zinnia thought to herself how she could definitely get used to this. It wasn't just the food, the candy, and the plants. It was the warmth of it all, the comfort, and new friends. Sure, they had jobs just like at New Life, but down there she felt a part of a whole. She felt important, needed. It felt like home, like family.

The next day in class they learned more history, and Atticus listed out what was to ensue in the weeks to come. This included a week of history, a week on religion, a week on traditions, art, languages, and holidays, and lastly, he was going to teach all about how the Underground operated. During the final week he taught them about the water, waste, food, and recycling systems. The sun pods were quite interesting. Apparently, being stuck underground had some disadvantages to their health. Vitamins could only do so much, so they had pods they laid in once a week that imitated the sun, giving them the vitamins they needed, just like the lights for the plants. Atticus also explained the inner workings of the heat room, and after their week on religion, the girls finally understood the 'Hell' reference. They also gained a sickening understanding of the name of the Little Angels Program. The last couple days were reserved for education on TOP's plans for taking back the cities.

This was what Zinnia had been waiting for. Exactly how close were they to this uprising? She got her answer when Atticus revealed that their plan was to destroy the transfer pods in less than five months.

At the end of class on the last day, while May and Lilly were laughing with some of the other people in the classroom, Zinnia pulled them aside, and with great earnestness in her voice, begged them to see the seriousness of what was to come.

"Okay, Z, I hear you. Just tell me what you want me to do," May said with a compassionate and serious tone.

"When we have our free time each night, I really want you both to sit down with me so I can tell you everything I've learned in the last month. I've done all the reading so you wouldn't have to. Tomorrow we go to our assigned jobs. Learn everything you can. Take notes. If you don't understand something, please ask for clarification, otherwise you're going to be dead weight, and could very well, actually end up dead. We have five months to get ready. Five months. That's nothing," Zinnia expressed anxiously. May and Lilly exchanged worried looks but agreed to take things more seriously.

Later that evening while the other girls were off doing their own activities, Zinnia lay in her bed, thinking about everything. Her mind raced out of control. Her anxiety was at an all-time high and nothing seemed to bring her any comfort. She decided to take out her PED and watch some videos she had stored from her parents. She missed them so much. Maybe seeing their faces would help her.

She watched a few videos from her mom first. Mostly video letters congratulating her on her achievements and an occasional birthday video. Her mom wasn't always the best with technology. She spent most of her time on the farm. Her father's videos were detailed and more frequent. Videos for every birthday, every holiday, every achievement, even videos of his progress at New Life, even though she barely understood what he was talking about. He pretty much sent her a video every day. She thought it was a bit excessive at times, but it made her feel loved nonetheless. Although it pained her greatly, she pulled up the last video her father ever sent her. She'd watched it a thousand times, but she couldn't watch it enough.

She grabbed hold of her lightbulb necklace and hit play. A man came up on the screen with a loving look in his eyes. His wavy, dirty blonde hair had platinum highlights and hung just past his shoulders. His beard was full with speckles of white throughout its wiry mane. Zinnia instantly felt comfort seeing his warm, familiar face.

"Hey Z, Dad here. Just sending you a quick note to let you know that I love you, and I'm not gonna make it home for dinner tonight. I'm getting held up at work, but I was able to score a special ration for you. My friend Rob will get it to you later." She stopped the video to think for a moment. She never realized it before but she never did get that special ration from her dad's friend. She never even met him actually. She continued watching the video. "I hear May is settling nicely into her apartment. I haven't had the chance to get over there and check it out yet. I bet it looks great. You remember when I took you to work when you were little? I wasn't supposed to but I couldn't resist a fun day teaching you all about what I do. You didn't understand anything, but as smart as you were, I thought it'd pique your interest and maybe you'd follow your old man's line of work one day. Anyway, I taught you all about the dome shield and how it worked. Of course, I know you were too young to remember any of that. I do believe I also taught you how to spell a few words that day. Shield, dome, electricity…glass. The secret is in the glass," he said and chuckled. "That sure was a nice day together, you and me. Hey, if you ever find yourself feeling stuck in life, remember that beautiful day we spent together and hopefully it'll give you just the right key to get you unstuck. Good memories will always keep us going. Love you, kid. Tell May I love her too."

"I don't get it. You were fine. Then you were transferred. I wish this wasn't the last video I was ever going to get from you. You would know how to help me. You always knew how to help me... I miss you so much, Dad," Zinnia said, as a few tears fell down her cheeks.

Later, while the girls were laying down for the night, Zinnia got up and slid into May's bed with tears in her eyes.

"Come here," May said as she hugged Zinnia tight. She didn't need to ask her what was wrong. She already knew. She was scared too. "Hey, no matter what happens, you have me. I'm right here and I'm not going anywhere. We're not going anywhere." She waved her hand in Lilly's direction, who was completely passed out and snoring. August was snuggled up with her cat, pretending she wasn't listening to their conversation. The girls didn't mind though. They'd grown to become good friends with August, even though she was overly obsessed with her cat.

"I just couldn't bear it if anything happened to you, to any of you. I have this intense feeling in the pit of my stomach. My arms feel cold," Zinnia said as she put her hand on her chest, letting out a few more tears.

"Okay, remember what I told you when you were young and mom fell off the tractor bot? You worried night and day until she got better. You couldn't sleep. You couldn't eat. Worrying isn't going to change what's happening. All it's going to do is make you sick. I know that I don't know what that kind of anxiety feels like, but I'll hold your hand through it and when you feel better, we'll go out there and kick butt."

Zinnia giggled as she wiped the tears from her face.

"Now get some sleep. We start our jobs bright and early. I love you."

"Love you, too."

May kissed Zinnia's forehead and Zinnia crawled back into her own bed, trying her best to take her sister's advice and calm her mind until she drifted off to sleep.

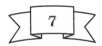

7

The rows of plants went on for miles on the grow level. Rations looked and tasted like cardboard, so to see food as anything other than light brown, gritty bars awakened Zinnia's senses. The fresh smells danced in her nose as she took in all the colors of the eggplants, squash, radishes, and bell peppers. She read the names of the vegetables as she made her way to the herb garden where she was told to meet Florian Astrid for training.

Florian was hosing the dirt on the floor toward a drain when she got there. Knowing she had to work with him turned her stomach. He was the most egotistical person she'd ever met, but she was stuck there for a couple of months. And with the "transfer-pod-take-down" happening in five, she decided she should make the best of it and learn as much as she could regardless of her company.

"Are you going to show me what you're doing, or am I just gonna stand around all day and watch you garden?" she asked after standing there for a few minutes being ignored by Florian.

"I don't know. You think you're ready to get your hands dirty? Cuz, I don't think so," he teased as he pulled a hose down from above the herb garden and started spraying the plants.

"For some reason your father thinks this is where I'll benefit most. Believe me, I'd much rather be—"

"Sticking your nose up in a book somewhere?" Florian interrupted.

"Are you calling me a snob? That's really funny coming from you," Zinnia snapped back.

"Dude, chill. Plants can only grow in a Zen environment," he said, putting his hands out over the plants as if he were casting a spell over them. "You're bringin in the negative energy."

"That's it! I'm going to your dad and asking to be moved right now! This isn't going to work!" Zinnia fumed as she turned to leave.

"Wait! Come back!" Florian chuckled. "I'm just kidding around with you. My dad will get so pissed at me. Just come back here. I'll show you what I'm doing... But I was being serious. The plants do grow better in a calm, Zen environment. I've seen it with my own eyes," Florian said as he pruned a few dead leaves from the basil plants.

Zinnia tried to relax a bit and took a few slow steps back over to him with her arms crossed. "Fine...but I mean it. We need to work together or not at all."

Florian winked at her as the corner of his mouth curled up into a cocky grin. "You got it, princess."

"Ugh!" Zinnia rolled her eyes, pushed up her sleeves, and started looking around the room for a rubber apron like the one Florian was wearing. "If you're not going to help me, I'll figure it out for myself. I'm sure there's plenty of stuff about gardening on my PED."

"You can read all the files you want on gardening but if you don't have a soul, you'll never make anything grow."

Zinnia started turning red, clenched her jaw and fists, and stared him straight in the eyes. "Did you forget that I only just learned what a soul supposedly is? Your insult holds no weight on me."

"Is that why your face is so red?"

Zinnia flipped around quickly as tears started falling down her cheeks. "You don't want to see me mad. I mean it," she said through gritted teeth.

Florian leaned around the side of her. "Are you crying?"

"No. Leave me alone!" She snapped, turning away from him.

"Oh, man. Don't cry. I'm sorry! It wasn't an insult, I swear! You have to have a soul to grow things. That goes for everyone. This is what I do. You want me to teach you, I'm teaching you," Florian explained, taking an apron out of a nearby closet and putting it over her head. "There ya go. Now you're ready to get your hands dirty. First lesson, have a soul, keep it Zen, get your hands dirty, and lighten up," he said as he tossed a pair of gloves at her.

***

Lilly once told her Nana Hopkins that she was going to bring laughter and sunshine to the world. How fitting that Seth said she would bring some sunshine to the tech level. That morning, she shot up out of bed, got ready as fast as she could, set her hair to purple, and flew out the door.

"Alright, see ya later, Lilly!" May yelled out after her, laughing and shaking her head.

The tech level was mind-blowingly huge. There were computers, television bots, music bots, cleaning bots, transport bots, communication bots, every bot you could imagine, and of course, tons of sun-lights and pods. The ground was made of concrete and there were desks randomly scattered around.

Lilly's eyes widened as she looked across the expanse of the room. "Hey Cypher," she said. "What's that over there? And that over there! Oh man, this place is so cool!" Lilly exclaimed as she darted from one direction to the next.

Cypher chuckled. "Hold on. Hold on a minute. I can't keep up with you. One question at a time," he said.

"Sorry! I have this hyper thing. It's no big deal," Lilly said and quickly bent down to grab a piece of metal off the ground. "Why is it such a mess in here?"

"Ah, we just get tinkering around and don't always have time to pick up. Some of the guys down here actually prefer their areas a mess. They say the chaos calms their nerves. Whatever that means." Cypher sighed as he rubbed the back of his neck. "Alright, um, you can start over there. I'll have you learn about the sun-lights. Those are needed the most around here so they take priority."

"Alright, boss. You tell me what to do and I'll do it. I can't wait to learn all this cool stuff!" Lilly exclaimed as she flashed her typical cheesy grin.

***

May was nervous about going to the surface after the cat attack. Working with Zon was the only thing motivating her to go. That alone made it worth it to her.

"Do we have to go all the way back to the vent hatch we came out of?" May asked as they walked down the long tunnel toward the ladder they took when they arrived.

"No, there is a checkpoint not far from the camp you set up on your way in," Zon answered. "We go to the checkpoint, wait for the transport bot, empty the medical supplies, put them in my pack, set the bot to return, and we go home. Simple."

"Okay, but what about the cats?"

"We have dogs," Zon stated, matter of fact, as they reached the ladder.

After he got to the top, he reached his arm down to help May up the last few steps. She gazed into his eyes as she stepped onto the floor of the tower. The small room left little space between them. She had to pull in close to get around him and out of his way so he could close the steel hatch behind her. She started to feel her heart beating in her chest as her cheeks turned pink. She waited for him to open the tower door and as soon as she was outside, she took in a deep breath of the clean air. She definitely needed it after that.

Zon pulled his whistle out from his shirt and blew into it. The dogs turned from their posts and came running up to him with their tails wagging. He let out a joyful laugh as he rubbed each one of them and fed them treats. May smiled, watching the joy on his face. Having never been around animals, this expression of love was foreign to her. It was something almost pure. She yearned for that love for herself. She continued watching them as she put her hand up to her chest.

"Here," Zon said, handing her some treats. "Give them some. They will love you forever." He smiled wide.

May got down on her knees and started feeding and petting the dogs too. She giggled as they licked her face. "This is amazing," she said, looking over at Zon with admiration.

***

After a long, eventful day the girls were completely wiped out. They met in their room for showers and a few minutes of rest before heading to dinner. When they arrived, August was lying on her bed, petting Cinnamon. "Hey guys! How was your first day in the workforce?" She asked excitedly.

"My day was great! I got to learn all about sun-lights! And Cypher, he's great too! I got him to laugh a couple times, which is awesome because he seems a little down all the time. But I have goals! I'll cheer him up and he'll be wearing a smile for at least a week!" Lilly exclaimed.

"That's a pretty lofty goal," May said, giggling.

"How about you? How was your day with Mr. Chunk o' Hunk?!" Lilly teased.

"It was...amazing," May said dreamily. "He has more than just a nice body. I saw a side of him that just blew me away. He has such a sweet, kind place in his heart for animals. It got me thinking, if he can have that much love for an animal, what kind of love is he capable of for a woman?"

May continued chatting with Lilly and August, while Zinnia got her stuff ready for a shower. She was silent, mentally exhausted, and crying always gave her a headache.

"What about you, Z? How was your first day?" May asked.

"I don't want to talk about it," she said before closing the bathroom door behind her.

The girls looked at each other with concerned expressions.

"Just give her a few. She always needs space when she's upset. I bet some food will help," May decided.

"That jerk Florian is probably to blame for this!" Lilly announced.

"Who? Florian? Oh, he's alright. He's probably just giving her a hard time because he likes her," August said, aloof.

May and Lilly looked at her like she was an alien.

After a few seconds Lilly chimed in, "So you're telling me that down here, when someone likes you, they give you a hard time?"

"Yeah, it's how some of them flirt, I guess," August answered.

"Huh, well I guess I've been doing it wrong all these years then!" May blurted out and she and Lilly burst into laughter. "That's absurd!"

"Yeah, it's kind of weird but that's just how guys are down here. Oh, and you have to pretend not to like them too much, or they get scared," August explained.

"Of what?! Someone liking them too much?" May asked, shaking her head with wide eyes, as if searching for the logic in her brain.

"I had a boyfriend once," Lilly announced proudly. "His mom made him dump me, though, as if he could catch my 'orphan,'" she added, shaking her head. "She told him I was trouble. I'm not trouble." She spaced off for a moment.

May gave her a warm smile. "Well, she's a jerk too, then. You have no say in where you come from. She doesn't know what she lost for her son by pushing you out of his life. Moms don't always know what's best for their kids. I was lucky mine let me scrape my knees a few times. We learn from our mistakes."

"Well, aren't those the most motherly sounding words I've ever heard." Lilly said, laughing. "Thanks, May."

***

Zinnia was finally beginning to get used to Florian's personality after spending a few weeks with him. She realized that was simply how he was and taking offense to everything he said was just exhausting. But she didn't think twice about snapping back when he was being over the top. In general, she knew he meant well, even though he lacked tact. She had even started teasing him back.

"How is learning how to garden going to help me with the transfer-pod-take-down anyway?"

"It's not, but we all need to eat," Florian responded.

Zinnia got agitated, grabbed a hold of her necklace, and started pacing around the room.

"Alright there, pacer. You really need to learn to relax," Florian teased.

She stopped pacing suddenly and looked up from her zone. *Pacer. Shortelle. I forgot about them. I wonder what they're doing. I hope they don't get hurt through all of this. They were so nice to me.*

Florian watched her as she continued to pace around the room. "Hey, if you want, I can show you some fighting moves," he said.

Zinnia looked up at Florian, flashing him a dumb expression.

"Or…how to shoot a wave gun," Florian added, trying to offer anything to help her relax.

"What's a wave gun?"

"It's a device that shoots out sound waves so fast it knocks people down. It's pretty powerful. Doesn't kill 'em though, and they're relatively safe for the handler. If it backfires it usually just knocks you down. Although, that depends on if you're holding it right or not. Tim Jacobs took one straight in the ear and now he can't hear out of it," Florian told the story with exaggerated hand movements.

"Well, you're going to have to show me the right way to hold it then," Zinnia decided.

"Will do," Florian responded while leaning his arm on a post above her. "Hey, maybe after I show you a few moves we could go hang out."

Zinnia scoffed. "I don't think so," she responded and uncomfortably tucked a loose strand of her curly blond hair behind her ear.

"Alright…just asking," he said as he put his hands up in the air and turned away from her.

"Is that how you ask all girls out on dates? Piss them off, make them cry, and then think, 'Hey, let's see if she wants to go on a date with me?'" Zinnia shook her head in disbelief.

Florian shook his head, too, and walked away.

"Ha! Looks like I'm not the only one who needs to lighten up!" Zinnia yelled out as she jogged to catch up to him.

Florian stopped and turned around suddenly, making her almost run into him. "You know your feisty side only makes me like you more, right?"

Zinnia scowled as he turned around and walked off again.

"Hey, come here. I want to show you something," Florian yelled back to her. She reluctantly followed. He took her to a small closet with brooms and mops resting up against the door. As busy as the grow level was, she was surprised there was an area hidden away with no one in sight.

Even though she'd rather not be gardening, she had to admit it was all very fascinating. There were separate rooms where they took seeds from the already existing plants and planted them in soil. They waited until the seeds grew little sprouts, which she learned was called germination. Then they took the seedlings to another room where they placed them in bigger pots. All the different plants required different kinds of soil too. After the vegetables and plants started growing larger, they had to control the directions they grew. Some grew up poles and some spread out along the ground. The watering even had to be different for each kind of plant and they all got harvested at different times.

Who knew there was so much to learn about growing food? It was completely different out on the farm. They only grew wheat, and there was only one way to take care of those crops. What really fascinated her were the fruit trees. Peach, pear, apple, plum, cherries, and oranges. The biggest challenge there was keeping the bugs away, although she couldn't blame them. The fruit was delicious.

"Since I'm the only one who sweeps and mops around here at the end of the day…" Florian pointed out, annoyed, and continued, "no one comes over here. It was easy to hide." He stopped in front of the door and said, "You can't tell anyone about this. Promise?"

"Uh…okay," she said hesitantly.

He opened the door and told her to get in quickly. He stepped in after her and closed the door behind him. Inside was a small bush with little brown flowers. She had never seen a bush with brown flowers before.

"I named this plant 'Open Eden.' It has special qualities. When you smell the flowers, it makes you instantly happy. Sometimes it even brings up pleasant memories, like from your childhood, granted it was a good one for you," he said, raising his eyebrows.

"Oh wow. That's amazing. How did you discover this?" Zinnia asked.

"I found it growing in the cracks in the west tunnels when I was helping my dad chart courses for the takeover. Here, smell one."

Zinnia hesitated. She wondered if they should be doing this, but she was intrigued. So, against her better judgment, she decided to smell it. She instantly relaxed and felt a surge of happiness as memories of her father flooded her mind. The feeling was so intense, so amazing, that tears started to fall down her cheeks.

"Woah. It's never made me cry before. What'd you see?" Florian urged.

"My dad. I miss him so much. It was a day we spent together when I was young...when he took me to work. I just watched a video not too long ago of him talking about that day, so that must be why that's the memory that popped up. I don't know." She paused to wipe her face. "He always used to say, 'The secret is in the glass.' I was too little to understand any of it though." She shook her head and changed the subject. "I don't know if this should be in your hands. It's too powerful for anyone to have uncontrolled access to." She stopped talking and thought for a moment and then continued on. "But... I did promise I wouldn't tell anyone. I'm warning you, if this causes any problems, I'm telling your dad."

Florian rolled his eyes. "What harm can it do? It's sitting in a closet that the lazies wouldn't touch if smeared avocados landed them on their butts."

"We'll see."

"Interesting part, if you pick the flowers off the plant, the effects only last for a few smells. Keep the flowers on the plant, unlimited Eden," he added, sailing his hand in the air.

***

May gained a little confidence each day working with Zon. They'd run into a few cats here and there, but Zon blew his whistle and sicced his dogs on them. One day, they were ahead of schedule so Zon decided to take her to a secret spot of his.

"Right through here," he said as he led her through some thick brush and down a small hill. "Here, give me your hand."

"Oh, wow! I've never seen a real waterfall before!"

"Good. You know what this is then."

"We weren't cut off from everything. I mean, we didn't have any waterfalls in the cities, but we learned about them in school," May responded, still in awe.

Zon brought her down to a few large boulders where they sat to enjoy the beautiful landscape. The rocks closest to the bank were covered in moss and branches hung down into the water. There were tree roots deep below the surface causing a ripple in the current. And as she sat there, captivated by the magical scenery, the sun peeked through the trees just right, causing a rainbow to appear in front of the rushing water.

"It's the most beautiful thing I've ever seen," May said, following the water with her eyes. Interrupting her daze, she suddenly heard an unusual sound from behind her. She turned quickly around to see where the noise was coming from.

"What is that?" she asked curiously when she spotted a strange wooden object in Zon's hands.

"This is a guitar. It makes music. Not like the digital noise you're used to," he answered while strumming the strings a few more times.

"Play a song for me," May requested with a half-smile and a twinkle in her eye.

Zon played for her and even sang a few songs. She was completely mesmerized. She couldn't take her eyes off of the motion of his hands. He saw her looking at him in admiration and he gave her a wide smile.

After watching the waterfall for a while longer, Zon got up and sat on a rock closer to her. "So, in the city, you're called a Lover?" he asked inquisitively.

"Uh, yeah. It's weird. I know you guys don't have spurs," May said, feeling embarrassed.

"And why don't you have a love?"

May's cheeks turned a deep shade of pink. "Well, it wasn't for lack of trying. I just couldn't find it. I got hurt every time." She looked at him and then quickly back at the waterfall. "But I haven't let my heart go cold. I'll find somebody one of these days. But anyway, you probably don't want to hear about that."

"Why not?"

"I don't know. Most of the time people don't want to hear about your love life, or your hurt, or failed attempts," May responded while rubbing the back of her neck.

"I want to hear about it. It's a part of you and who you've become. It's through our trials that we gain our strength. That goes for here too." Zon put his fist up to his heart. "The poison of pain needs to come out, not stay in."

May looked away as a tear fell down her cheek.

"I knew love once. She was taken from me by another man," Zon continued.

"Oh, Zon. I'm so sorry."

Zon looked off in the distance. "There is a deep pain in love. Heartbreak is so common that it is often disregarded as something detrimental to your health. To the world, it's not an important pain, not damaging or dangerous."

May agreed. "And people are usually annoyed by the subject, especially when you're going through it because you don't shut up about it," she said, laughing nervously.

Zon picked up his guitar and lifted it into the air. "Music…one of the most beautiful things in this world doesn't shut up about it, and we listen to it every day."

"I think I just fell in love with you," May said dreamily. Zon let out a bellowing laugh and May giggled in embarrassment as her cheeks turned pink again. Zon stood up.

"Come. I want to show you something," he said, reaching his hand down to help her up. He led her back up the little hill and off the rocks. They ended up at the top of the small waterfall. Zon walked over to the ledge and, without hesitation, dove off the cliff above the water. May let out a tiny scream and put her hands up to her mouth. She ran to the cliff to look over the edge and could see him in the water.

"Come on! Jump!" Zon yelled up to her.

"No! I can't!" she yelled back to him.

"Yes, you can! Step on the edge, close your eyes, and jump!"

May paced around for a few seconds. "Oh, my gosh. I can't do this. I can't do this," She paused and looked back over. "Okay. You can do this, May. You can do this."

She stepped to the edge of the cliff. Her heart was beating harder than it had ever beaten before. She took a deep breath, closed her eyes, and then dropped down to her butt. "Nope! I'm not doing it, Zon! Sorry!" She yelled down to him.

Zon let out another deep bellowing laugh as he made his way back to the rocks.

8

"Cypher! Come here, please!" Lilly yelled from approximately twenty feet away. She was sitting cross legged on the ground with parts and pieces all around her.

Cypher slowly walked over to her, shaking his head with a half-smile. "Yes, Lilly. What can I do for you?"

"I did everything you told me to do and the light isn't coming on." She flipped it over and back again. "Light me up!" she said, putting the light up above her head to hand to Cypher.

Cypher leaned far down in front of her, grabbed the light, and flipped it over again. "I think you're plenty lit up already." He cracked a smile again. "It's right here. Just flip that switch before you clamp it down."

"Ah, okay. I get it. Flip the switch, then clamp the lamp."

Cypher exhaled, almost choking. "You're weird," he said, standing back up.

"I know. That's what happens when you're raised by an old lady. You end up with a bunch of old lady jokes. She was funny." Lilly reminisced happily.

"I thought you said you were in the orphan system."

"I was...after she died. Nana Hopkins. She was already old. She adopted me from the Little Angels program after my parents died in a Thrill Seeker accident. Here, I have a video of her telling me the story," she said, standing up to pull her PED out of her pocket. "It was always my favorite story. She recorded it so I'd always have it, and it'd be just like her telling it to me after she was gone."

She hit play on her PED and a wrinkled old lady with gray hair and a warm smile appeared, sitting on a chair in front of the camera.

"It's running, Clair. Go ahead," a voice said from behind the camera.

"That's her friend, Benny. She was never really good with technology," Lilly told him.

"Lilly, my sweet Lilly. This is for you for when I'm gone. Don't you cry for me. I lived a long, happy life, and because of you, an even longer, happier life. My little ball of sunshine. You had the cutest little pigtails. You were just four years old when I watched you talking to everyone in that line. The worker tried to hold your hand to keep you by his side, but you weren't having that," she said, bobbing up and down from a quiet laugh.

"You gave out smiles like candy to the people waiting for their transfers. You had no idea why you were there in that line. I had just lost my husband to a transfer. You see, he was a bit older than me, closer to 200. I still had a few years left. He was just tired and couldn't do it anymore and I tried but I couldn't live without him, so there I was in that line, right across from you. You saw me looking at you and without hesitation you waved and smiled your cute little smile. That smile," Claire said, nodding her head toward the camera with a big smile.

Lilly smiled back as a tear fell down her cheek. Cypher looked at her and she quickly wiped it away.

Claire continued, "I was never able to have children of my own and William never wanted any, so we never considered adoption. That day I did something I never thought I'd ever do. I stepped out of that line and I knelt down in front of you. You stuck your hand out and grabbed ahold of mine. And then you petted my hair and examined my purse." Claire stopped to laugh. "Aw my heart." She put her hand up to her chest and shook her head. Tears started to well up in her kind eyes. "I asked the worker what I would need to do to take you home with me. He said it was a simple screening process and he took both of us up to the adoption office. I sent my signature and the required credits, and that was it. All of my New Life action logs were spotless. You became my little Lilly that day and, well, you remember the rest."

Lilly stopped the video, wiping another tear from her face. "She passed away by herself, not by transfer, when I was 20. I wasn't old enough to be on my own yet so I ended up in the orphan system for the last 10 years. That's how I got a number for a last name." Lilly paused for a moment, lost in thought. "You know, before I came here, I had no idea what an angel was. Now that I know, there's no doubt that Nana Hopkins was my guardian angel."

Cypher put his arm around her shoulder.

"Well, that's my story. What about you? Why are you moping around here all the time?" she asked, stepping back from him so she could see his face.

Cypher expelled another breath of air. "You really don't have a filter, do you?" he said, shaking his head.

"I don't know. What's a filter?" she asked curiously.

He laughed. "Never mind. I lost someone, too, not too long ago."

"I'm sorry," Lilly sympathized.

There was a small pause and Lilly blurted out, "We all lose people. Nothing we can do about that! You never get over it, but loss is a part of life. It's why we gotta cherish the time we're given. I'm not saying you can't be sad, but it can't pull you down forever! Look at me." She pointed to herself and then put her hands up in the air. "You can lose people, because we always do and always will, and we can still be happy."

Cypher smiled again. "Thanks, oh wise one."

"Here! I have an idea! Let's get some sun!"

"I haven't really been using the sun pods lately," Cypher admitted, rubbing the back of his neck.

"Well, there's your problem, silly! Vitamin D! We need it! It makes you happy! But anyway, no, I'm talking about the real thing!"

Cypher raised his eyebrows and objected. "What? No one goes out there. It's not safe."

"Malarkey! I came from up there. Granted, the forest is way nicer than the city, but I mean it. We're going."

Lilly couldn't remember the way out so Cypher had to lead them, disagreeing with it the whole time. There was no way the door guards were going to let them out. Cypher, of course, told Lilly this but she was insistent.

"Oh, I got it! Okay, this is what we're gonna do… I'll go over to the black hole and hang off the railing and make the guards think that I'm going to fall and that I need help—"

"No! Absolutely not!" Cypher cut her off.

"It's fine! Trust me! Up there," she said, pointing up, "my spur is Thrill Seeker. That means I spent my whole life pulling stunts like this. We did every sport, rock climbing, anything that requires upper body strength!"

Cypher shook his head, turned his back to her, and started to walk away. "I'm not going to be responsible for you falling down that hole and dying!"

"Well, you aren't responsible for me. And you can't stop me! You open the door after the guards come to help me," she said as she ran over to the railing without the guards seeing her, popped herself over, hanging on as tight as she could and yelled, "Help! I'm gonna fall! Help!" before Cypher even had a chance to object.

"Oh crap!" he yelled, sprinting for the steel door after the guards ran to help Lilly.

He pulled the door open with all of his might, and the guards turned swiftly around. Lilly jumped back over the railing and kicked both of them in the back of the knees, causing them to drop to the ground. As they fell, they lost grip of their wave guns and they were shot back from the backfire.

Lilly let out a loud laugh and ran to the door. She and Cypher worked together to close it as fast as they could and they booked it down the tunnels.

"You're nuts, Lilly Hopkins!" Cypher yelled as they ran.

Lilly looked over at him, stunned and filled with joy at the same time.

They reached the ladder to Greenwrich Tower and Lilly paused to look at Cypher. "Are you ready for this?"

"I don't know." Cypher hesitated, nervous about what he'd see for the first time above ground. "But it's too late now."

They reached the top of the ladder and Lilly yelled down to Cypher, "Hold on! We gotta open the floor door!" She pushed up and a beam of light shot down onto Cypher's face. He winced and put his hand up to block it.

"Oh geez. I can't see," he complained.

"Oh geez, you're about as fun as a fart in a ZGS!" Lilly teased as she pushed the door all the way up.

They got outside of the tower and Lilly eagerly turned to watch Cypher's face. She couldn't wait to see it light up.

Cypher took a few steps away from the tower and looked around as his eyes slowly adjusted to the light. He noticed the green trees, the blue sky, and little purple, orange, and yellow wild flowers. He saw little animals scurrying about. It took his breath away.

He laughed as he felt the warm sun on his face and took in the biggest breath that he could. All the wonderful smells he had never smelled before, all the bright colors lit up even brighter by the sun. The shadows… They were so big! Birds flew above him and he felt a happiness he'd never felt before. He stood there for a few moments soaking it all in.

Lilly stood by his side with a gentle smile. It really warmed her heart to see him happy.

This little moment was interrupted when they heard a sound coming from the tower. "Oh no, the guards followed us out here!" Cypher said as he started looking around for a place to go.

"Here, let's go this way!" Lilly yelled and darted for the forest.

They eventually found a giant fallen tree with a hollowed-out center, large enough to hide in. They jumped inside and waited, peaking above the broken layers of bark to make sure they hadn't been followed. After a while, when they thought the coast was clear, they emerged and stepped lightly as they looked in every direction.

"Boy was that a close one," Lilly said, wiping the dirt from her pants. Cypher nodded in agreement.

They took a walk around the area, being careful not to wander off too far, in fear of getting lost. They walked and talked for hours. Lilly talked more about Nana Hopkins and how she'd been super lonely since losing her. Cypher talked about his loss too. His story broke Lilly's heart. The person he had lost was his girlfriend, Sarah.

"Someone was horsing around and thought it would be funny to try to balance on the railing you hung from," Cypher said, swatting at a low hanging branch on a tree. Lilly immediately felt bad. "Sarah saw this kid slipping and she ran over to catch him, but he pulled her over and they both fell. I watched the whole thing happen. It happened in slow motion and I can't get the vision of her falling out of my mind." He looked down at the ground and kicked at a weed. "I haven't been the same since."

"I understand that. I lost everyone I ever had when I lost Nana Hopkins."

"But you have Zinnia and May, right?"

"Well, yeah, and they're great... They just have so much going on all the time, what with losing their dad and all," she reasoned, shrugging her shoulders.

"You lost your parents too. Twice," he reminded her and then lightly punched her arm.
She smiled up at him.

"You're alright, Cypher. I like you," she said, lightly punching him back. "Well, we better get back before Seth pops." She looked up suddenly as a thought entered her mind. "Before Florian's Pop pops!" she blurted out and laughed, almost too loud. Cypher exhaled and shook his head.

Once they made it back to the tower, Cypher turned to Lilly and stopped her before they went back in. "I have an idea, Lilly. Let's take that loss, our loss, and let's toss it up to the sky right now, and let it go."

He put his face in the air and his hands out, and she did the same. She immediately felt a peace flood over her. She felt included in this magical moment, like this was exactly where she was supposed to be, where she was always meant to be. Everything she had gone through, brought her to this moment.

Cypher put his arms down and looked at Lilly. "Thank you. I'm glad I met you."

Lilly got a cheesy grin across her face like always. "We're going to be the best of friends! And if I can make you laugh, well that's just a bonus."

***

Lounging around the rec room had become one of Zinnia and May's favorite things to do. Neither of them had Lilly's energy so after a long day of work, they'd rather rest than join in on the thrilling activities Lilly was into. The Underground had large gyms, swimming pools, movie theaters, bowling, and various other classic activities. A few levels up there were some of the more modern gaming systems. They also had team sports for old games like baseball and soccer. Every weekend there was some sort of game happening and each level had their own team. Lilly ended up assigned to the fourth level and their team's name was the Sunflowers. Her upcoming soccer game was against the Goldfinches.

Zinnia and May liked to participate in most of the activities, but not sports, and not after work.

"How is everything going with Zon?" Zinnia asked while she snacked on some popcorn. "This stuff is delicious. It keeps getting stuck in my gums, though. It's really annoying but I can't stop eating it."

May smiled and got a dreamy look on her face. "He is amazing. I got so lucky working with him. He just gets me. Like on a level no one else has."

"What? I get you!" Zinnia objected, tossing popcorn at her.

"It's different. He understands my pursuit of love," she said, throwing the popcorn back at her. "I mean, I actually want to slow down and get to know him instead of just jumping in head first like I always do. I guess if I get to know him first and decide we aren't a good match romantically, then at least I'll still be able to keep him as a friend. I like who he is. I want to be around him. He has a sort of wisdom about him, which is definitely something I haven't seen in any of the other guys I've tried to get to know. The other day, he jumped off a cliff! He tried to get me to do it too but I was like, 'No way!'"

"What? He jumped off of a cliff?" Zinnia asked, leaving her mouth wide open.

"Yes! But he jumped into the water! It was fun to watch," May said and sighed happily. "How's it going with Ego?"

"It's actually not too bad. He's still a jerk, but I'm not taking everything so personally anymore. Once I got used to him, it's actually fun teasing him back. He hasn't told me too much about himself. Apparently, he doesn't know his mom. Never has."

"What about his cousin, Luke? Didn't he say their moms are sisters?" May asked.

"Yeah, they are, but he didn't know Luke and his mom either. They met after Luke got down here a few years ago. After talking to Seth one day, they put it together. Seth had never met Luke either, but he knew his mother at one point."

"Oh, yeah, now that you mention it, I remember Luke saying something about that when we first got here," May added, stuffing some popcorn in her mouth.

"Hey, I'm going to find Lilly. I feel like I haven't seen her much lately," Zinnia said, standing up and picking up the popcorn kernels that landed on the ground.

"Okay. Sounds good. I'm going to see Zon. He's going to show me the art room. He says there are tons of different paintings, sculptures, and apparently books filled with something called poetry…whatever that is. It's all so fascinating."

Zinnia smiled as she got up to leave. "I'm glad you're learning about all this stuff. It makes me happy."

She left the room, thinking to herself how nice it was to hear May talking about anything other than love, and guys, and heartbreak. Not because she didn't like talking about that stuff, but she hated seeing her sister with such a broken heart all the time. She was wary, of course. May getting involved with another guy was always a little scary. She dreaded the thought of having to watch her get her heart broken again, but she knew there was nothing she could do. May was going to do what she wanted and you can't tell someone not to do something. They never listen. They always have to learn the hard way. It's just too bad that other people's lessons have to be heartaches for you as well.

***

Zinnia found Lilly jumping up and down on something that bounced her high into the air. She watched her do all sorts of flips as she ascended repeatedly. Lilly noticed her after a few minutes, jumped down, and greeted Zinnia with a big hug. "Hiya, Z! How've you been?"

"I was going to ask you the same thing! What have you been up to? I haven't seen you much lately."

"Ah, yeah. There's so much to do here! I've just been busy trying out all of these activities. Plus, I'm trying to give you some space. I know how much you like studying and all," Lilly said, looking around at everything going on in the large area.

"Yeah, I like studying, but I like hanging out with my best friend too. Hey, so I have a secret," Zinnia said, lowering her voice and leaning in close to Lilly's ear. She knew she shouldn't tell, but she missed her friend and they'd always had their secrets together. That's what best friends do.

"A secret!" Lilly blurted out.

"Shhh!" Zinnia put her hands up to Lilly. "Come on. We have to go to the grow level. You're gonna love it."

When they got to the broom closet, Lilly stopped. "Um, that's just a cleaning closet. Why are we going in there?"

"The secret is in there," Zinnia said, as she opened the door and motioned for Lilly to go inside quickly. They both entered and Zinnia closed the door behind them.

"What is that? This is the secret? A bush?" Lilly asked, confused. "It sure is an ugly bush."

"This bush is called 'Open Eden.' Florian found it in the tunnels. When you smell the flowers, it makes you happy and you sometimes get flashbacks of happy memories." Zinnia felt a nudge in her heart as she remembered the memory she had when she smelled the flowers before.

"That's so cool! Can I try?" Lilly asked and without waiting for a reply, grabbed at a flower on the bush.

"Wait, wait, wait..." Zinnia stopped her before she pulled the flower off of the plant. "You have to leave it on the plant to keep its potency."

"But it works off the plant, too?" Lilly asked.

"Yeah, just not as long," she answered.

"Cool." Lilly plucked the flower off the plant and put it up to her nose. She inhaled deeply and immediately exhaled with a huge smile. "Nana," she whispered, staying there for a moment in a dream-like state.

Zinnia interrupted her daze. "How is that? Pretty awesome. Huh?"

"I mean, I'm not a stranger to happiness, but that was like hyperdrive happy! I saw Nana Hopkins when she took me out of the Little Angels line. She looked a lot younger than I remember. Of course, I was only four," she said, laughing. "Ah man, Cypher could probably use some of this."

"No! Lilly, you can't tell anyone about this. I promised I wouldn't tell anyone, and if Florian finds out he'll be pretty upset. Not that I care how he feels. I just don't want to get in trouble for not reporting this."

"Alright, Z. You have my word," Lilly said, nodding her head firmly and drawing an X across her chest. "Can I at least bring one tiny little flower to him?"

"No, Lilly!"

"Okay! Okay!" She laughed.

"Hey, Cypher! Look! I just put together 12 sun-lights!" Lilly exclaimed.

"You really picked this up fast," he said, impressed.

"Thank you! I owe it all to a great teacher!" She grinned.

"I don't know about all that," he responded glumly as he walked back toward his desk.

Lilly put the sun-light she had in her hands down and chased after him. "Heya, what's wrong?"

"I don't know. Is there ever a real reason for anything to be wrong?" Cypher asked and plopped down in his chair.

"Woah, Debbie Downer. Negative Nelly. Cynical Cypher! Well, I don't know if that one works but it sounds cool!" She laughed. "But no. Seriously, what's wrong?"

"I don't know. I'm just down. I don't have any energy. I just want to go back to bed and stay there."

"Have you been using the sun pods? We talked about this," Lilly questioned, squinting her eyes at him.

"Yes, Lilly. They don't do anything. The truth is that yes, losing Sarah made me sad for a long time, but I've always been sad…even before her. She helped for a while," he explained.

"Hmm...then your depression is probably chemical and not situational. Cypher, that's good news! We can fix that! I mean, we can at least try," she said excitedly. "I may not be super smart but I know all about mental health!" She lit up as she spoke.

Cypher squinted one eye as he listened to her.

"You're not going to live as long as other people if you don't take care of up here," she said, tapping her temple, "and here," and then pointing to her chest.

"Well, what if I don't want to live as long as other people?"

She jumped right back into her speech. "You gotta charge forward even if you don't want to! Run straight ahead! Don't think about it and don't stop! Eventually, when you feel better, you'll want to," she finished with a pleased look on her face. "Come on. I have something to show you," she said, yanking him out of his chair.

"Where are we going, Lilly?" Cypher asked, as she dragged him along.

"We will need to talk to the doctor about your depression, but I have something that I think will fix you up for a little while," she said, smiling. "But it's a secret. You can't tell anyone. I just can't watch you being all sad any longer."

Lilly took Cypher to the little closet with the bush. She put it up to his nose and told him to smell. Cypher's tense shoulders relaxed instantly as he let out a long sigh. Lilly beamed at him.

"How did you find out about this?" Cypher asked, taking another smell of the little brown flower. "Can I take a few of these?"

"I don't see why not. Just try to take some from the back. I don't want Florian to find out we took these."

"Florian did this? That jerk! Holding out on his friend like this," Cypher said, shaking his head.

"I'm honestly shocked you're just now finding out he's a jerk," Lilly said, laughing. Cypher gave her a sideways look.

"Apparently he found it in the tunnels. And apparently that crazy feeling lasts longer if the flowers stay on this ugly thing," she said as she poked the bush and shrugged. She looked up at him quickly and asked, "Hey did you see anything? Like memories? These things bring up happy memories too! I saw my Nana Hopkins."

"No. It just made me feel happy for a second. These are amazing," Cypher said, looking down at the flowers in his hand.

"Well, come on. We better get out of here," Lilly said as she began pushing him out the door.

He put the flowers in his pocket, turned around, and put his hands up between him and Lilly. "Okay, okay. I'm going."

Later that day, Cypher went to his bathroom for a shower and took the flowers out of his pocket. He wrapped them in a washcloth and hid them at the bottom of the towel basket, but not before taking one more smell. An instant calm came over him. He laid in his bed and enjoyed his Eden. He laid there thinking about Lilly. He had never had a true friend before. Florian didn't count. He could never have shared this side of himself with him. He felt comfortable around Lilly. She was a little crazy, but in a good way. He smiled thinking about her.

A few days went by before he went back to smell the flowers. He felt a pull in his gut. He didn't know what it was or understand it. He just felt like he had to smell them. He *needed* to smell them again. He dug them out from the towels and breathed in, but nothing happened. He sniffed over and over again, but it did nothing. After trying to get them to work for a while, he finally threw the flowers and dropped to the ground, burying his face in his hands. He rubbed his head and took big breaths as tears began to fall down his cheeks. He wiped them away and sat there for a while, searching his brain for a solution. He just needed one more flower to get him through the next few days, before he could get in to see the doctor. After that he would forget about them completely… *What could she possibly do for me anyway?* he thought. *The sun pods don't even work. Lilly showed me outside… It was beautiful, but even that didn't help.* Excuses and justifications circled his mind, eventually leading him to the decision that he had reason enough for it. He'd just take a couple flowers from the back again, to make it not so noticeable. He deserved it. He needed it.

Cypher got to the broom closet as fast as he could and shut the door behind him. He picked a couple of flowers right away and breathed in as hard as he could. His head got light. He instantly relaxed as memories of Sarah flooded his mind. He had lied about not having a memory before. Those were his memories. He wanted to keep them for himself.

He hid the flowers in the towel basket again, visiting it every day. Once in the morning, and again after he was done with the day's bot building.

After a few more days, the flowers stopped working again. In desperation he went back and took more. He kept doing this until he realized that if he kept taking flowers, he was going to pick the plant clean. He thought about how to get more and after hours of justifying his need for the Eden plant again, he remembered what Lilly had said about the effects lasting longer if the flowers stayed on the plant.

"That's it!" He blurted out loud. "I'll just uproot some of the plant. There's absolutely no way anyone would know who did it. There are at least four people who know about the plant. It could be any one of us," he reasoned, pacing around the bathroom. "I'll do it tonight after everyone is asleep."

***

The next morning Florian stormed quickly over to Zinnia, who was watering the green beans. "Have you been taking flowers?" he asked angrily, lowering his voice when he got to the word "flowers." "Half the plant is gone!"

"No. I haven't been in there since you showed it to me," she lied. Her mind immediately jumped to Lilly and she felt her cheeks get warm.

"Well, my plant has been picked clean! And part of the bush itself is gone. I don't know if we'll get flowers again! I've never let the plant lose all of its flowers before. I don't know enough about it yet," he said, fuming. "You're the only one I've told!"

"Maybe someone found it. The room isn't locked," she argued.

Florian took a deep breath. "That's a big fat maybe, Zinnia." He said her name harshly.

"I'll look around. I'll figure it out," she insisted. Her heart was pounding in her chest. She left right away, heading straight for the tech level.

Zinnia marched quickly over to Lilly when she got there. "Lilly, can I talk to you out there please?" she asked as she pointed to the door she had just come through.

"Sure thing!" Lilly smiled nervously.

"Have you been picking flowers off of Florian's Eden plant?" she asked in a panicked tone.

"No! I would never. I kept your secret, I swear!" Lilly lied.

"Lilly, you're the only one I told, and I'm the only one Florian told. One of us picked the flowers and it sure as heck wasn't me!" she yelled as she tried to calm herself down.

"Um, okay. I might have, kind of, accidentally told Cypher about it," she admitted, looking down at the ground. "But he only took a couple, I swear!"

"Lilly, how could you!? I told you not to tell anyone and now he's taken half the plant and all of the flowers!"

"He took half the plant?" Lilly asked nervously.

"Yes! Florian doesn't know if he'll get flowers again! Why would you do that?!" Zinnia demanded angrily.

"My *friend* needed help!" Lilly snapped back at her.

"What's that supposed to mean? '*Friend*,' like I'm not your friend..."

"Well maybe I don't feel like you are! You'll never know what it feels like to have no one! To only have yourself to rely on! Well, I had a chance to be there for my friend and I took it! Why do you think I'm always trying to be there for you? Maybe, just maybe, I'd like that from you once in a while. When was the last time you bragged about our friendship, showed me off like you're proud to have me as a friend, or hugged me when everything was falling apart?" Lilly asked, fuming, and she didn't give her a chance to answer before turning her back and storming off.

Zinnia stood there in disbelief with her mouth open. She'd never seen her friend like this. Lilly had never yelled at her before. She felt hurt and confused. After a few minutes of standing there, she decided that she really needed her sister right then. She dragged herself with a heavy heart and tears streaming down her face.

***

Lilly stormed over to Cypher when she got back into the tech room.

"Cypher, Zinnia just yelled at me and I yelled back at her, which I never do, and now I'm really upset. She said someone stole half of the ugly bush and all of the flowers. Zinnia has never lied to me, so it had to have been you. Please tell me why you would do that."

"I'm sorry, Lilly. I've just been feeling so low lately. It helped me. It really helped me, but only for a little while. I needed more and then I remembered you saying that if the flower stays on the bush it doesn't fade. I didn't take the whole thing."

"That's no excuse! I told you to go see the doctor. You're taking the easy way out. I guess you really don't want to get better." The tears started to well up in her eyes.

"You could never understand," he said as he walked away.

Lilly started to cry as he left the room.

***

Worried someone was going to go looking for it, Cypher headed straight to the plant. He had put it under a sun-light in another closet that wasn't being used, hoping that some flowers might bloom. He also made a locking mechanism to keep the closet door closed. When he got back to the plant, not only had the flowers bloomed, but the plant had doubled in size!

Of course! If this plant can flourish in dark tunnels, then it must be strong and resilient. Give it more sun and it grows wild. He thought for a moment and remembered how good he felt with the real sun on his face. He wondered, *Maybe, if I take it outside it'll keep growing fast and then I'll have a never-ending supply of flowers.*

He started formulating a plan in his head. It was Lilly who got them out of the Underground before. How was he going to do it again? He headed back to the tech level and got to work right away. Lilly watched him from across the room but kept working on building bots. After a couple of hours of tinkering with spare bot parts, Cypher finally created the perfect thing to help him get outside.

He took his contraption and went to the closet that was hiding the bush. He plucked off some of the flowers and put them under a drying bot. Then he crushed them up, put them into a small ball, stuffed it into a bag with the plant, and put it on his back. He snuck up closely around the corner from the guards that were standing in front of the door to the tunnels, took a deep breath, and threw the ball in front of them. They looked around but didn't see anyone, so they bent down and picked it up. After a couple of seconds, the ball popped open and a small cloud of dust puffed out of it and into the guards' faces. They stopped instantly, relaxed, and dropped to the ground, stuck in a daze. Cypher then ran to the door, slipped out, and closed the door quickly behind him.

"Yes! It worked! These flowers are amazing!" he yelled, as he ran down the tunnel, laughing.

He got out of the tower as fast as he could. He didn't know how long a powder version of the flowers would last, but he wasn't going to stick around to find out.

***

Lilly looked around the tech level as her shift was ending and felt a knot in her stomach when she realized that Cypher had already left. She went from level to level looking in all the places she'd seen him go before. After having no success in tracking him down, she headed straight for her room, hoping maybe May might have seen him or could at least help her find him.

As she entered the room, she saw Zinnia with tears in her eyes, hugging May. Still upset from their fight, she let out a heartless, "Oh."

This hit Zinnia in the gut and she turned and ran into the bathroom, crying even more.

"Lilly, what's up with you? You don't seem like yourself. Talk to me," May insisted as she sat on her bed and patted it, telling Lilly to sit down too.

"I just wanted to help him, like I've always helped Z. She doesn't appreciate anything I've done," she said, sitting next to May on the bed.

"You know that's not true. She loves you. You two have been through everything together. We had no idea that you've been bottling up all of these feelings. How can she fix something she doesn't know she's doing? This plant situation is nothing. You two have been through way more than this. I mean look where we are," May pointed out, putting her hand on Lilly's.

Lilly giggled as a few tears fell from her cheeks. "True… I didn't know I was bottling them either."

Zinnia opened the bathroom door and leaned up against the doorway, holding onto her necklace. "I didn't know you felt that way, Lilly. I know I've been wrapped up in this takeover and stressing about it. I guess I just thought you were indestructible. You always seem to have it together. I didn't think you needed any sort of strength or validation from me. I barely have enough for myself," she said, looking away. "Nothing ever seems to scare you, and everything scares me."

"I am scared. I'm scared all the time, but I do what has to be done anyway. Plus, I always try to be there for you." Lilly told her in a nicer tone.

"You're right. You have always been there for me. I'm sorry I didn't think about how you must be feeling with all of this. I'll work on getting out of my head and being there for you more."

May motioned to Zinnia to join them on the bed. "Being there for others pulls us out of our self-pity."

Zinnia sat down and instantly burst into laughter. "Where'd you read that, May?"

May joined in the laughter too. "In one of those magazines in there," she answered and pointed toward the rec room. "But hey, I'm guilty of it too. Do you girls want to talk about guys? I mean, I haven't thought to ask if you're holding onto any feelings of love. Are you afraid to talk to me because I talk about my love life all the time?" she asked teasingly.

"Ugh." Both Lilly and Zinnia rolled their eyes and stood up.

May hopped up quickly. "Hey, come here you two," she said, putting her arms around both of them. "I love you girls. We will get through this. No more of this fighting business. Deal?"

"Deal," they agreed in unison.

Lilly suddenly remembered why she went to May in the first place. "I'm worried about Cypher. He left the tech level before the shift was over. He's been depressed and he was using the flowers to feel happy. He went crazy over them ugly things. I tried to get him to see the doc but he wasn't having it."

"Do you have any idea where he might have gone?" Zinnia asked.

"I looked everywhere I could think of...*here*," she said nervously.

"What do you mean, '*here*'?" Zinnia asked.

"Like down here," she answered, pointing down a few times. May and Zinnia looked at each other.

"Wasn't he born down here? Can he even go up there?" May asked.

"Well, yeah, he was fine. He loved it actually. Cypher and I sorta got in trouble for leaving the Underground. They said it was too dangerous to go above ground because New Life has bots patrolling. We got extra cleaning duty," she said, looking down. "But it wasn't a punishment! They said it was a 'learning opportunity,' and it was actually part of the reason you haven't seen me around much lately. I was too embarrassed to tell you."

"Let's go," Zinnia said, as she headed for the door.

"Where are we going?" Lilly asked as she followed her.

"Outside."

"I don't know how we're gonna get outside. I distracted the guards last time. They aren't fallin' for it again," Lilly pointed out.

"We'll figure that out when we get there, but we need to find Florian first," Zinnia added.

10

Florian was angry with both Zinnia and Lilly when they told him everything that happened, but he agreed they'd better go find Cypher. They headed for the tunnels and tried to work out a plan. May offered to try to convince the guards that she was supposed to meet Zon outside. Only Runners are allowed up and she wasn't technically a Runner yet. She went outside every day anyway. Who knows, maybe it would work.

They got to the door and immediately saw the guards sitting on the ground in a daze with a small metal ball in front of them. One of the guards started rubbing his head and looking confused. Lilly saw this and whispered, "Come on! Let's go!" waving at everyone to follow.

They pushed their way through the hatch and exited the tower quickly. Once outside, they stopped dead in their tracks. In front of them stood Cypher, seemingly frozen in place. He was staring at what looked like hundreds of vines with the brightest flowers of every color they had ever seen, stretching across the ground and stopping once they hit the shadows of the forest's trees. They looked down and saw the plant that Cypher had taken, rooted into the ground.

At this point, Zon and his dogs arrived and the dogs started barking erratically at the plant, growling, and frothing at the mouth. He blew his whistle and yelled at them to back up, but as they were backing up, the dog closest to the plant dropped to the ground and began shaking.

Zon covered his mouth and nose, sprinted over to the dog, picked it up, and hurried to get away from the plant as quickly as he could. As this was happening, Florian stepped in front of the girls and put his arms up backing them away from the plant. May broke away from Florian's barrier and ran over to Zon as he cradled the dog in his arms. Tears began streaming down her face as she dropped down to the ground beside him.

"No, come on! You're okay! Come on. Wake up. Wake up!" Zon yelled over and over again as he hugged his dog.

"What's happening to him?" May asked. The sight of Zon in so much pain was crushing her.

"I don't know," he answered. He started wiping the saliva from the dog's mouth.

Suddenly, the stiff shaking body lying in his arms, relaxed, twitched, and then let out its final breath.

Zon looked down at his dog's face and cried out in agony, "No! Ah, no! Nooo…" His deep bellowing cries carried out far and echoed through the trees, causing the nearby birds to scatter from the branches they were resting on.

His mourning was interrupted when he heard the others gasping and crying out. Cypher had dropped to the ground and was now shaking and frothing at the mouth too. Florian crouched down to the ground as he reached to grab Cypher's leg and dragged him away from the plant.

Zon set his dog in May's arms, ran over to Cypher, picked him up, and quickly headed for the tower. The others opened the door and followed him down the ladder.

May set the dog down next to his pack who immediately lowered themselves to the ground and began howling. They started licking him, putting their chins on top of him, and poking him with their noses. May took a few steps toward the tower, but turned back to look at them once more. She watched as they mourned over their friend and her heart hurt as she heard them crying nearly all the way down the ladder.

***

The group filled Dr. Sherlie Windon in on everything that happened. The plant, the dogs, Cypher's bizarrely intense desire for the plant, everything.

"It's no secret that dogs' noses are stronger than ours. It must have hit them faster than it hit Cypher," Zon reasoned.

"Get out of the way!" Doctor Windon yelled as she hooked Cypher up to a bunch of different machines the girls had never seen before. "His lungs are failing. I don't know if we can fix this. We used our last lung bots last week!" she stressed as she continued caring for him urgently.

Right then, Lilly stood tall and boldly offered, "Take mine."

"Are you kidding me?! Get out of here!" the doctor yelled at the girls and Florian immediately pushed them out of the room.

"Lilly, what are you doing!?" Zinnia demanded once outside of the surgery room.

"What?! I'd do it for any one of you."

"That's sweet, Lilly, but now is not the time for heroics," she said as she grabbed her necklace and started pacing around the room.

"I have an idea!" May said quickly, pulling out her PED. "I was given contact with the inside guy, Rob. I'll message him and tell him we need lung bots, and tell him it's an emergency!"

"Isn't the need for organs always an emergency, May!?" Zinnia yelled in frustration.

"Z! Chill out!" May yelled back.

Lilly nodded her head quickly. "Yes! Do it, May! Tell him it's for Cypher! He's gotta know who he is since he's been sending him bots!"

She got her message sent to Rob and reassured them, "He usually gets back to us pretty quick."

After a few excruciatingly long minutes of waiting, a message dinged on her PED. She opened it quickly and read out loud. "I'll see what I can do. I had to slow down on the amount I was taking. One of my guards noticed and then notified me that bots were going missing. I'm sorry to hear about Cypher. Stand by."

"If he's able to get the lungs, Zon and I will have to run. You two stay here and..." She paused for a few seconds, looking back and forth between Zinnia and Lilly and with a piercing seriousness in her eyes said, "Pray."

After a few more moments, a message came in confirming that Rob had successfully acquired lungs. Lilly burst into tears of relief.

"Stay here. I'm going to get Zon."

May slipped quietly into the surgery room and tapped Zon on the shoulder. He turned around and went out with her.

"Rob got lungs. We need to go now," she insisted.

"May, I'll go. You stay here with your sister. I'll have to run. You won't be able to keep up."

"I can! I've done this run with you a bunch of times! I'll keep up! I promise!" she begged.

He looked into her eyes and saw the unwavering passion within them. He knew there was going to be no changing her mind. "Let's go," he said as he jetted off quickly.

May followed him, setting off into a full sprint. She steadied her breathing, determined to keep up. She wouldn't accept it any other way. The sun was starting to go down now and she could feel the cool air on her face.

"Cover your mouth!" Zon yelled back to May as they exited the tower and prepared to pass the plant. They were suddenly shocked to see hundreds of birds nestled on the plant's flowers.

May waited until they were far enough away from the plant before yelling out to Zon, "What was that?"

Zon yelled back, "I don't know but we don't have time to stop. We'll have to worry about that later!"

Zon blew his whistle and the dogs set off running too. A small group of them bolted ahead of the others to lead the pack. They heard the screeching of feral felines fading in and out as they ran past overgrown patches of thick forest. They looked up as something flying over their head caught their eye. There were hundreds of the colorful birds soaring right above them.

Zon yelled back to May, "I don't know what they're doing!"

"Aren't they warning the forest creatures about the cats?" she yelled to him.

"Normally that's the case, but they've never run with my pack like this before!"

May and Zon's running stirred up such a commotion that hundreds of cats started jumping out, slicing and slashing, as they launched themselves aggressively at them. The dogs did their best to fight them off, but began to slow down as too many cats jumped out ahead. All of a sudden, the birds started diving down, stabbing effortlessly through the cats as their beaks severed them in half one by one. This was so mind-blowing that May and Zon couldn't take their eyes off the blood bath unraveling in front of them. Then the birds started circling around them like a tornado, keeping the cats out of the tube-like barrier they had created. As they reached the checkpoint, the birds didn't leave their side for a second.

"Now we wait!" Zon yelled out over the deafening screeching and flapping of the circling birds.

After what felt like hours, they saw a break in the birds as the arriving transfer bot lowered down into Zon's hands. He took the lungs out, set the bot to "return," and began the race back to the tower, with the dogs repositioning themselves into their protective formation. The birds continued to circle around them, fighting off the cats as they went. The run back to the tower felt longer than the run to the checkpoint had been and May felt a deep tugging in her gut, just hoping they weren't too late.

They were shocked once again when they arrived at the tower and saw that with the sun down, the plant's colorful flowers had shriveled up and some of them had turned back to the ugly brown color they were before. Some had dried up completely, spilling their dust on the ground as if they had been set on fire and all that remained was ash. Again, they didn't have time to stop. They exchanged confused looks before entering the tower.

They made their way back to the surgery room and were greeted by a crowd of worried friends. Those who were lying or sitting down immediately jumped to their feet as they caught sight of their arrival. Seth patted Zon on the shoulder as he headed straight for Cypher. May went over to Zinnia who had been holding Lilly's head in her lap.

Now they wait again.

After hours of coffee, sleep deprivation, and the early morning bustling of the crews, the doctor stepped outside of the surgery room, looking exhausted but relieved.

"The lungs attached successfully. He's taken to them quickly and is now recovering," she said as she wiped the sweat from her forehead.

The entire room burst into cries of joy and relief while hugging each other.

"Oh, thank you, Jesus!" Roberta Blake yelled out.

"He'll need to rest. He should wake up by tomorrow. In the meantime, I suggest you all go rest after that stressful night," the doctor said and started shooing everyone away from the door.

Everyone took turns shaking the doctor's hand or patting her shoulder as they left, giving her many thanks. Zinnia approached her after everyone had said their goodbyes and asked her opinion about the plant. Completely exhausted, she answered that she didn't know enough about it, but after some sleep they would reconvene to discuss their observations and come up with a plan on how to handle the plant going forward.

After everyone got some much-needed rest, Lilly and Florian decided to go visit Cypher. Lilly was so antsy to get in to see her friend, she could hardly contain it. She wanted to jump up and down and squeeze him really tight, but she knew she needed to stay calm so she didn't break him.

"How are you doing, friend!?" she asked, standing on her tippy-toes and clasping her hands up to her chest.

He coughed a couple of times, looking sleepy but happy to see his friends.

"Hey, bud. You really scared us all for a minute," Florian began while holding onto the railing attached to Cypher's bed. "Need you, dude. Can't be goin' off on your own like that."

Cypher looked at Florian apologetically, cleared his throat and said, "I know. I don't know what came over me. It's like the plant took control of me." He adjusted uncomfortably. "I guess it took me nearly dying to get away from it." He laughed weakly.

"It's not just you, Cypher!" Lilly interrupted. "Sam Sanders, back at New Life, got hooked on junk food so bad he had a heart attack and almost didn't make it! Those darn Foodies," she remembered, shaking her head in disbelief. She quickly changed the subject as if she was bursting with curiosity and information she needed to get out to him. "Hey, that little ball thingy you used to get past the guards was sure neat! How'd you do that? How did the plant root into the ground like that? Did it just fall out of your hands?"

Cypher winced as he shifted again to give his airway more room to breathe. "I put a timer on a bot and filled it with dried, crushed up flowers. It exploded in the guards' faces and I ran out. And yes, it just fell out of my hands and rooted."

Florian furrowed his eyebrows and asked curiously, "How'd you get more flowers? You had just taken the plant that morning and there weren't any more flowers left from what I could tell. Even if there were a flower or two, I doubt that would have been enough to fill that ball you made."

"I put it under a sun-light that morning and when I got off my shift the plant had grown," he answered.

Florian thought for a few seconds. "I was afraid to put it under a sun-light. I didn't know what it would do so I was taking my time with it. This might actually help us, bud. You're a genius. Well, we're gonna get out of here and let you rest. Right?" He looked at Lilly when he said this.

She nodded quickly, pushing herself up onto her tippy-toes again. She wrapped her arms around herself and said to Cypher, "Air hugs!"

Cypher laughed lightly and nodded in her direction.

Later that day, Seth called a meeting with all of those involved in the events regarding the Open Eden plant. He was clearly upset about everything that had happened but pushed past his immediate emotions.

"What I want to know is where this plant came from, who had it in their possession, and how it put Cypher in the hospital. How did a plant this dangerous go unnoticed?"

Florian cleared his throat and answered, "It wasn't dangerous at first. That's why I named it Open Eden. It makes you happy for a few seconds when you smell it."

"Nearly dying is worth a few seconds of happiness?! Is that what you're telling me, Florian?!" Seth snapped at his son.

"I had no idea it would bloom and grow that fast under the sun! It had brown flowers in what I'm assuming was its dormant state. I was still studying it," Florian quickly replied, defending himself.

"I'd like to get a few samples of the dormant plant when we're done here," Doctor Windon added with raised eyebrows, nodding in Florian's direction. Florian nodded back.

"You should have told me about it. This has stirred up quite the commotion." Seth shook his head and looked down. "The strange bird behavior still doesn't make any sense to me," he added before sitting back in his chair and tossing his pen down on the table.

"If I may say," Zon spoke up, "we saw the birds resting on the flowers on our way out of the tower. I think the plant that nearly killed Cypher somehow made the birds stronger, faster, and smarter. I've never seen them behave like that before."

May leaned forward at the table and nodded her head in agreement.

Seth looked around at each person in the room and with great seriousness announced, "I'll be addressing the Underground at dinner."

Zinnia felt those faithful chills down her spine as everyone stood up. She felt deep down in her gut that this was the time she had spent all of those hours preparing for. She was scared. She just hoped that her sister and best friend were ready for what was to come.

After Roberta Blake was finished with the dinner prayer, Seth appeared on the screen to address the Underground. Zinnia assumed he was going to announce their advancement into New Life, but to her astonishment he did no such thing. He informed TOP all about the plant and everything that happened. The only thing he left out was Cypher's name. It shocked her that this situation wasn't being kept a secret, showing her once more the intriguing togetherness of this community.

"Nothing has changed our course of action and I want you all to continue on as planned. We will let you know as soon as we have more information about the plant. Thank you," Seth said as he finished his speech.

As per usual, Lilly was the only one with any sort of energy the next morning. She hummed to herself happily as she put on her fiber optic hair extensions.

"Lilly, I'm begging you. Please bottle some of that energy so we can have some," May pleaded through profuse yawning.

"You know, exercise gives you energy! Supply and demand! You gotta use energy to get energy!" Lilly proudly educated as she selected the rainbow setting on her hair.

"I am not looking forward to today's gardening. Who knows what kind of mood Florian's going to be in after getting yelled at by his dad," Zinnia said as she zipped up her jacket.

"Alright, time to start the day. See you all at breakfast. I'm going to see if August needs any help," May announced as she headed for the door.

May had finally received her official "Runner" badge after proving herself capable of handling the outside. Zon gave his recommendation and, considering they saved Cypher's life, the Underground agreed.

After breakfast May headed outside to help Zon feed the dogs, but he wasn't in the usual spot when she got there. She pulled her PED out and called him.

"Hey, I'm here for work. Where are you?"

"I'm around the corner. Walk north," Zon said through the PED before disconnecting the call.

"Okay…" she said, looking around confused. She was still getting used to navigating. She eventually made her way to a large cement enclosure with a cement roof that was covered by a veil of weeds, moss, and other greenery. It surrounded what looked like a garden, only there was mostly just dirt inside. Zon's dogs were standing guard around it. Inside she found Zon standing over a pile of dirt, holding a shovel. She looked up from the dirt and could see the somber look on his face.

"Come here. I want to show you something," Zon said, setting his shovel against the wall. "Have you seen this before?" he asked.

"No. I haven't."

"This is called a graveyard," he said, holding his arms up and looking around the cemented area. "This," he said and pointed his hand down to the pile of dirt, "is a grave."

She looked at him more confused than ever but didn't say anything.

"This is what we do with people, or animals, when they die. We bury them."

"We don't bury…well, obviously not animals…but we don't bury people," she said.

"I know. This is why I wanted to show you. Where you come from, people are thrown into trash compactors and disposed of as if they are nothing more than the garbage you throw away every day. Human beings have stopped believing that lives have any sort of meaning."

"That can't be true. Zinnia and Lilly's lives have meaning. Your life has meaning," May said passionately as she reached over and grabbed Zon's hand, stepping in closer and looking up at him.

"Well, I know that," he said, laughing. "Do you know now that yours does too?"

Her heart started to beat faster in her chest. Embarrassed, she began to pull away but Zon pulled her in closer and wrapped his arms around her, holding her in a soft embrace. Calm flooded over her as she started to feel strangely safe and protected. She melted into him, wishing she could stay there forever.

***

Florian set new sun-lights above a row of sprouting tomato plants. He had spent a good part of the morning thinking about what Cypher said about the plant growing under the sun-light. How would the sun-light make the plant grow but not to the extent it grew once outside in the real sun? His dad gave the rest of his plant to Dr. Windon so she and some of the TOP scientists could run tests on it. He just hoped they would come up with some answers. He was sure he wouldn't be included in anything now that the plant was out of his hands, especially after keeping it a secret from his dad.

"Florian, I need your help with the peas. They're growing too big for the support," Zinnia said as she tried to tie up a bunch of the vines.

"I see that as the opposite of a problem," Florian responded sarcastically.

"What's up your butt? You've been grumpy all morning," Zinnia pointed out.

"Wouldn't you be if Lilly almost died? Or your sister?"

"Of course, but I didn't take you as being the down-in-the-dumps kind of person," Zinnia laughed lightly. Florian went silent for a while and Zinnia started to feel uncomfortable. She'd never seen him so serious, so somber.

After a few minutes, he seemed to come out of his daze. "It's my mom," he said. "My dad always told me that she wasn't a good person. She didn't care if people got transferred. Said she'd pushed for it even…said she pushed for me…" He stopped talking suddenly and Zinnia felt like he was trying not to show her too much emotion, trying to hold back tears.

"I don't want to be like her," he added, changing in an instant from sad to angry. "I've been thinking about the bomb Cypher made to knock the guards down. We could make a bunch more and use them when we go to take down the pods. That way we'll have more than just the wave guns. If we don't have to fight as much with our fists, maybe less people will get hurt. The more people we can save, the better."

"And…I definitely didn't take you as the want-to-save-people's-lives type," Zinnia laughed again, still feeling incredibly uncomfortable.

"Seriously? When did you become the laughs-at-serious-subjects type?" Florian rolled his eyes at her before tossing down his gloves and walking away.

She jogged after him and stopped suddenly when he turned around, almost running into him. "I'm kidding. I think that's a great idea. You should talk to your dad. I'm sure he'd love the idea too."

"Doubt it. Doubt he'll listen to anything I have to say after that crap," he responded in defeat.

"Let's just see what Dr. Windon and the other scientists say. They will have a better idea of what we're dealing with. I think you should just talk to your dad. He can't stay mad at you forever.

"We'll see," he grumbled.

***

Dr. Windon and the scientists were able to run tests on the dormant plant and were now discussing the possibility of running tests on the mature plant with Seth in the meeting room.

"—that means we would have to take another piece of the plant out into the sun. It might be risky, but if we can build a box around it big enough to create a shadow but still allow a small amount of sunlight in, we might be able to control its growth while also containing its toxins," Dr. Windon suggested.

"Well, I trust you will be more than capable of carrying out this experiment successfully and without any harm to your team. I'll leave this in your hands, Dr. Windon. Please let me know if there is anything I can help you with and thank you for keeping me informed," Seth said as he shook her hand and smiled warmly.

Florian approached him as he was heading back to his office and said, "Dad, can I talk to you for a minute?"

"What do you want, Florian? I'm busy cleaning up your mess," he replied, clearly still upset.

This hit Florian hard in the gut. A lump of guilt got stuck in his throat but he cleared it and began. "I was thinking…about Cypher and how he got past the guards. The ball he made shot out a cloud of flowers that he had dried and crushed up. I was thinking that maybe we could build more of those flower bombs and use them when we take down the pods. That way we'll have more than just the wave guns."

Seth thought about it for a moment. "That sounds like a good idea, but we still don't know enough about the plant. We would need to do some more tests. Who's to say the powder doesn't also take root?"

"I don't think that will happen. The effects of the brown flowers only work off the plant for a few days it seems. Dried, and obviously inhaled, they knocked down the guards and only kept them down for a couple of minutes."

"I guess we could have Dr. Windon run a test on the powder to make sure it doesn't take root and grow," Seth said before entering his office and closing the door behind him.

Florian was still hurt, but he was happy he listened to him, for the sake of the citizens of New Life. He loved that his dad had always been able to separate his personal emotions from business.

***

"Good afternoon, Ms. President. I'm here to report," Colton announced firmly as he entered Sophia's office.

"Please... Colton, be quiet. I have a migraine. Can't you see that my office is dark?"

Colton looked around the room for a moment. "With respect Ma'am, why not go to your home and rest?"

"There is work to be done and no one to do it," she said slowly while pressing her fingers against her temples.

"What about President Liam?" he asked.

"He's off with his family...again." She stood up and slowly started pacing around the room, hoping that the movement would distract her from her pounding head. "Well...report."

"No news so far about Dr. Waters' daughters. One of the guards in transfer storage noticed supplies going missing and decided to keep an extra watch on the supply room. He reported seeing Officer Bailey taking lung bots from the room, so he felt it necessary to notify me."

"Bring the medical supply manager in for questioning. Do the questioning yourself," Sophia said, sitting back down in her chair and resting her head on her arm.

Colton walked behind her and began rubbing her shoulders. "You're so tense. I really think you should go home and rest."

"Colton, what have I said about this at work? You know Liam could walk in at any moment and that would be the end of us," she said while turning her chair and painfully looking up at him.

He bent down and kissed her forehead. "I know…but I mean it. Go home and rest. How will you lead us if anything were to happen?"

She thought for a few moments and exhaled. "Perhaps you're right. I'll just take a little nap. Let me know what you find out from Mr. Bailey," she said as she rose up from her chair, walked to the door, and held it open for him. She gave Colton a loving smile as he stepped into the doorway, and he returned the look as he exited the office.

***

Rob Bailey had been undercover for years. He'd never had a problem getting medical supplies and bots to the underground until now. He worked closely with other undercover TOP members, and supplies went from one person to the next very quickly via bots that had been disconnected from the New Life system.

Rob entered Colton's office. "How can I help you?" he asked.

"I've been given a report from one of your guards that supplies have been going missing. The issue was brought to your attention, but you didn't see it as a problem?" Colton asked and waited for Rob's answer.

"After he mentioned it, I began to keep a better watch on things and haven't noticed a change. I dismissed the guard's concerns due to the fact that I was already in the middle of an inventory count."

"Why would an inventory count be necessary? If all supplies are logged, tracked, and filed according to regulations, there would be no need to count. Unless, of course, you yourself have noticed supplies going missing." He raised his eyebrows suspiciously. "In which case, why have you not reported the possible missing supplies yourself?"

Rob started to feel uneasy and swallowed the lump in his throat. "Uh, it was just a precaution. The extra security and the extra people around—"

Colton abruptly interrupted. "The extra security would keep supplies FROM going missing, wouldn't you say, Mr. Bailey?" Colton demanded, clearly starting to get angry. "And what is this I've heard about you taking a lung bot out of storage?"

Panic began to settle in and he frantically searched his mind for an excuse. "I was having the lung bot tested. I had gotten word that one of them didn't attach to a patient," he blurted out, trying to hide his nervousness.

Colton stared at him for a few moments. "I want you to know, I see something very wrong when a guard comes to me about my supply manager," he said seriously, standing up from his desk. After a few seconds of locking eyes with Rob, he continued, "I want those numbers when you finish with your inventory. You will do the inventory with the help of my guards, and I want the report on the lung bot not attaching. I've never heard of such a thing before."

Rob nodded his head and stood up, trying to conceal his trembling, and left Colton's office panicking inside. He searched his mind for something, anything, that he could come up with to solidify his excuse.

***

Cypher had been released to return to work. Organ bots sped up the healing process and in two days it was as if nothing had happened.

"I think I better work on making more organ bots. I've been too wrapped up in sun-lights," Cypher decided as he sat at his desk to get the day started.

"What other bot projects you got goin' on around here?" Lilly asked, looking around the room.

"Well, you've seen most of them. I have a few side projects I just haven't had the time to work on with the upcoming events and all. After what happened, I really need to stop dragging my feet," Cypher admitted, rising from his desk and walking toward the back of the tech level. He led her to a large sliding door and she stared up at it, wondering why she hadn't noticed it before.

Once inside, Lilly turned her head straight up and her jaw dropped open at the countless number of bots hanging on long towering walls. There were thousands and thousands of bots and bot parts. Cypher continued walking toward the back of the stock room with Lilly following closely behind.

"Back here I have a flybot I'm almost done building, a few different organ bots I've been working on... Rob got me the blueprints for the flybot and a ZGS. Obviously, he couldn't sneak either of those out," he said, taking a cover off the flybot and sending dust everywhere. "We can't really do anything with a ZGS at this point, unless we need antigravity for some reason. So that one isn't really a priority."

Lilly's eyes were wider than ever. She started walking around the massive room and inspecting every bot she came into contact with. "What are those?!" she yelled out as she pointed to the corner of the room where there were enormous machines with sharp points on the top and a solid tube encompassing them. Right behind them were gigantic bay doors. "Where do those doors lead to?"

Cypher laughed at how excited she was. "Those are the drills we're using to come up from the tunnels into New Life. We don't need to work on those though. They're already done. More than done, actually. We made a few extra just in case. The doors open up and the drills drive back onto a lift that takes them down to the subways. We'll be loading them onto the trains and..." He stopped when he saw the confused look on her face. "Trains are kind of like ZGSs but they are attached to the tube instead of hovering and don't go as fast."

"Ahhh..." she said as a light came on in her eyes.

"The different trains will take the drills to certain checkpoints and when we get the signal, each drill will start drilling," he continued. "The drill is...well, obviously it's the sharp point at the top and the tube around it will catch the dirt and debris, and the tube behind it will take it back down the subway we came through. The dirt has to go somewhere," he said matter-of-factly.

Lilly walked behind the drills and inspected them too. "How are these short tubes going to take all the dirt all the way back through the subways?"

"Oh, those extend out pretty far, but we have more tubing we'll be taking with us."

"So, does that mean the dirt is going to clog up the subways? How are you going to get back through?" she asked, concerned.

"I don't know," he chuckled. "I guess a few of us don't think we're coming back."

"WHAT DOES THAT MEAN, CYPHER!?" Lilly yelled at the top of her lungs, turning a deep shade of red and lifting herself up onto her tippy toes in a futile attempt to get closer to his face.

"Oh geez, why are you yelling, Lilly?" he asked, covering his ears.

She stared at him with intensity, and he felt like he was being scolded by his mother.

"Okay, sorry…" he said, looking frightened.

"Too soon, Cypher. Too soon!" she said, still staring him down.

"Apparently… I won't do it again, Mom," he teased, not taking his eyes off her. "Anyway, I was just kidding. They won't clog up the tunnels completely. Roberta's team still has to travel down the subways afterwards to help the citizens."

Being the happy person she was, Lilly couldn't hold her serious demeanor for long. She broke down and punched his arm with a smile and let out a long breath. "Don't talk like that. I can't stand to think about losing you again." She shook her head as if trying to shake out the bad thoughts. "How are you feeling by the way? I mean emotionally and whatnot."

"Oh, I'm doing fine. The doc gave me meds. They're pretty fast acting. I just mostly feel stupid and pretty embarrassed about all of it," he admitted while rubbing the back of his neck and turning a slight shade of pink. "I'm glad you came looking for me, Lilly," he added seriously. "I don't know what would have happened. I feel horrible about Zon's dog." Tears started forming in his eyes but he held them back.

She suddenly got an excited look on her face and changed the subject. "Can you show me the subways? Can you take me that way?" she asked, pointing toward the bay doors. "I'm sure Zon doesn't hold you responsible. No one could have known that was going to happen."

"I guess I can show you," he said as he went to the panel next to the door and pressed a button.

Lilly whipped around and hopped up and down a few times, waiting for him to pull the bay door up.

"…and thanks. That makes me feel better. Still feel bad about the dog though."

He raised the bay door just enough for them to go under and they stepped onto a massive elevator without walls. Lilly looked around and noticed the panel had an "up" arrow.

"This thing goes up too?" She looked up and saw a ceiling a good distance above them.

"Uh, yeah, that leads outside but it's been sealed up. Too big of an opening. They thought it would leave us too vulnerable."

"That makes sense," she said, nodding her head.

It didn't take long to get to the subway level, and they entered into an enormous room made of cement and tiles that had cracked over time, exposing dirt and tree roots.

Lilly eyed the train ahead but could only see the top half. "Wow! That train is HUGE!" she yelled.

"Yeah, before New Life took over, the trains and tunnels had been rebuilt to four times their original size. Some of the original trains already had two levels but eventually they all did, and were widened, of course."

She noticed there was a group of men with electric saws cutting at the sides of the train.

"What are they doing?" she asked curiously.

"They're cutting off the top and sides to make room for the drills. Eventually we'll cut this upper platform off too," he said as he walked ahead toward the workers. "Hey, what's up, Casey?"

"Ah, nothing much. We got the upper ten cars cut. Ten more to go," a guy wearing a dirty white t-shirt and jeans answered, exhaling and wiping the dirt from his brow.

"Awesome. Movin' right along," Cypher responded, putting his hand up for a high five. "We'll get out of your hair. Just showing Lilly around. Lilly, this is Casey. He's leading the train revamp down here."

"Nice to meet you!"

He nodded in her direction. "You too," he said with a smile.

Lilly and Cypher waved goodbye and made their way back to the tech storage room.

"This train will be heading east. Seth and I are on the East Team, and we're leading the Presidents' capture. We'll be drilling right outside of the New Life facility and charging straight up the capitol building."

"Sounds like you have the most dangerous job," Lilly said with concern.

"Yes and no. Florian is on the South Team, and that team is blowing up the transfer pods. I personally think that's more dangerous, having to use explosives and whatnot. There'll be tons of guards in every direction, though, so no team is safer really. Zon's on the North Team. Their job is to clear the people out while the South Team prepares to ignite the explosives."

"Have you ever used explosives before?" she asked worriedly.

"No. No one has really. They've tested them of course but other than that, they haven't actually blown anything up."

Lilly thought about it for a few seconds and wasn't sure what else to say so she changed the subject. "Well, what do you say we work on some of these projects you've been putting off, eh? How about that flybot? That seems like a lot of fun! Plus, it'll get your mind off stuff," she suggested excitedly.

"Sure. Why not?" Cypher said with a half-smile.

"Alright, that's the spirit! I love learning this tech stuff!" she yelled as she did strange hops and skips on her way to the flybot.

Back at New Life, in the employee cafeteria, Shortelle was rambling on about the inconvenience of the extra added security over the past few months, after Zinnia, May, and Lilly escaped the city.

"The guards have been watching the library like the computers are about to turn into an army of rogue bots. I mean, why me? I worked with her for one day," Shortelle complained in an irritated tone, after setting her food tray at the table and sitting directly across from Pacer.

"It's not just you, hun. They're everywhere." Pacer got a disgusted look on his face, set his fork down, and pushed his tray away. "Oh hunny, no. This cherry pie is almost as horrible as the chocolate cream pie disaster that happened that one year. You know what I'm talking about? Anyway, I could make this way better, just saying," he boasted while shaking his head.

"Pacer, look. Theo just walked in," Shortelle said as she stood up and waved her hand in the air. "Hey, Theo, over here!"

Theo made his way through the crowded cafeteria and sat next to Pacer. "Hey," he said unenthusiastically.

"Any news on Zinnia and her sister yet?" Shortelle asked.

"Nothin' yet," he answered with an exhale.

"Well, how long are all these guards gonna be up in our faces? It's getting really old. Why all the fuss over a couple of girls? People go missing all the time."

"Their dad is…"

"Dr. Waters. We know that. Why does that matter?" she interrupted, getting increasingly more annoyed.

"He was the leader of the Glass Project…" he said, lowering his voice. "Apparently he hid the blueprints to the Glass System and wiped all the files before he disappeared. I listened in on a conversation between my dad and President Sophia. I do that every once in a while. Anyway, if anything happens and it goes down, they won't be able to get it back up, and the old electricity can't sustain everything for long.

"What does any of this have to do with his daughters?"

Theo got a worried look on his face. He was suddenly afraid he'd said too much. What if his dad found out he had gotten this information and was now sharing it? After debating it in his head for a few seconds, he went against his better judgement and decided to finish anyway.

"They've gone through all of his files; every single one of them. They've gone through all of Zinnia's files and all of May's. They can't find anything anywhere. Somehow, they've been able to keep things running without it shutting down. Anyway, they figured all they could do was keep a close eye on them and hope the blueprints pop up somehow."

"Well obviously not close enough," Shortelle responded, rolling her eyes and getting up from the table to throw her garbage away. She made her way back to the table and added, "If they don't knock it off soon, I quit."

"Oh hunny, you know that's not going to happen," Pacer responded, pulling his cherry pie close to him again and taking another bite. "Ugh, I don't know why I keep thinking this is going to start tasting good," he said and pushed it back away from him.

***

Lilly swept into her room excitedly, ready to tell everyone about the drills Cypher had shown her, but stopped instantly when she caught sight of something in August's arms.

"I got you something, Lilly," August exclaimed excitedly with a smile from ear to ear.

"Oh my gosh! You never said they were so cute when they're babies!" Lilly yelled out as she rushed over to August, scooping up a tiny kitten and putting it up to her face for a kiss.

"Oh yeah, they're cute. My Cinnamon here was the cutest of them all. Weren't you, lovey? That's right, yes you were. You were the cutest little fluff ball," August baby-talked while hugging and kissing Cinnamon. She nuzzled her face in the cat's chest. "But your kitten is pretty cute too," she added, pulling her face out from the cat's chest.

"Kitten? That's its name?" Lilly asked seriously.

August laughed. "No, silly. A 'kitten' is what she is. You get to name her yourself," she beamed.

Lilly didn't hesitate for a second. "Pigtails!"

"That's an interesting name."

"Nana said I had the cutest pigtails." She sat on her bed, petting the kitten's tiny body over and over. "And now I have the cutest pigtails again," she added, baby-talking as well.

August giggled. "Well, that works."

"Now I know why you always have Cinnamon with you. Oh man, too bad I can't take her to work."

"I know, right? I wish that all the time," she agreed with a frown.

Lilly went out to the rec room and showed her new kitten off to the people relaxing and playing games.

"I can make her a sweater if you want. I'm the best stitch there is around here. I once sewed 30 shirts in one day. Try and top that!" Luke bragged. "Those towels you use," he said, putting his thumb up to his chest, "I probably made 'em, since I'm the fastest." He had a pleased look on his face. "Toby models my clothes for me. Don't you, Toby?" he announced, embarrassing Toby and turning his cheeks pink.

A girl who was lounging on a couch brought her magazine down from her face and lifted her head above the back of the couch. "Quit embarrassing him, Luke!" Molly's fiery hair and short stature matched Toby's perfectly.

"Oh, he doesn't mind. Do you, Toby?" Luke asked, ruffling his hair.

Toby shook his head quickly, still looking embarrassed.

"I mean it. Leave him alone," she said, standing up.

"It's okay, Molly," Toby said.

"No, it's not. Why do you hang out with this creep?"

"Everything embarrasses Toby. Don't you see? Without me, he'd be a total loner. We're friends, so mind your own business," Luke said, putting his hand on Toby's shoulder.

"Whatever! Mom wants you sitting with us for dinner tonight," she told Toby before leaving the room.

Lilly went over to Luke. "I think a sweater would be great!"

"You're going to have to make a bunch," August added. "Cats grow really fast."

"Not a problem," Luke responded. "But you're going to have to do something for me first."

Lilly looked shocked. "Me? What could I do for you?"

"I heard you're a Thrill Seeker at New Life. I want you to give Toby here some strength training lessons. When we bust into the city, I want this little turd holding his own. I mean, I can take care of him like I always do, but I can't have him dying on me, you see?"

"Haven't you guys gotten any training?" she asked, confused.

"Yes, but he needs extra work. He's tiny, see?" Luke stretched his arms out the length of Toby's body.

"Well, sure! I don't mind! Back at New Life I actually taught rock climbing classes. That's a lot of upper body strength!" Lilly exclaimed. "When do you wanna start?"

"Uh, right away. He's getting nervous. Sooner the better," Luke answered, shifting his eyes. Lilly didn't buy it for a second. She knew it was really Luke that wanted the training. She was fine with it. Hopefully it did help them both.

"Sounds good to me," she said, quietly laughing.

***

Zon decided to take May to a huge music room on level 247. There were many music and art rooms, but this was by far the biggest one.

"This is a piano," he said, sitting on a bench and playing a few notes to a song.

She was immediately intrigued. "That was the most beautiful thing I've ever heard," she said with wide eyes as she stepped in closer. "Can you play more? Like the rest of the song?"

Zon let out a laugh. "Sure."

He continued playing the song as May watched dreamily. She was lost in the song, but most of all, she was lost in Zon's amazing musical talent and how good he looked playing it.

"This is one of my favorite instruments," he said after he finished the song.

"I can see why," she responded, still lost on a cloud. She looked around the room and caught sight of a large wall crowded with many shiny instruments. "And what are these over here?" she asked before walking over to the wall.

He got up from the piano and stood beside her. "These are wind instruments. Here, I'll show you," he said as he pulled down a flute and played a couple of notes. "Here, you try."

May took the flute and after he showed her how to hold it, she attempted to play a note but was confused, and slightly embarrassed, when nothing but an airy noise escaped the long tube.

Zon let out his usual bellowing laugh and her cheeks turned pink. "It's okay. It takes many years of practice to play these instruments. Long ago, people would dedicate their whole lives to mastering them. They created beautiful symphonies and played together in magical orchestras. Then technology took over and they were no longer needed. They became ancient artifacts."

"How did TOP get so many? They don't have these in the museums at New Life," she asked curiously.

"When New Life took over, TOP took as many instruments, books, and works of art as they could. They had already destroyed most of them at that point, and TOP knew the world of creativity was about to disappear forever. Diversity, gone. Authenticity, nonexistent. Originality, imagination, color…lost forever," he finished, seemingly lost in thought.

May looked into his eyes and grabbed his hand again like she had in the cemetery. "I feel lucky that I get to see so much beauty and color here. Thank you for showing me and teaching me all of this."

"I feel lucky that I get to see so much beauty, too," he said, returning the loving look in her eyes.

That slight shade of pink filled May's cheeks again and she felt her heart begin to beat in her chest. She had never met anyone so kind, honest, and loving. She yearned for that love as she felt a tugging inside. It was okay that she had been hurt so many times. All of that was worth it to be able to stand in front of this man now.

Zon grabbed her other hand and drew her in for another hug. After a few seconds, he pulled back to look in her eyes again. "May, if it's alright with you, I'd like for us to advance into an intimate relationship together."

She got a serious look on her face and thought for a few seconds. "Are you sure you want to do that? What if it doesn't work out?" she asked, getting worried as she remembered all of the failed attempts in her past.

"Then we will be friends," he answered.

"How could we be friends once our hearts have gotten tangled up?"

"If our hearts have gotten tangled up, then we are working out," Zon responded with a soft laugh.

A smile spread across her face. They continued to look at each other lovingly and then after a few moments, Zon lowered his head down and gently kissed her. It was the softest, warmest, most affectionate kiss she had ever had and she knew instantly that she wanted this for the rest of her life.

*****

Dr. Windon and the other scientists gathered around the table in the meeting room again, discussing their findings on the mature Eden plant. They updated Seth on their progress.

"We've done some tests and the mature plant is putting off an incredibly high level of a toxin none of us have ever seen before," Dr. Windon began. "Cypher inhaled a large amount of this toxin, obviously the reason for his lung failure. We believe that the birds benefited from it somehow due to their more efficient one-way airflow system. While conducting the experiments, the birds acted strangely again. They were not in the vicinity, but as soon as the boxes containing the plants were brought outside, they circled the area and landed on the surrounding trees. They stayed there watching us the entire time. Their behavior is unexplainable. The only suggestion I have is to keep our eyes on the birds and keep the plant out of sight.

"We also learned that only the plant roots and grows. Just the flowers by themselves do not. We wanted to run some additional tests in the lab but in order to do that we needed to make sure we kept the plant in its mature state. Taking it into the tower would have caused it to turn to dust, so we decided to test it out under a sun-light. We weren't sure if the flowers would revert to their dormant state like they had after the sun went down the day Cypher almost died, but they didn't. The plant stayed mature under the sun-lights and we were able to take it to the lab. Upon further testing, we discovered that only the flowers are toxic; not the vines" Dr. Windon concluded.

"Thank you for the update. Dr. Windon, Florian has brought an interesting idea to me. He believes that we may be able to replicate the flower bomb Cypher made to get past the guards. His idea is that we use them to safely stun the guards at New Life, and hopefully that'll give us a little more of an advantage when we enter the city," Seth said, looking for Dr. Windon's opinion.

"That is an interesting idea. We would need to run more tests. Could you bring Florian here for further discussion? I'd like to get more details. Maybe Cypher, as well, if he's feeling up to it. How about we meet here after dinner?"

"Will do," Seth answered, nodding his head at Dr. Windon before leaving the meeting room.

After dinner, everyone got together to discuss the idea and agreed to run tests the next day. Florian was to grow the plants under the sun-lights and dry the flowers. Cypher was instructed to make a couple of the flower bombs. In the morning, they would load the bombs and test them out.

The next morning, they met outside with all of the items needed for the experiment. They decided it would be best to do it outside just in case anything strange happened. Cypher pulled out one of the bombs he made, and Florian brought out the dried flowers he had put in an empty pot from the grow level.

"Okay, Cypher, please show us what you did," Dr. Windon instructed.

Cypher opened one of the flower bombs, put a small handful of crushed, dried flowers into the ball, and set a timer on the outside to go off in ten seconds. "Who's going to hold this? No offense, but I don't want to go near this plant again," Cypher admitted with an embarrassed look on his face.

Florian grabbed the ball and said, "I got ya, bud," and he took a few steps away from everyone.

When the time was up, the ball popped open and a puff of dust blew into Florian's face. He waited for Eden to hit him but was puzzled when nothing happened. Everyone looked around at each other confused.

Cypher walked over to Florian, grabbed the ball and turned it over a few times trying to find the malfunction.

"I don't think it's your bomb, Cypher. It did what it was supposed to," Florian said as he turned to Dr. Windon. "Well, what now? It didn't work."

"I'm not sure," Dr. Windon said, trying to search her brain for an answer.

"Well, that's that," Seth concluded as he patted Florian's shoulder. "It was a good thought."

Cypher kept turning the ball over, also searching his brain for an answer. He started asking questions. "Okay, wait... I made the bomb the same way I did before. Florian, what exactly did you do with the flowers?"

"I put a small plant under a sun-light. When it was done growing a few flowers, I picked them off and put them under the dryer. When they were done drying, I put them in the pot and brought them up this morning," Florian answered, going through the steps in his mind to make sure he hadn't left anything out.

"This doesn't make sense," Cypher continued. "Okay, when I did it before, I set the plant under a sun-light, went to work, and when I came back it had grown flowers. I made the bomb, went back to the plant, picked the flowers, dried them, crushed them, and put them into the ball. What did we do differently?"

Florian suddenly lit up. "That's it! You picked them, dried them, and put them straight into the ball. I picked them, dried them, and didn't put them into the ball until this morning. They sat out all night. Maybe that's just how the dried flowers work off the plant. If they stay on the plant, they never lose their potency. We need to put the crushed, dried flowers straight into the airtight ball," Florian finished with a pleased look on his face.

"You're right," Cypher agreed. "That's it."

"Well, then it's settled," Seth chimed in. "Let's try this again. Florian, grow some more flowers, pick them, dry them, crush them, and put them straight into the ball. Then bring them back up here. Let us know when you're ready and we'll head up."

Everyone nodded in agreement as they headed off to their duties. After completing the tasks, everyone met back outside with the flower ball.

"Okay, we're ready," Florian said as he put the ball in front of him.

"Actually," Seth interrupted, "I was thinking about it and I'd like to test this out. I'd like to have a better idea of what we're dealing with here, if it's alright with everyone," he said, looking from face to face to make sure it was okay with them. Everyone nodded.

Florian agreed and passed the ball to Seth. Seth turned the ball over a few times looking for the switch and Cypher leaned in to point to the timer. "Here. Right here. We'll set it for ten seconds."

They all stood around anxiously. Ten seconds seems like an awfully long time when you're standing around waiting.

After the ten seconds were up, a cloud of dust puffed into Seth's face. He instantly relaxed, so much that he nearly fell over, but Cypher and Florian caught him. They set him down gently and waited for the effects to wear off so he could share his experience.

Seth sat in his daze, lost and unresponsive, as his mind traveled in time to a place he had long forgotten; a memory he had pushed back into the farthest parts of his mind. It wasn't a bad memory, just one he hadn't thought about in a very long time. A painful, and yet comforting memory.

The room was filled with sunlight. The window was slightly cracked open, letting a small breeze into the room. She was there, the sunlight glistening off of her skin, little strands of her beautiful dark hair waving in the breeze. It wasn't the tidiest hair, considering all the hard work she had just done. Wrapped up tightly in her arms was a tiny baby boy. Florian was a little smaller than most babies, but he had the biggest eyes and he matched his mother's complexion perfectly. She held him tight with tears of joy in her eyes. Seth's heart was so full. He looked lovingly at his beautiful wife and the precious creation they had just made together. She looked down at Florian and then back up at Seth as she stretched out her hand to hold onto his with the most loving smile.

And just as quickly as the memory had flooded into Seth's mind it floated away, leaving him with a gaping hole in his chest. He realized he had shed a tear and wiped it away as he looked around at the faces staring intently at him. He began to stand up and Florian reached down to help him, all the while remaining quiet as his dad regained his bearings.

Once he raised all the way to his feet, he nodded his head, smiled warmly, and patted Florian's shoulder. "These will work," he said and walked quietly toward the tower, disappearing into the tunnels, leaving everyone in a somber cloud of Open Eden's undeniable capabilities.

Rob ran back to his desk outside of the supply rooms. He didn't know what he was looking for, but he rummaged through his desk anyway. He dug through everything in a panic, stopped for a few seconds when he heard some of the guards walking past his office, and then rummaged some more. This had never happened before. Everything had always run so smoothly, practically seamless.

The blueprints are safe. I made sure of that. The girls are safe. I made sure of that, he thought to himself after sitting down in his chair, putting his face in his hands, and resting his elbows on his knees. He was at a loss. What could he do? He sat there for a few minutes feeling completely hopeless. Finally, he decided he should at least get word to the Underground, and hopefully he'd find a way to get out of this. If not, he knew he'd be locked up, questioned, possibly tortured, and eventually transferred.

"Seth, they're on to me. I may end up heading that way but I'm going to do everything I can to stay in the city first. I'm going to fabricate a report on the lung bot I took, and hopefully that will buy me some time to electronically alter my inventory numbers. I don't know how I'm going to do that with the guards watching my every move. This isn't a matter of supplies anymore. This is an assessment of my loyalty. One wrong move and I'm done."

"Wouldn't it be a wiser choice to leave now while you still can?" Seth asked, concerned.

"I can't do that, Seth. I can't leave here. I'm closer to the office than any other TOP members. If I can save my position, it's worth the risk for our people. I could never forgive myself if I didn't try."

"Fair enough. But you should know...no one would blame you for walking away. You have helped the Underground in countless ways. It isn't necessary for you to give up your life."

"I understand what you mean, but you should know, I'm going to keep helping until I can't anymore."

***

"Alright everyone! Shut up!" Florian yelled over the hundreds of people on the grow level, where everyone had gathered to assist in the production of the flower bombs.

"We're going to split into teams." He raised his arm in the air to point over people's heads. "You, you, and you, over there... You, not you...and you, on that side. Okay, split down the center here. This team is gonna follow Cypher to the tech level to make the flower bombs. The rest of you are staying here with me, where we'll be growing Open Eden. After we have enough flowers, and Cypher and his team have made enough bombs, we will be drying, then crushing and putting the powder into the bombs. Got it? Oh, and everyone growing the plants has to wear these," he said, holding up strange looking masks. "The docs and science nerds want us to protect ourselves," he added mockingly.

Lilly was sent off with Cypher, of course, since she'd already been working on the tech level, along with August, Luke, Toby, and Molly. Zinnia, May, and Zon stayed with Florian's team.

"Hey, you," Florian nodded in Zon's direction and waved for him to follow. "You know about growing. You run around with all the trees up there and stuff, right?"

"Not exactly," Zon answered flatly as he followed him.

"Good. I need you to run this team. We'll separate into two groups. We'll need to uproot, split, and replant after each split. We'll have to split the first one, put both halves under the lights, then split those two after they grow, and so on and so forth. You run that half of the plant and we'll run this half of the plant, and we'll just keep doing that." He went through the steps with exaggerated hand movements.

"Then we'll divide the two groups into four and those two groups will go back to the head of the line and start picking the flowers off to dry them. Then Cypher and half of his team will bring in the bombs, crush the flowers, and put them straight into the bombs. And they'll stack 'em up in that storage room over there," he finished as he grabbed the plant and started to uproot it.

Meanwhile in the tech room, Cypher had everyone gather specific tools and parts and instructed them on how to put the pieces together.

"There's a door on this side. Once it's been loaded, it will shut automatically so make sure you move your fingers out of the way. That's to ensure it's airtight and sealed before the flowers lose their potency. Nothing to it really," he said, flipping the bomb he had in his hand over a few times. "So, if we each make 10 a day, that should be enough, if my calculations are correct. We're only invading the New Life capitol and I think 10 is about all you can carry anyway. After we've made the first batch, half of us will head down to the grow level and load the bombs with the crushed flowers."

"Hey, Toby!" Lilly called out when she saw him and Luke a few rows behind. "I was thinking we could get together after this. Is that cool?"

"That's cool," Luke answered for him. "We'll be there."

Lilly laughed. "You're like his translator bot!"

***

After finishing his conversation with Seth, Rob decided he was going to meet his guys to inform them and set up a plan of action. He stepped out of his office but was immediately stopped by Colton and a few guards, including the one who had reported him.

"What, did you really think we wouldn't have bugged your office the second your loyalty was in question?" Colton demanded after grabbing Rob by the throat, spitting in his face as he yelled at him. The guards grabbed him by the arms and put him in handcuffs.

"Where are you taking me? Let me go! You can't do this!" He kept yelling as they dragged him away from his office.

Theo saw this unfolding as he was walking by and decided to follow. After putting Rob in a glass cell, Colton went up to Sophia's office to inform her. Theo took a different elevator and waited quietly until Colton was in the office. He put a sound amplifier against the door to listen.

"The guard said he made a call and was talking to a TOP member named Seth."

With a shocked expression on her face, Sophia looked up from the work on her desk and began turning a slight shade of red. "What?!"

Colton continued, slightly confused by her reaction. "Rob mentioned being closer than any of the other TOP members."

Sophia stood up, enraged. "How did this happen? How did a TOP member get so close? The Underground is getting stronger. We need to take action, and we need to find those girls!"

"Our surveillance bots have been searching around the area the girls escaped from but something has been blinding the bots. We can't tell what it is. It looks like something is flapping in front of them. It looks like..." He hesitated for a second. "...it looks like birds."

"That's the most ridiculous thing I've ever heard, Colton!" Sophia yelled. "Get more bots out there! I don't care what you have to do! Just do it!"

"Yes, ma'am," Colton responded with a clenched jaw before heading for the door. He exited the office and ran right into Theo.

"What the hell are you doing here, Theo?!" he yelled as he grabbed him and slammed him up against the wall.

"I, I, I..." Theo stammered.

"I, nothing! Move!" Colton yelled, grabbing Theo's arm and yanking it as hard as he could. He pushed him down the hall and away from Sophia's office.

"What is this Underground? Is that where May and her sister went?"

"Shut up! I told you to shut up!" Colton yelled and then punched him in the back of the head, knocking him down. "Get up!"

Theo's face smacked into the ground and his lip busted open. He stood up as quickly as he could, wiped the blood, and jetted forward to avoid another blow from Colton.

***

Lilly had Toby and Luke meet her in the sports activity room where the trampolines were.

"I thought it would be fun to practice some moves on this. That way when I knock you down it won't hurt so bad," she said after doing a flip in the air.

She spent a fair amount of time teaching Toby some moves. Naturally that meant Luke was also getting the training, although he kept making a verbal note that this was all for Toby and that he knew all of this stuff already. Lilly just kept nodding her head and agreeing and focused all of her energy on Toby. They decided to meet every day after working on the flower bombs, and after she'd decided he was good and ready, she'd move to training him on the ground. In the meantime, right as she was in the middle of showing Toby the throat punch, Molly, who was on her way to the batting cages, saw them wrestling around and stormed up to them.

"What do you think you're doing?!" she yelled up at them, fuming.

"What do you want, dictator?" Luke sneered.

"Funny you should call me a dictator when you're the one dragging Toby around, making him learn combat moves with Ms. Thrilled over there! I told you he's not going and Toby, get down from there right now!"

"And I told *you*...he is going and there's nothing you can do to stop it!" Luke stood tall, staring Molly right in the eyes. She looked back and forth between Luke and Toby, and when she realized Toby wasn't moving and wasn't going to, she broke down crying and ran back the way she came from.

"Ms. Thrilled..." Lilly mumbled to herself, shaking her head, and then called back to Molly, "It's Thrill *Seeker!*"

***

"I'm so excited! I can't wait until you guys see the New Life escape celebration!" August exclaimed as she and the girls headed toward the dining hall. "They call it 'NLeave Celebration.' There's music, dancing, food! Oh man, so much food..." She said, practically drooling. "There's even a play about the New Life escape. I can't wait for you to see it! I almost cried when I saw it last year but it had a happy ending. Well, beginning, I mean," she chuckled.

"Oh, that sounds wonderful!" Lilly responded, joining in on the excitement. "I'd love to see what kinds of food there is. Hey, do they have desserts like Foodies make up there?" she asked, pointing up. "Don't get me wrong, the desserts here are delicious but those Foodie desserts were the best!"

"Totally! There's almost every kind of dessert you can think of. This is the only time of year when they open up the kitchens to let people make their own personal recipes! Some recipes have been passed down from these families, generation after generation. I personally loved Roberta Blake's peach cobbler! Pierre made creme brulee. Inessa made medovik! Anatoli made baklava! Huan made egg tarts! Ivy made a pavlova—," August paused when she saw the confused looks on the girls' faces. "That's a meringue, marshmallowy thingy. It's good."

"I still can't get used to hearing all of these exotic names," May said, shaking her head and smiling. "I've been looking forward to this actually. Zon said the play is put on by the children," she added, looking over at Zinnia, who was walking along silently holding her necklace. "Hey," she said, swatting Zinnia with her NLeave Celebration program. "What's up with you?"

"We're running out of time. That's all. Just seems like a waste of time going to this thing," she answered gloomily.

"Ah come on, Z," Lilly jumped in. "That's the point! We need a little fun before things get all discombobulated around here! You can mope all you want but that's not going to change anything! Enjoy *one* day. You can have a day. Am I right?" she asked in May and August's direction. They both nodded.

"Absolutely," May agreed. "Have some fun and we'll get right back into preparing for the capitol takeover tomorrow," she added, squeezing Zinnia's shoulders.

Zinnia cracked a small smile. "Okay. I'll try to have fun…but I mean it…back at it tomorrow."

Everyone nodded.

"Hey what's that?" Zinnia asked May when she spotted a tiny tube hanging around her neck.

"Oh, this is a dog whistle. Zon gave it to me. He's going to show me how to use it tomorrow and I'm so excited. It's what he uses to direct them."

They arrived at the dining level and everything was dancing around happily. Kids were skipping and hopping with glowing sticks and hand-made jewelry, families were baking in the kitchens, groups of kids were doing crafts. There were circles of people playing instruments and singing. The girls felt a small bit of excitement bubble up inside. Lilly's eyes were wide as usual.

"Each level has a dessert competition and then the winners of each level get to compete. They always make two batches. One batch is for the judges on the level and the other batch is for the Underground competition, if they win. Otherwise, the rest of it goes to us!" August exclaimed excitedly.

The girls partook in some activities. Lilly did some crafts with the children. She loved it and really missed teaching the rock climbing classes. Zinnia hung out with May while Zon played music around a circle with some other musicians. She was totally impressed and could see now why May loved it so much. It was beautiful.

They eventually took their seats for dinner and it was more amazing than the girls could have ever imagined. The family recipes were rich with culture and diversity. There were so many flavors they had never tasted before. It was hard for them to believe that there were even more treats to enjoy before the end of the event.

"Hey, who is that?" May asked as she spotted a completely bald girl in the far corner of the room. She didn't even have eyebrows.

"Oh, that's Darla. She was working in the lab trying to come up with a gun that kills hair follicles. Don't ask me why, but for some reason she had this idea that The Fountain of Youth was found in the hair follicles and that if she could cause them to close completely it would speed the aging process up again. Well, the gun backfired and she hit herself with it," August said, taking another bite of her falafel.

"So, does that mean it worked? Is she going to live a shorter life?" May asked, completely intrigued.

"Well, no one knows. We'll just have to wait and see, I guess," August answered. The girls shook their heads in disbelief as they returned to their delicious meals.

After dinner they watched the play performed by the children about the retreat from the cities on the wall screen. They learned even more about how New Life came to power and how TOP created their sanctuary out of old subways, military bunkers, and secret doorways hidden below condemned communication towers. It was a bloody battle that killed many people. Once they started raising children who were in line to get transferred as their soldiers, the New Life army grew too big for even the thought of a revolution. The children, taken as soldiers, knew nothing else. They became trained robots with no emotion. Most believed that they were actually robots.

After the play was over, they jumped right into the dessert competition. Jose's churros won first place on their level, and after that the Bajwa family won the TOP competition with their gulab jamun.

They all sat at their tables, stuffed and ready to call it a night, but before the event was to come to a close, there would be a few words from Seth.

"We wouldn't normally end such a wonderful event with such a serious topic but we have decided since it is more likely that everyone would be in attendance, we should take this opportunity to discuss the upcoming takeover."

The girls looked at each other nervously and Zinnia, who had been resting her chin on her arms, sat up tall to listen.

"You have all prepared and we cannot ask for more than that. You have been shining examples of what it means to be a family, a team…a friend," he said firmly with a gentle smile. "Soon we will begin our journey down the subways. There have been some new projects that not everyone is aware of, and we were able to find some good out of the plant that nearly cost a life. Florian, Cypher, and a large group of your peers have been building bombs for each person to bring with them."

A symphony of gasps and chattering began to echo throughout the underground.

Seth's body bounced lightly from a silent laugh as he patted his hands in the air, instructing everyone to settle down. "It's not what you think. These bombs contain the dormant crushed flowers from the Open Eden plant. We will use them to stun the guards, in addition to the wave guns we have. This was Florian's idea and I couldn't be prouder. After some tests, they were deemed safe enough for the handler. We will be going through a quick tutorial on how to use these flower bombs. Florian, Cypher, take it away," Seth said before stepping out of the view of the camera and handing the microphone bot to the boys.

Florian and Cypher went through the tutorial and each level was given the opportunity to ask questions. After that was through, Seth got back on the screen to finish up with the plan of action.

"I'd like to turn everyone's attention to the map."

A map appeared on the screen with hundreds of tunnels branching out in every direction. The girls had no idea the Underground was so big. There were a few more black holes that they could see and they wondered how many other underground colonies there were.

"Our teams will be taking these routes surrounding the New Life facilities," Seth said while highlighting the different tunnels they'd be using. "The teams will be walking to these points over here, where they will then board the subways that will take them to the drill points. Hopefully we have built ourselves strong drills.

"Going forward, I would like for our fighters to start gathering your weapons. Gardeners, harvest your current crops. Cooks, start preparing the meal plans. Water treatment workers, start bottling the water. Techs, gather your bots. Preachers, teachers, and medical staff, get ready. We're going to need you. Remember, this is just the start. There will be more battles ahead. For all of the newcomers, you are to stay here. This infiltration has taken years to plan and we could not, in good conscience, send you into battle ill prepared."

"What?! No! I've been preparing!" Zinnia blurted out and the people around the room looked at her.

"Z, this is a good thing," May tried to reassure her.

Zinnia sunk down, slightly embarrassed that the whole room was now staring at her. August added, "Hey, that means I'm staying here too. I haven't been here very long either."

"And what are we supposed to do? Once this round of crops is harvested, I'll have nothing. And then what? We just sit around and wait?" Zinnia asked as she stared off into the screen.

Zinnia decided to relax in her bed and flip through the book she found in her sister's apartment. Some things made more sense now, especially the religious parts. She found all the different beliefs very fascinating. There were so many of them and she had only ever known about one. Well, they didn't exactly call it a religion. She felt like it could be considered one. You die or you transfer and then you go on to the next life. There was complete comfort in that to people, but not to her. She hadn't really thought about her own afterlife before. All she knew was that the whole thing made her uncomfortable. She felt scared. She just kept wishing she wasn't so afraid. She thought about what Lilly said about using energy to get energy. Maybe the same thing applied to courage. Be afraid and do it anyway, and then maybe after a while she wouldn't be so scared.

She noticed there were five pages oddly placed in no specific order throughout the book. They had charts and graphs that didn't seem to have anything to do with the religions she had read about. They didn't make any sense to her at all. She had been hoping she'd learn something in the Underground that would reveal the meaning, but there was nothing. Maybe Seth would know. She hesitated to bring it to him, though. He was busy, and who was she anyway? He probably didn't even remember her. There were so many people down there.

She was thumbing through the pages over and over, examining them from top to bottom, when she accidentally dropped a piece of popcorn right in the crease of the book on the first page containing the graphs and charts. She tried to grab it but ended up pushing it further into the crack. She had to pull the book open wider than she would have liked to open a real, old fashioned book in order to get it out. As she had it pulled open, she noticed a tiny letter on the bottom left corner of the book on the other side of the seam. She brought it up to her eye to get a closer look and saw the letter "G." Her eyes widened and she quickly flipped to the next page containing graphs and charts and found the letter "L." The next page had an "A" and the last two pages each had an "S," all together spelling out the word "GLASS."

Zinnia pulled up her PED and called May right away. "May! I found something in the book Dad left for us! It's a code of some sort!"

"What do you mean 'a code'? Hold on, we'll head up. I have Zon with me."

***

"Since you're 'in the know,' Theo, I'll be needing your assistance. Your father here," Sophia nodded in Colton's direction, "will have you taken to one of our prisoners, Rob Bailey. I want you to watch over him. He will need constant supervision, even though we have him secured behind the toughest Glass Project walls this place has ever seen, thanks to Dr. Waters. This Rob Bailey is capable of horrible things and has been a big threat to New Life."

"Didn't realize I was a guard," Theo said under his breath, before getting a punch in the arm from Colton. "Ow!"

"Boy, when did you get that mouth on you?! What makes you think you can talk to our president like that?!"

"That's enough, Colton," Sophia said gently. A soft smile spread across her face without losing eye contact with Theo. "Have the guards take him down to the office holding cell."

Colton gave the guards the order, and after they left the room, he went over to Sophia and wrapped his arms around her, bringing her in for a kiss.

After their kiss Sophia pulled away so she could see his face. "Colton, I want you to know your efforts haven't gone unnoticed. After things settle down, I plan to move you to another department so we can be together."

"That won't bring us together! That would take me away from you more! You spend all of your time here!" he responded angrily.

"That temper of yours isn't going to help us right now. Your son is being held, guards are everywhere, I can't seem to get these mothers to stop breeding...and what are we to do about these girls? The Glass Project? Is that temper going to keep the lights on, Colton?"

"No," he responded, still red in the face.

"Now go away. I have work to do," she commanded, walking to her desk and waving him toward the door.

He stormed out of the office, punching a guard on the way out.

***

Lilly entered their bedroom, sat down on her bed, and delivered Zinnia an ear full. "Hey Z! You wouldn't believe the day I just had. I was teaching Toby some combat moves and his sister, Molly, shows up with her hair pulled back and she's carrying a stick. I was like, 'What're you carrying that burning material around for?' and she was all, 'If you're going, Toby, I'm going.' So now I'm teaching three people combat moves, only Luke won't admit that he's getting the lessons too because, well you know, he's a turd. I guess the stick is for fighting but I've never done anything with sticks so I told her we'd have to figure it out together. She was fine with that. She's pretty cool actually. She just cares about Toby a lot and doesn't really like Luke."

"That's great. I'm glad you're here Lilly! May is on her way up. I found a code in the book I found in her apartment," Zinnia said, opening the book and showing her the hidden "G."

Lilly's eyes widened as usual, and she was about to ask for more information when May and Zon entered the room. Zinnia took the book from Lilly's eyes and put it in front of May's.

"The letters spell out 'glass,'" she said.

"I forgot you even had this," May said as she took the book and started examining it. She flipped to each page with the graphs that Zinnia had bookmarked, found each of the letters in the far corners, and studied the pages for a few moments.

Zon reached around May and pointed to a symbol on page G. It looked exactly like the New Life symbol, only the bird from the box that held the book was faintly in the background. "This symbol is on all of the undercover bots working with the Underground so TOP members know they can trust it. Rob tracks them on his end."

"This symbol was on the box that was holding this book," Zinnia responded. The girls looked closely at the symbol and could see the bird with the perfect "T" for wings.

"Like I said before, the birds are the watchers of the forest. It's been that way for a long time. It's only recently that they have become so powerful, because of that plant," Zon reminded them.

"Rob?" Zinnia asked, suddenly remembering what Zon had said before. "Dad said his friend, Rob, was going to give us a special ration in the last video I have from him. He never did give us anything."

"Except for this book," Zon added. A light came on in the girls' eyes.

"Yeah, Zinnia, don't you remember me sending a message to Rob for the lung bot the night Cypher almost died?" May asked.

"Yes, I remember that. I was a bit preoccupied, though…stressing out and whatnot. I didn't pay attention to his name. I guess I just thought this came from Seth," Zinnia answered. "I didn't realize that this book was the 'special ration' Dad was talking about in the video. He was sending us messages but we didn't even realize it. I need to watch that video again," she added before pulling out her PED and holding it up for everyone to see.

"Hey Z, Dad here. Just sending you a quick note to let you know that I love you and I'm not gonna make it home for dinner tonight."

Zinnia paused the video and looked at May. "He knew, May. He knew he wasn't coming back." May put her hand on Zinnia's shoulder.

She hit play again. "I'm getting held up at work, but I was able to score a special ration for you. My friend Rob will get it to you later. I hear May is settling nicely into her apartment. I haven't had the chance to get over there and check it out yet. I bet it looks great. You remember when I took you to work when you were little? I wasn't supposed to but I couldn't resist a fun day teaching you all about what I do. You didn't understand anything, but as smart as you were, I thought it'd pique your interest and maybe you'd follow your old man's line of work one day. Anyway, I taught you all about the dome shield and how it worked. Of course, I know you were too young to remember any of that. I do believe I also taught you how to spell a few words that day. Shield, dome, electricity…glass. The secret is in the glass. That sure was a nice day together, you and me. Hey, if you ever find yourself feeling stuck in life, remember that beautiful day we spent together and hopefully it'll give you just the right key to get you unstuck. Good memories will always keep us going. Love you, kid. Tell May I love her too."

"Did you hear that? How he emphasized the word 'life'? The key to get us unstuck. There has to be a reason he brought up those words. Dome shield, electricity, glass," Zinnia contemplated as she started pacing around the room, clutching her lightbulb necklace.

"The numbers under the symbol," Zon said. "They look like coordinates."

"Yes! Coordinates! I learned about those in a class once!" Zinnia yelled out.

May and Lilly looked at her confused.

"I've never heard of that. What are coordinates?" May asked, slightly annoyed that there was always something Zinnia learned from a class she took somewhere.

"They are numbers that point to a specific place on a grid. Here, let me show you on my PED," Zon said and took his PED out of his pocket.

A surprised look spread across Zon's face after he entered the numbers. "These are the coordinates to the bot passthrough. It's where the bot enters the city...the tunnel I told you about when we first met, that goes far below the city wall."

"We need to check it out," Zinnia said seriously.

"The city is very far away," Zon reminded her. "The bots travel very fast to the checkpoint that May and I go to every day."

Zinnia got a disappointed look on her face. "Well, maybe we could at least take a closer look at the bot!"

May looked up at Zon. "Yeah. We could do that. Right?"

"Perhaps, but not today. When we get to the checkpoint tomorrow, we will call you," he said, looking at Zinnia. "And we can examine it together. Make sure you are on a break. We should keep this between us for now."

"Sounds good," she said and they all nodded in agreement.

***

First thing in the morning after breakfast, May and Zon headed out on their run for the day. Their plan was to inspect the bot to see if there were any clues.

Once outside the tower, they swung open the door and ran right into a large gang of elk who were surrounding the area. The elk were instantly spooked, and as they started to run, the colorful birds darted off of their branches like they'd done so many times before, and began making geometric shapes in the sky. The elk immediately calmed down and stopped running.

May, completely blown away as usual, asked, "What just happened?" She stood motionless, afraid to scare the elk again.

"They warn, but they also let the creatures know when it is safe," Zon answered as he headed out in the direction of the checkpoint.

Once they arrived, they sat and waited for the transport bot. They sometimes had to wait an hour or two depending on the day. That day, though, it seemed like they'd been waiting a long time. They had time to talk about all the different dog breeds that Zon had in his pack. May's favorite was the tiny Yorkshire terrier that she decided to name Wendell. He didn't need it, but May liked to carry him around sometimes. They even spent some time practicing with the whistle, but after the fourth hour Zon picked up his belongings and said, "Something is wrong. We need to get back to the Underground."

When they got back, Zon went straight to Seth to report that the bot never came.

"I was worried something like this might happen," Seth said, shaking his head and letting out a long sigh. "The last time I talked to him he said that the presidents' guard was on to him. I should have tried harder to convince him to leave while he still had a chance."

"Do you think they arrested him?" Zon asked.

"There's no way to know for sure. We're just going to have to keep moving forward. Hopefully he is still alive when we get there," Seth said as he stood up from his desk. "Tomorrow we move out. I'll be announcing it tonight."

***

Zinnia had been examining the pages for hours. Paragraph by paragraph, chart by chart, the diagrams, the pictures. She had been staring at the pages for so long, her eyes kept going in and out of focus as she started getting sleepy. She laid her head down on her arm and kept her eyes on the book. The page started to blur and her mind drifted off as her eyelids began to close. Before they closed all the way, she saw something. She popped her head up and opened her eyes quickly but what she thought she saw disappeared. She was confused. She laid her head back down and stared at the book again. She let her eyes unfocus. After a few seconds she saw it again. Some of the letters were slightly raised. But not actually raised, it just looked like they were raised. She focused her eyes and the letters disappeared again.

"This couldn't just be my imagination, could it?" she asked out loud as she grabbed a piece of paper and a pen (something she was still getting used to). She started writing down the letters on each page and was again blown away when she realized that there were hidden messages within the floating letters. On page "G" the letters spelled "get out" with the "G" being the letter in the corner. Page "L" had floating letters spelling "lights out." Page "A" spelled out "access files." The first "S" page spelled out "shield," and the final page spelled out "save the kids."

Zinnia ran to tell the others but was told about Rob's possible capture, so she decided not to bother anyone with what she discovered. She'd wait until later.

***

Seth showed up on the screen at dinner and began his speech. "The time is now. We will be heading through the tunnels first thing tomorrow morning. You all have your gear, your wave guns, and stun bombs. It is our plan to capture the presidents and then we will broadcast a nationwide live video from their office. We will bring the truth to the people of New Life about the lies they have been fed. It is my hope that they will turn to us for guidance and leadership. It will be a shock for them. We are prepared for that. It is our goal to bring the truth with as little violence as possible! And we hope that they will see our intentions as honorable.

"Following the infiltration, if all goes well, our support teams led by Roberta Blake, will go into the cities, set up camps, and offer assistance to the people who might be having a hard time dealing with the shocking new information. This will also be a way to call out to the other underground colonies. We have contact with the neighboring colonies, but we are hoping to get them all involved and eventually expand out to the rest of the world. We can't say for sure, but if we have colonies here in America, we believe the other countries do as well. We need to prove to them that this is possible. We need to prove to them that we can rise up! That we do not have to stay under anymore! If we can do it, so can they!

"I'm proud of every one of you. It is your courage and strength that has gotten us this far and what will take us through to the end. I will pass you off to Roberta. Enjoy your dinner." Seth finished his speech with his usual kind smile, and there was chattering heard around the Underground until Roberta said the dinner prayer. Dinner seemed awfully quieter than usual, and Zinnia was still thumbing through the pages of the book.

"Zinnia, you need to eat," May said in her usual concerned tone and startled Zinnia out of a deep zone.

"Huh? Oh…yeah… I will. I'm just thinking about this book still. I found a few more clues in it," Zinnia said and grabbed her fork, without taking her eyes off of the book.

"What did you find?" Lilly asked.

"Each page has a phrase hidden in letters that only appear if you unfocus your eyes," she said as she lifted up her piece of paper to show the phrases to them.

"Any idea what it means?" May asked.

Zinnia just shook her head slowly. "I've been trying to figure it out, but I can't and it's giving me a headache."

"Just put it away for now. We'll look at it again later," May told her, sounding all too motherly.

***

Cypher, Florian, Zon, and the girls spent the last little bit of time they had together after dinner in the rec room. It felt calm and quiet, but their minds were very loud.

"Well, I for one have had a blast teaching Toby, Luke, and Molly some combat moves. I hope it serves them well," Lilly said, breaking the silence.

"I'm sure it will," Zinnia responded with a warm smile. "I know it was a little unreasonable to think I was gonna go with you guys. I'm glad, though. I just wish I didn't waste so much time stressing about it."

"Yeah, I guess I should have told you that. My bad," Florian teased with a smirk. Zinnia glared at him, causing Zon to let out a bellowing laugh. Pretty soon everyone in the room was laughing too.

After the laughter died down May added, "I don't know what's gonna happen after all of this is over. I guess we won't be running anymore."

"That all depends on how this goes," Zon replied. "If we are successful, we will be adjusting our jobs, yes. We won't need transport bots because we will have unregulated access to the city. If we fail, we will more than likely have to go in different directions for supplies… We might possibly lose that connection all together."

"I'll miss you," May said as she broke down in tears and buried her face in his chest.

"Hey," he said, pulling her up so he could see her face. "I'll be back. I promise."

"I'll make sure I get him back to you," Cypher added, sending a warm smile in her direction.

"I don't mean to sound like I'm saying goodbye forever, but it's been nice being here with you guys. I'm happy that May has you, Zon, and I'm happy that Lilly has you as a friend, Cypher. Get back here safe, okay?" Zinnia said, finishing the conversation before the time arrived for them to head to bed. The time for their lives to completely change again.

15

The morning came and it was time for The Original People to travel down the tunnels. They packed their bags and gathered their wave guns and stun bombs. The South Team packed their explosives and workers loaded the trains with the drills. The people staying behind hugged their loved ones. Everything would happen in just this one day, but it felt like they would be gone forever. May was crying, of course, and Zinnia felt sad for her. She saw Lilly punch Cypher lightly on the arm and then reach up as far as she could to hug him. He looked silly having to bend down so far. It was time to go. The teams headed in different directions down the tunnels and just like that, they were gone, leaving a quiet and empty feeling in the Underground.

"What now?" Zinnia asked as everyone wiped tears from their eyes.

"We go to work I suppose," said August. "May, you can come with me to the kitchen if you want."

"Thank you, August, but I think I'll go to the grow level with Z," she responded sadly.

"Ok sounds good to me. Lilly?"

"I still have work to do on the tech level. I'm almost done fixing the fly bot that Cypher and I were working on. I just have a few screws to tighten," she said, looking sad.

They all parted ways and Zinnia and May headed to the grow level together.

"I decided I was just going to keep growing the dormant Open Eden plant but Dr. Windon took what we had left. I guess she didn't trust it just laying around here. I get it," Zinnia said, shrugging.

"What can we work on instead? Hey, how about you show me what a typical day looks like for Zinnia Waters?" May suggested with a smile. "Besides, I really need a distraction. I'm going crazy right now."

"That sounds like a great idea to me," she answered and handed May a rubber apron and gloves.

Meanwhile, Lilly stacked the remaining empty flower bombs on the tech level and spent the rest of the morning finishing up the flybot. At lunchtime, everyone was eager to get to the dining room so they could get an update on the infiltration. When they got there, they saw the drills working quickly on the wall screen. Each team had a camera set up, live streaming their progress. Dust and rubble was pumping down the tubes. Some of the drillers had turned toward the camera and put their thumbs up, sending nervous giggles around the dining room.

"Everything is going according to plan so far. We're almost to the top. We know this is making noise up there, so as soon as we're through, the drills will drop down and we'll be rushing up," Casey said before he put his thumb up to the camera and turned back to the drilling.

The girls watched nervously, holding hands. "I can't go back to work. There are knots in my stomach and I can't focus anymore," Zinnia said, shaking her head, almost in tears.

"Shhh…it's okay, we can stay here and watch. It's fine. I'll stay here with you. No worries," May said in a soothing tone, even though she had the same knots in her stomach.

Zon was on the North Team and they could see his team was almost through, so they had stopped to wait for the others to catch up. Seth and Cypher were on the East Team and had stopped too. All that was left was the South Team with Florian and the TOP members who would be blowing up the transfer pods.

Once they were all stopped, Seth turned to the camera and said, "In just a few moments we will be breaking through. This is where we turn the cameras off."

They knew ahead of time that they'd only be broadcasting up until the drilling stopped. Given they didn't know how it was going to unfold, Seth thought it better they didn't watch. He knew it would be too stressful, so they were to wait for updates through the radio.

"We will keep you updated the whole time. Say your prayers. We're heading up!" he yelled right before the cameras shut off.

***

After the cameras shut off Seth yelled, "Go!" and all at once all of the drills powered back on and broke through the rock above them. Light suddenly entered the tunnels as the drills pulled down and a large solid cover closed over the top of them creating a platform for the TOP members to climb on top of. People were simultaneously stacking multiple ladders all around the drills and were now running up them as fast as they could go.

As soon as they reached the top, guards began running at them with their own weapons. They weren't as kind as TOP's. Bullets were flying through the air and TOP members were falling to the ground one by one as they charged forward toward the New Life facility.

***

Zon exited the tunnels as fast as he could, with his dogs following closely behind. He had trained them to climb ladders and it wasn't a struggle for their strong bodies to pull themselves up. He fought with all of his might. Being a Runner had certainly helped him. He had speed above all else. He dodged the guards left and right and only had to fire his wave gun every once in a while. When he had gotten a moment to breathe, he noticed they were not at the point they had set their target for. Their aim must have been off just slightly because his group had landed on the other side of a Thrill Seeker Mountain. He pulled out his PED and dialed Seth who didn't answer, of course.

He spoke into his radio to the people in the Underground. "Our mark was calculated wrong!" he yelled. "I'm going to run south. There aren't too many guards around this area so it shouldn't hold us back much. If anyone hears from Seth, let him know. We're going to head to the ZGSs."

May stood up from the table. "That's good right?? There are less guards! That's good!" she said nervously, shaking. Zinnia stood up and grabbed her hand.

***

Seth and Cypher exited their drill point and headed into the New Life facility. This was the most heavily guarded so their team had the most TOP members. They started throwing their flower bombs and shooting their wave guns, but they could see they were only knocking down the guards for a few seconds.

"I doubt they have good memories slowing them down!" Seth yelled over the loud gunfire.

Cypher agreed and started fighting with his fists. He wasn't as strong as Seth but he was tall enough to knock the guards down from the top. It turned his stomach when he realized he just knocked down a child. He couldn't have been more than 20.

"We just need to get up to the office! Let the others fight! We need to head to the elevators!"

Seth and Cypher got past the courtyard but were stopped by two guards who were blocking the elevators. Seth fired his wave gun at one of the guards and it pushed him back only for a second. Cypher then hit the guard down with the back of his wave gun causing him to crash into the side of the elevator. The other guard grabbed Cypher around his waist and Seth kicked the side of his knee, causing him to collapse. They both hopped on the elevator and Cypher quickly pressed the up arrow.

Meanwhile, Shortelle and Pacer were watching in horror as they ran behind the glass tables and chairs in the front courtyard. Pacer was screaming as Shortelle tried to get him to calm down.

"What do we do?!" Pacer yelled.

"Just stay down!" Shortelle yelled back.

***

Florian was on the South Team with Molly, Toby, and Luke. They powered through the crowd as hard as they could. Florian was carrying the explosives with a few other guys, while guards were charging at them. Molly kept smacking them with her stick but, just like the wave guns and flower bombs, could only knock them down for a few seconds. Luke and Toby were fighting beside her with only their wave guns and flower bombs.

"These are utterly useless!" Luke yelled out.

"Keep trying! Don't stop! It's all we have!" Molly yelled back.

Zinnia could hear this happening and began pacing around the room, only stopping every couple of steps so she didn't miss hearing something important. Frustrated, she eventually stopped her pacing and blurted out, "What were they thinking?! Didn't they realize that the guards had better weapons? Obviously, they didn't just use wave guns. Idiots!"

"Z, calm down! You're not making this better! Shut up!" May yelled at her.

"Both of you, stop fighting!" Lilly yelled when she saw the horrified looks on the faces of the people in the room.

Zinnia sat down and rocked back and forth, trying to control her breathing.

"Oh, great," May said. "Now is the perfect time to have a panic attack!"

Lilly glared at May and sat down beside Zinnia, who was crying, and breathed with her to try to help her steady it.

After a few moments she started to calm down and May sat next to her and apologized. Zinnia wasn't mad at her. She knew how inconvenient her panic attacks could be. She just hugged her and they didn't say anything else.

Florian, Molly, Luke, and Toby made their way to the south entrance of the New Life facilities. They got to the door as a bullet zoomed right past Florian's head, causing him to fall down. Luke reached down to help Florian but a bullet hit him right in the shoulder and he screamed out and fell to the ground himself. Molly, who had been standing in front of Toby, reached out to try and catch Luke, but ended up leaving Toby exposed, allowing a bullet to hit him right in the chest. Molly screamed out as she whipped around and dropped to the ground where Toby had landed. Luke crawled over to them as Molly held Toby in her arms.

"I told you not to make him come!" she yelled as she pushed Luke away. "Go away!" she cried.

"Toby! Toby! Get up! You're okay!" Luke cried out.

"This is your fault you...you...you demon! Get away from him! Don't touch him!"

He didn't listen to her and kept trying to get to Toby, whose eyes were now closed. "I didn't mean it, Toby! You're not the loner! I am! Toby!" Luke sobbed and Molly stopped trying to push him away.

This angered Florian and he yelled at the other guys holding the explosives to go ahead without him. As the guys got the door open, he dragged Toby inside and dragged them behind a large glass pot holding a fake plant just inside the door. He reached inside his pack and pulled out a clotting chemical and reached for Luke's arm but Luke smacked Florian's arm away.

"Help him!" Luke yelled.

Florian grabbed his arm again and yelled, "Knock it off, you idiot!" and poured it on his shoulder before going over to Toby. Luke rolled around on the ground in agony.

Florian pulled Toby up and checked to see if he was still breathing and he was. He ripped open his shirt and saw that the bullet had gone straight through him, making him exhale in relief. He poured the clotting chemical on Toby and yelled at Molly to stay with them. Then he ran and grabbed a thick glass table and dragged it in front of them. It was too heavy for him to lay on its side but he hoped this would help block them a little.

The noise he made from dragging the table attracted the attention of a nearby guard who started running toward Florian. He decided he'd better move before the guard saw the others behind the table, and he darted forward in the direction of the elevators. The guard ran after him and tackled him to the ground. Florian rolled over and tried to reach for his wave gun but realized it must have fallen off outside, so he decided to reach for the guard's gun instead. He was able to grab it and he aimed it at his head and fired it, killing the guard instantly. He crawled away from him, and looked back in shock. He quickly jumped to his feet, threw the gun down, and ran away.

Meanwhile, Zinnia listened nervously while holding onto her necklace. Most of the people in the room had left. She knew she shouldn't keep listening too, but she couldn't leave. She just couldn't! Overwhelmed, she suddenly stood up and yelled, "I can't do this! This can't happen!" and she stormed out. May and Lilly ran after her.

"Where are you going?" May asked, catching up to her.

"We need to do something. I can't sit by as people die. They're all dying!" she yelled.

"I know, Z, but what could we possibly do??" Lilly asked, running behind them.

"I have an idea," Zinnia answered.

***

Zon and his team worked fast to run over the Thrill Seeker Mountain. It wasn't a huge mountain, but it was steep enough. A few guards chased him as he ran along the top. His dogs suddenly jumped at them and knocked them off balance, sending them over the edge. He turned to run right but got stopped by another guard, so he decided to run the other way. He pointed his wave gun behind him and shot it, but he lost his footing and it sent him forward and over the edge too. He tried to grab the edge but ended up slipping through a tiny crack into a small covered valley, getting scraped up from head to toe on the way down.

He heard his dogs whining far above him. He could just barely see the guard looking down from the top as his dogs pounced on him, knocking him down the crack Zon had just fallen through. The guard didn't have time to grab onto the side and his body flipped upside down, sending him head first to the ground. With a loud thud and crack, Zon could tell that the fall had broken his neck and killed him.

Zon stood up, dusted himself off, and looked around, unsure of where he was. All he could see were thick bushes and boulders all around him. He started looking for a spot to get out. He circled the area and couldn't find anything, so he tried standing up on a rock to get a better view. Still nothing. He decided to sit down and rest for a moment, and after a few seconds he looked to his left and saw a shaded area that looked too dark to be just a normal shadow. He got up and walked toward it. As he got closer, he noticed that it was an entrance to something.

Overcome with curiosity, he went inside and traveled down a long tunnel. After a while he came to a large, open area with a bunch of beds on the ground, tables and chairs against the walls, and maps pinned above the tables. He looked around but didn't see anyone. *This is strange*, he thought.

After scanning the room for a few minutes, he walked to the other side and saw a ladder. As he went up, he took one last look at the strange room behind him. The ladder took him to the top of the mountain again. As he got there, he opened the hatch door very slowly and saw that there was no one around there either. There was just a small cactus, strangely out of place.

He closed the hatch and blew his whistle, and his dogs came running his way from a distance. They started licking his wounds and he had to tell them to stop as he petted them and handed them the treats he had saved in his pocket. Then he looked for a way to get down the mountain. He pulled out his PED and decided which way he needed to go. He tried to call Seth one more time, but he didn't answer.

***

"Start grabbing people, Pacer! You gotta get them out of the way! Isn't this something you get trained to do, being in HR and all?!" Shortelle yelled as she started dragging the people who were standing around scared, not knowing what to do.

"No, hunny, no!" he screeched. "I don't even know what this is. What is this?! I don't know!" he cried.

"Stop being a baby and help me!"

"Okay…." he said, whining, and he ran over to a little girl and her mom and led them behind a glass planter. "Stay here, okay, little girl and mom?" He patted their heads as he ran to grab the next person. "Can we stop yet, Shortelle?"

"No!" she said before she saw a guard pointing a gun in her direction at a TOP member. "Oh crap!" she yelled and dropped to the ground to dodge the bullet. "Okay, maybe you're right. I'm getting out of here!"

They ran for the door but were blocked by a guard who had closed the exit and was standing in front of it. Shortelle stopped and looked at the guard nervously as the guard shook his head. She put her hands up and Pacer grabbed her off to the side.

"Okay, I guess we're stuck here," she said as she and Pacer crouched down on the ground.

***

Seth and Cypher got out of the elevator on the top floor and were stopped again by a large foyer full of guards. Of course, the entrance to the office was going to be heavily guarded. They wondered where the rest of the East Team went. Given they'd realized their defenses were limited, they had the heavy realization that they might not make it to the office. They stood there, frozen. One of the guards charged at them and they were pushed back onto the elevator. Cypher immediately pushed the button, sending them back down to the courtyard.

When they got to the bottom, the door opened up and Florian jumped onto the elevator.

"What are you doing here, Florian?! You're supposed to be going to the transfer pods!" Seth yelled, out of breath.

"I sent the others. I had to stay behind to help Luke and Toby. They both got shot!" he yelled back, trying to catch his breath as well.

"Are they okay?" Seth asked.

"Luke will be fine. Toby, I'm not sure. The bullet went straight through, though, so let's hope so."

"We got to the top level, but the entire entrance is blocked by guards! We don't have a way through," Cypher added.

"Sure, you do," Florian responded, pulling out an explosive from his belt and flashing a cocky grin.

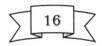
Zinnia ran into her room with May and Lilly following closely behind. She yanked her drawer open and grabbed the book.

"What do you need that for?" May asked as she watched Zinnia run around gathering stuff.

"Grab a coat…or whatever. We need to get to the city," Zinnia ordered as she headed for the door.

"Wait, what?" May asked, stopping Zinnia before she could leave.

"Yeah. What are you thinking, Z?" Lilly added.

"We need that plant, and we need to get to the city!" she answered as she tried to tug away. "If you don't want to come then, fine. Stay. But I'm going and you can't stop me."

"Stop it, Z! I mean it!" May yelled. "I'm not against you. You know darn well that we aren't going to let you go by yourself, but you gotta talk to us."

"Okay," Zinnia said, calming herself as she stopped trying to leave. "We need to get to the city with the plant. We need to make it grow so we can use the mature plant. The dormant plant isn't working!"

"How on earth are we going to do that?" Lilly blurted out in disbelief.

"We need to get to the science lab, get the plant and the masks, and take it to the city wall. We'll grow it and load the bombs when we get there. That way we can keep it hidden in the shade during the trip. Less exposure that way."

"How are we going to get there? Or *in* there?" May asked

"I don't know. I haven't thought that far. Let's just get the plant first and head up to the tech level for the extra bombs. Okay?"

"Okay, then," Lilly agreed. "Let's do this!"

The girls ran to the science lab and peered through the window. They could see two scientists working under their microscopes. They scanned the room, searching for the plant.

"It's right there!" Lilly said excitedly.

"Shhhh!" Zinnia said, putting her finger up to her mouth.

Lilly covered her mouth quickly and then uncovered it to mouth the word, "Sorry."

They saw both the dormant and the mature plant in glass cases on the far wall. The mature plant had a sun-light over it.

Suddenly May realized something and said, "How are we going to bring it with us? How are we going to keep it covered, or in the shade, or whatever?"

"Good point," Zinnia admitted, as she turned around and crouched below the window.

"What about Zon's pack? It's a box. I think it's big enough to hold it and it's solid," May recommended.

"That's a great idea," Zinnia agreed.

They headed toward Zon's room to find his box. May ran over to his bed. "He keeps it down here!" she yelled as she reached below it. She grabbed the wooden box and saw his walking stick and decided to grab that too. "Here, got it."

"Great, let's go," Zinnia said, heading for the door. They got back to the science lab and saw that the two scientists were still in the room.

"We can try the distraction method again," Lilly recommended. "You and May distract them, and I can go for the case."

"That could work actually," Zinnia agreed. "Okay, May, you go that way and take that stick with you, and Lilly and I will go in that door. Oh Lilly. Just grab the dormant plant. We will grow it when we get there."

They all nodded in agreement and headed for the two doors. They entered the room at the same time and both of the scientists stood up.

"What's going on?" one of them asked, looking back and forth between May, and Zinnia and Lilly.

"We just need to get something," May said, holding the stick up.

"What are you going to do with that stick?" the scientist closest to May asked suspiciously.

They started walking towards May and Zinnia. Lilly jetted out from behind Zinnia and ran for the case while Zinnia went toward the scientist closest to her. He saw Lilly going for the case and turned away from Zinnia. Lilly got the case open and reached inside just before the scientist grabbed her and flipped her around with her arm still behind the glass.

"I can't let you take that," he said as he tried to close the case with Lilly still half inside of it.

Lilly was stuck. She couldn't figure out what to do. Suddenly, she got an idea. She quickly grabbed a flower off of the plant, yanked her arm out of the case, and shoved it in the scientist's face, causing him to drop to the floor. The other scientist turned away from May and was about to run to help him when May smacked her as hard as she could with the stick, causing her to trip over a chair. The girls quickly ran out of the lab with Lilly carrying the plant, and raced up to the tech level.

Lilly ran all the way to the back wall and yelled behind her, "Follow me! The bombs are back here in the storage room!"

The girls got inside the storage room and closed the door behind them. Lilly looked for something big to put in front of the door. She didn't really think the scientists followed them, but she did it just in case. After barricading the door, she ran to the extra supply of bombs and realized they didn't bring anything to carry them.

"Shoot!" Zinnia yelled. "What now?"

Lilly searched around the room and remembered that there was a cover over the flybot. She ran to it, pulled the cover off, and started cutting it with a sharp piece of metal she found on the floor.

"Lilly, you're a genius!" Zinnia praised, making Lilly stop and laugh for a second.

"You're the genius, my friend! I'm resourceful," she responded in a proud tone.

"Yes, you are," Zinnia replied, enjoying her friend's proud moment.

May added, "You know what I just thought of? Once we put the mature flowers in the bombs they'll turn to dust!

"You're right!" Zinnia yelled. "Shoot! Oh, I got it! The sun-lights. I saw a sun-light over the mature plant in the lab. It must be keeping the plant mature! We can put one in each ball!"

Lilly blurted out, "I know where they are!" and she ran to one of the rows of bots, grabbed a handful, and ran back to them.

"Okay, let's load these up!" Zinnia said, grabbing a bunch of the bombs and setting them on the ripped off piece of flybot cover.

After they put a sun-light in each bomb, they tied the cover up in a knot with all the bombs inside it. They stood there for a moment, not sure what to do next. Now it was May's turn to ask, "What now?"

"What about the tunnels?" Zinnia suggested. "They went down the tunnels to get there. The spot they drilled would still be open, obviously. We could find a way to get down it really fast. What about that flybot? Does it work?"

Lilly answered, "Yes, it works! It just had a few screws loose, but we've already tested it out and it flies great. The tunnels are a no-go, though. The flybot won't be able to fit through the holes they drilled with the drills blocking them, but we can drill ourselves!" she yelled as she ran toward the bay doors.

"How are we going to do that?" May asked.

Lilly got the bay door open, pointed to one of the extra drills, ran inside of the elevator, and yelled at the girls to follow her. Once everyone was inside, she showed them the button on the elevator, pointed up, and told them that it used to be open, but it got closed off because Cypher said it wasn't safe to have such a large opening to the Underground.

"Okay, let's get moving guys. They've probably already told someone what happened in the science lab and I bet they're looking for us," May urged.

They loaded the plant into Zon's box, the bombs into the flybot, and pushed it closer to the bay doors. Then they drove the drill onto the elevator and Lilly showed them where the "on" switch was. They hit the "up" button on the elevator and stopped it as soon as they were close enough to the top. Lilly told them to extend the tube out to the side of the elevator so the rubble would fall down below. She climbed on top of the drill and locked the tube that was around the tip of the drill into place on the ceiling. She jumped down and with the others, held the tube steady as they pressed the "on" switch and braced themselves for the weight of the debris traveling down the tube. Since it was a short distance to the outside, it happened very quickly and took barely any strength. They were all impressed at how smooth it actually was. After they saw light, they stopped the drill and brought the elevator down again. They drove the drill back into the storage room, and then they hopped on the flybot.

Lilly looked at the girls and said, "Uh, sorry, but Cypher is the one who drove this. I don't know how."

"It's okay, Lilly," May said. "We used to fly these on the farm. It's the only form of transportation we had out there."

"Oh good," she said and hopped in the passenger seat.

"May, you hold this in the back. I'll drive," Zinnia instructed as she handed May the pack with the Open Eden plant. "You guys ready?" she asked, exhaling and then taking a deep breath in.

"We're ready," they answered in unison.

Zinnia drove the flybot forward onto the elevator, pressed the "fly mode" button and flew straight up the shaft. When they reached the top, the sun's warmth hit their faces like a blanket straight out of the dryer. It was a beautiful day. Zinnia could see that a light rain had fallen and covered the trees and their changing colors. She could hear the birds singing and the creatures running about. It felt like it had been years since she had been outside, even though it had only been a couple of months. The sweet aroma of wild flowers filled her lungs as she breathed in each refreshing breath of the cool, clean air.

"Oh, I miss home," Zinnia said as she inhaled deeply again. "I miss Mom more."

"Me too," May agreed.

Zinnia flew above the trees, turned west, and pushed forward as fast as she could. As soon as they got going, May started screaming in the back seat. Both Zinnia and Lilly looked back and saw vines and flowers from the Open Eden plant quickly growing out of the cracks of Zon's box and the flowers turning to dust as soon as the shade from the clouds touched them. Each time they came out of the shadows the vines grew faster and longer.

May coughed and frantically yelled, "I gotta get rid of this!" She was about to throw the plant over the edge, when all of a sudden, the colorful birds appeared and started diving down one by one, snipping off the pieces of the vines as they grew. Zinnia then drove the flybot down to get below the cover of the trees and out of the sun. May coughed a couple more times and dusted off the ash from the plant's dead flowers. And just as quickly as they got under the cover of the trees, they ran into another problem. After a few seconds of flying through the forest, they started hearing an all too familiar sound, screeching and meowing from the feral felines getting louder and louder as they went.

"Oh no, not again!" May yelled, clutching Zon's pack.

"Just keep going, Z!" Lilly yelled out over the noise.

Just as she finished her sentence a cat jumped into the flybot and started clawing at Zinnia. Lilly grabbed it and threw it out, but suddenly more cats jumped on the front of the flybot and Lilly couldn't reach them to knock them off.

"Here! Take this!" May yelled and handed Lilly Zon's walking stick.

Lilly began knocking them off of the hood one by one, but they kept coming. Every once in a while, one would land in the flybot and she'd have to act quickly to get it out. Pretty soon there were just too many and she couldn't keep up.

"We gotta fly up again, Z! I can't keep them off anymore!" Lilly yelled over the screeching.

"NO!" May yelled back. "I can't breathe up there with the plant trying to grow!

"I agree," Zinnia yelled. "We can't. It's too dangerous!"

"Well, this is too dangerous too! At least up there we have the birds helping us!" Lilly yelled, as she looked up and saw the birds circling above.

May looked up and shouted, "That's what they were doing the night we had to get the lung bot for Cypher! Right before they…"

Suddenly the birds funneled down, weaving in and out of the trees, creating a tornado around the flybot. They began diving around it, severing the cats in half with their beaks as they went. Zinnia and Lilly's mouths dropped wide open in shock, but they kept flying as fast as they could go.

"Where are we going?" May yelled out.

"I was thinking maybe we should get to that passthrough! There's gotta be a reason why Dad would want to lead us there! I don't remember where the entrance to the ZGS tunnel is that we came through. Do you?" Zinnia asked, looking at Lilly and May. They both shook their heads. "Okay, then. That's the best idea I have."

Zinnia quickly handed May the book and May yelled out the coordinates so Zinnia could set the navigation. When they arrived at the passthrough they got out of the flybot, with the birds still circling around them. May handed the book back to Zinnia and she went to the page with the "G."

"Get out," she said. "I think Dad intended us to use this book to get out of New Life. Remember in the video he said, "If you ever find yourself stuck in life… He put these coordinates on this page. He wanted us to come here."

"What about Seth's video and the instructions that got us out when we left?" May asked.

"I can't say for sure, but I don't think Rob knew that this was in here. Don't you think he would have given it to Seth had he known?" she asked seriously.

"I suppose so," May answered.

"Dad put the clues in this book, knowing I would have eventually figured it out. Rob knew Dad wanted us to find the Underground, and he instructed him to give us this book so we could. Maybe Rob put the web address at the end of the book for us to find, not knowing that Dad had already mapped out a plan for our escape."

The girls shifted their gaze to the wall and saw the small bird symbol, like the one on the box and in the book. They didn't see a handle or a door or anything so they looked around the area.

"Zon said the passthrough goes deep below the wall through a tunnel. We just need to find the entrance," Zinnia said, looking around the ground.

Lilly started picking up rocks and May began pushing bushes to the side. After a few minutes with no success, Zinnia decided to stand against the wall where the symbol was. She opened the book to look for more clues. On the "G" page, there was a small tree at the end of a line on a graph. Zinnia held the book up. A light came on in her eyes. "This graph is a hidden map! See?" She brought it down so it was parallel with the ground and drew a line from where she stood to the tree on the graph. She looked back up and pointed to a tree. She ran over to it and found another bird symbol, this one sticking slightly out, that had a small handle on it. She pulled open the handle and saw a small keypad on the other side. She noticed a number next to the picture of the tree in the book and typed those numbers in the keypad. They heard a click and a noise behind them on the ground, as a square opened up. It wasn't big but definitely big enough to fit a person. Zinnia and May looked at each other nervously.

"Oh geez," Lilly said as she sat down and put her legs in the hole. "No monsters here either." She smiled and shook her head as she dropped down into the hole. She stuck her head back up and said, "it's big enough for us to crawl through. Come on."

They dropped down into the hole and Zinnia held her PED up for a light. She noticed a little button on the inside of the small tunnel and pushed it, closing the opening behind her.

They crawled forward a little way, and then the tunnel dropped down again and kept doing that for a few hundred feet. After a while, they got to the lowest point, which happened to be a bit bigger than the rest of it. This spot was big enough for them to stand up in. There was a stone wall that had another keypad and a screen on it. Zinnia walked up to it and took the book out again to look inside. She scanned the first page over and over but couldn't find anything that made this room make any sense. They sat down for a moment to rest.

"Here, let me see," May said, putting her hand out for the book.

Zinnia handed it to her and took a deep breath in and rubbed her face. Lilly examined the small room. There were some tools and electrical parts laying around.

May looked at the first page and then flipped to the next one. "What about the next pages?"

"Those are for different things, I think. The first one is about getting out of the city. The second page says, 'Lights out' and is equally as confusing," Zinnia said, feeling defeated.

May noticed another graph on the "L" page, stood up, and held it up with the screen in the background. She reached forward and tapped on the screen a few times, thinking that maybe it was like their PEDs. The graph had a picture of a light bulb at the end of the line, just like the graph with the tree. She tapped on the screen in the same place the light bulb was on the graph in the book. The screen suddenly lit up, displaying a numeric code. Zinnia stood up and put her hand out for the book so she could look at it.

Zinnia suddenly got excited. "Dome shield, electricity, glass! This is the control panel for the Glass Project! Dad must have moved it! I remember this screen!"

May and Lilly got excited too.

"What do you think he wanted us to do with this?" May asked.

Zinnia typed the numbers to the kill code into the keypad, and before she pushed the last digit she said, "Lights out."

Suddenly, there was a loud rumble and the ground shook. The girls heard a crowd of screams as the city's electricity shut down building by building. They looked at each other nervously.

"One more thing. There's another symbol here," Zinnia said as she pointed to the screen and opened the book again. "I saw this symbol on the first 'S' page.

This page had information about Italian Renaissance architecture and had a diagram and a mathematical equation for the dome on the top of a church. She clicked on the symbol on the screen and a different screen popped up. Zinnia typed the numbers from the math equation into the box and once again, they heard a loud rumble and more screaming.

"What was that?" Lilly asked.

"The dome shield. I just disarmed it. I don't know if this is what you wanted us to do, Dad, but we did it," Zinnia said as she shined her PED's light forward and headed in the direction of the city.

17

Florian hit the "up" button in the elevator, shooting them to the top floor. As soon as the door opened, he lit his explosive, threw it into the foyer in front of the office, and hit the "down" button as fast as he could. As the elevator was flying down at top speed, they heard a loud explosion, the elevator shook and screeched to halt, and then the lights went out. They turned around and looked down to the ground from approximately the 200th floor and saw that all the lights had shut off everywhere. They pressed the button a few times, but the elevator door wouldn't open. They stood there, confused.

"That wasn't us, was it?" Florian asked.

"No," Cypher answered. "There's no way that one explosion would shut down the entire New Life facility. This is something else."

They looked down again and could see people running around screaming and falling to the ground everywhere.

"This isn't what I thought was going to happen," Seth said, shaking his head. "They claimed this was a place of peace. We knew better, but they wanted to uphold that image to the people. I never expected this kind of reaction."

"I don't know, Dad, but we need to get out of here. Here, help me with the door," Florian said as he tried to pry the elevator door open.

***

Down on the basement floor, where they were holding Rob and Theo, guards swarmed around and passed through, grabbing guns from a storage room nearby.

"Hey. Hey, Theo," Rob said, trying to get his attention.

Theo went over to the cell and was about to ask what he wanted, when the guard assigned to watch them yelled at Theo to stay away from him and to sit back down.

"Am I a prisoner?" Theo asked. "Because if I am, then that means President Sophia asked you to hold me down here against my will. Is that what's going on here right now?"

"Be quiet and sit back down, I said!" the guard yelled as he stood up and walked toward Theo.

"Sounds to me like that's what's going on," Rob said before getting a mean glare from the guard.

"If I have to tell you two to shut up one more time, I'm going to press the shock button and shut you up myself," the guard threatened.

Rob immediately turned around and sat down. He'd had about all he could take of the electric shock that flooded the cell, knocking him down and keeping him down for hours at a time. At first, they just used it while they were trying to get information out of him. After a while, it became a fun game the guards would play to see who could keep him knocked down the longest.

"An electric shock would shut *him* up maybe, but not me," Theo said, stupidly challenging the guard.

"There's an empty cell behind you," the guard responded, holding up his gun.

Theo growled angrily. "This is stupid! Call my dad! There's obviously something going on out there. He wouldn't want me stuck down here defenseless!"

"Your dad is the one who told me to hold you down here, idiot!"

Theo finally sat back down in defeat. He had no idea what was going on, but it was no shock to him that his dad had finally dumped him off. He knew there was no use in fighting it. His dad hated him…and he wished he could hate his dad too, but he wasn't like him.

All of a sudden, there was a loud rumble. The ground shook, and the lights flickered and went off. Theo and Rob looked at each other and then at the guard. Rob quickly pushed his cell door open and both he and Theo ran at the guard, knocking him down. They took his handcuffs and cuffed him to the nearby bench, and stood there for a moment, looking at each other.

"Thanks for the help," Rob said before running off down the hall and disappearing.

Theo decided he'd track down his father, even though he put him down there. He needed to figure out what was going on. He started to leave but then he stopped and thought for a few seconds. Knowing there was a chance his dad could turn on him, he looked at the guard, reached down, and grabbed his gun, even though he had no idea how to use it.

***

Zon finally made his way to the ZGS tour car station. It was a ghost town and the ZGSs didn't seem to have any attendants anywhere. There were absolutely no citizens around and only a few guards here and there. Zon had lost his other team members and he just hoped they'd already made their way to the New Life facility. He ran to the tour cars and opened the doors one by one, instructing his dogs to get in.

A guard suddenly ran up behind him, flipped him around, and pointed his gun in his face. Zon ducked down and kicked at the guard's knee as hard as he could, knocking him to the ground and causing his gun to fire. He heard a high-pitched yelp and whipped around just in time to see one of his dogs fall to the ground. Zon yelled out angrily and jumped to his feet. He was about to go after the guard but his dogs beat him to it. They ripped him to shreds as he screamed out in agony, pulling off chunks of his flesh, piece by piece, until he stopped moving.

Zon blew his whistle and motioned to his dogs to keep loading into the ZGSs, while he caught his breath. There was not a moment to cry this time.

Once the rest of the dogs were loaded into the tour cars, Zon set the destination in each ZGS and closed the doors. He got into his tour car and sent them off down the track.

They were flying at full speed when the lights suddenly flickered off and the ZGSs dropped from their hover inside of the tube track, sending the spheres rolling and crashing into each other. Zon's car smashed into the car in front of him.

"What now?!" Zon yelled out angrily as he worked to get his door open between the two cars.

When he got out, he saw that the entire track had shut down and all of the spheres had fallen out. The lights were off everywhere, not just on the track. He climbed over each sphere to get to the dogs and pulled each door open, letting them out onto the track. He stood for a moment, trying to figure out how he was going to get there.

"Well, I guess we run," he said and he blew his whistle, sending his pack down the tube track as fast as they could go.

***

Zinnia, May, and Lilly exited the small tunnel and saw chaos all around them. There were TOP members laid out everywhere. "They never had a chance," Zinnia said, wincing at the sight.

She pulled her attention away from the battle and opened the book again. She stood against the wall and held the book parallel to the ground, following the line with her finger. She pointed up and there was a tree on that side too, confirming her suspicion that it matched the other side perfectly, with the tree being the end point on the graph. After walking over to the tree and locating the keypad, she entered the code in the book and the small square on the ground closed.

The girls looked up as something grabbed their attention. The birds had crossed over the wall and were now circling and protecting them again.

"The bombs!" Lilly yelled. "We need to get the plant to grow so we can fill them with the flowers!"

May pulled Zon's pack off of her back and held it up. "I got the plant!"

Zinnia looked at the plant and then looked at the ground for a place to set it so it could grow in the sun.

"What do we do after it grows?" May asked.

Zinnia, still looking around, stopped. "We fill the bombs. But...oh no..."

"Oh no, what??" May asked, nervously.

"We forgot the masks!"

"Oh no..." May responded. "Oh no!"

Zinnia started panicking.

"Zinnia, stay with me!" Lilly yelled.

Zinnia calmed herself down and thought for a few moments, still looking around. She suddenly perked up.

"The birds!" she yelled.

"What about them?" May asked.

"We can lay out the bombs, set the plant to grow, and they can pluck the flowers, and put them into the bomb!" Zinnia exclaimed. "Like they were doing on the way here above the tree line. They've been helping us this far!"

"That's asking an awful lot from birds... I mean, how on earth do you plan on conveying that plan to them?" May asked with an exasperated tone in her voice.

"I don't know! What's making them help us now? How do they even understand that we need help? There's something bigger going on with them. I just don't know what it is yet. Let's just set everything out and see what happens. I feel like they understand us. I just feel it," Zinnia said, pleading with them to understand.

"Sounds good to me," Lilly said.

"Okay. Let's give this a shot," Zinnia said. They opened all of the bombs they had and set them on the ground with the open doors facing up.

Then Zinnia took the plant from May and walked out from the tree's shadows to set the pack on the ground. She barely had time to move away before the vines shot out of the cracks of the pack. They broke through the box and started growing wildly out of control, extending out over any area that had sunlight beaming down, with parts of the plant dying as soon as it hit the shadows.

"Get back!" May yelled as Zinnia fell onto the ground. She dragged herself away from the plant and jumped to her feet to run back to May and Lilly.

They watched as the plant grew the bright colorful flowers. It seemed like it wasn't going to stop growing! There was too much sunlight around!

"Shoot!" Lilly yelled. "What do we do?!"

"I don't know!" Zinnia replied as they all covered up their mouth and nose.

Suddenly, the circling birds dove down and cast a shadow around the ends of the vines to stop the plant's growth. And without any instruction of any kind, they began plucking flowers off one by one and dropping them into the flower bombs.

Lilly burst out laughing excitedly. "Oh my gosh! Look at them go!"

All three of them started cheering and laughing, but only for a few seconds. They had work to do.

The girls loaded up their pockets with as many bombs as they could carry and watched as a group of the birds flew down, ripped the plant out of the ground, and carried it away. There was still a large group of them circling the girls, and there were birds who had grabbed extra flowers and were now flying with them in their beaks.

"What now, Z?" Lilly asked, still wearing an impressed look on her face.

"We have to help them!" she yelled over the sound of the birds. "We need to get into New Life! We need to get the bombs to the TOP members and give them a fighting chance!"

The girls ran toward the courtyard doors and quickly pulled one open, only to be met by the guards that had stopped Shortelle and Pacer from exiting before.

"Quick!" Zinnia yelled to Lilly.

Lilly had already set the flower bomb to open after five seconds and just hoped that was the perfect amount of time for them to get out of the way. She clicked the button and threw it at the guards. They were about to run off to the side when Shortelle yelled out to them.

"Over here! Over here!" she yelled and the girls ran over to her as quickly as they could.

Suddenly they saw the nearby guards drop to the ground and start frothing at the mouth, shaking uncontrollably.

"What was that?!" Pacer yelled in a shrill voice.

Zinnia turned around to face Shortelle and Pacer. "I'm glad you guys are okay. I was worried about what might happen to you," she said, out of breath.

"Oh, you were worried about us, were you?" Shortelle asked sarcastically. "Well, thanks so much for your concern! All of this is your fault!" she yelled.

"I know…and I promise I will explain all of this to you later, but right now we need to get downstairs to find Florian. We gotta get these bombs to him so he can use them. They're getting killed out there."

"The stairs are blocked by guards," May said to Zinnia and Lilly.

"I don't know who Florian is, but whatever. Anywhere is better than here," Shortelle said as she rose to her feet, pulling Pacer up with her.

"How do we get downstairs?" May asked. "We dropped the power so I'm guessing the elevators aren't working."

"Of course…" Shortelle said, rolling her eyes. "Of course, that was you guys. Freaking A, man. Come on," she ordered, walking off and waving at them to follow. "I know a way down."

Shortelle brought them down through a bot hall. They were narrow spaces between the walls where the bots traveled to get to their jobs. Some of the bots had shut down with the power and they had to climb over them. Pacer looked at them as if they were dead bodies too.

They got to the bottom level and exited the bot halls right into the cell holding room, where Rob and Theo had been detained, and saw the guard cuffed to the bench. He spotted the badge on Shortelle and Pacer's uniforms and begged them to let him out. They just kept walking with disgusted looks on their faces.

"Which way do we go now?" Lilly asked.

"Here…" Zinnia said, pulling out her PED.

She brought up a map and found where they were, and she could see points that looked like basins. The map on her PED only showed the floor layout in green lines, for some reason, with no detailed pictures of any kind. *For extra security maybe?* she wondered. She wasn't exactly sure what the transfer pods looked like but she imagined they might be in the shape of bathtub basins.

"I bet these are the transfer pods. Florian should be there already." She pulled her PED down and headed toward the basin-looking things.

"Yeah, I think you're right," Shortelle agreed and followed.

They wound through many halls and it seemed like they were going to get lost, but Zinnia kept moving forward, determined to get there. With the power out, none of the doors were holding them back. They noticed there weren't any guards around anywhere, and they were a little confused by it.

"I really thought we'd run into more guards down here considering the TOP members are here to destroy the transfer pods," Zinnia said, shaking her head and looking around.

They finally turned their last corner to the room with what looked like large basins on her PED and stopped immediately in their tracks, completely horrified at the sickening scene before them. Rob was there, as frozen as they had just become, with his mouth wide open. He didn't even realize that a tear had fallen down his cheek. He was just stuck and couldn't move and now so was everyone else.

The sound alone made May turn around and vomit. Pacer turned around and puked too and then passed out. The screams were deafening. There were children of all ages hooked up to machines in beds, in baths, on the walls. Some of them were cut open with their organs exposed. The children in the baths were struggling to keep their heads above the water as their machines failed to keep them breathing. The children that hung on the walls had tubes coming out of every orifice. The machines keeping them unconscious had shut off, and it was clear that some of them had died. Some had choked on their vomit, others were gasping for air, and some were crying with tears streaming down their faces. The kids who were alive noticed them standing there and looked at them with begging and pleading in their eyes.

Shortelle angrily ran over to the baths.

"No! Don't," Rob yelled. "You could kill them."

"They're already dying!" she yelled back as she reached into the bath, pulled the child out of the strap holding her shoulders down, and pulled her above the water. There was a tube attached to her belly button and Shortelle realized that if she pulled her all the way up, the tube might come out, and she didn't know if that would kill her or not.

"Damnit!" She looked the girl in her eyes and said, "Just stay here. I can't pull you all the way out, but I promise I will find a way. You just wait. I have to help the others too." The little girl nodded while she wiped the tears from her eyes.

Zinnia, May, and Rob ran over and helped as many as they could but after a few minutes Zinnia looked over at Shortelle and shook her head. "I need to get to Florian. It's the only chance we have. We need to get people down here to help."

Shortelle nodded, out of breath. "You go. We'll stay here with them."

Zinnia grabbed May's arm and nodded to Lilly to follow.

"Rob, are you coming with us or staying here?" May asked.

"I need to find my guys. I'm sorry," he said in Shortelle's direction.

She shook her head and said, "Go. It's okay. Go." Rob nodded at the others and left. Pacer had finally come to and looked over at Shortelle with tears streaming down his cheeks. "I'm staying here with you, doll face," he said to her sadly.

"I'll come back, I promise," Zinnia yelled as they left the room, still sick to their stomachs.

18

Seth, Cypher, and Florian had finally gotten the elevator door open and saw they were on the 201st floor. They noticed right away that this was a residential level so they ran down the hallways looking for another elevator or stairs to bring them back up. After climbing the 49 floors it took for them to reach the top, they opened the door and were immediately met with black melted soot and body parts that looked like they had been put into a blender with the top off. They covered their mouths and coughed as the smoke filled their lungs.

Out of nowhere, a loud buzzing filled the hallways and the lights came back on. Seth and Florian looked around confused.

"It's the backup power," Cypher said through his coughing. "Which way?"

"This way," Florian responded as he started walking over the bodies toward the Capitol Office.

"We can't go in there unarmed. We already know these things do nothing," Cypher pointed out as he held up his wave gun.

Florian bent down to grab a guard's gun and said, "We aren't."

"Florian, you shouldn't pick that up. It's dangerous," Seth warned him seriously.

"It's dangerous not to have it! Dad, this is it…all of the training and all of the planning. We're here and we're getting our butts kicked out there! We have to stop this. We won't get another chance. People have died and they're going to keep dying unless we end this. Capture the presidents, broadcast to the nation, blow up the transfer pods, and hopefully, if all goes well, we get all of the other underground colonies and the citizens of New Life to join us. None of that will happen unless we get in there and capture the presidents!"

Seth nodded reluctantly. "Okay. But Florian, there's something I need to tell you. Something I should have told you a long time ago…"

Before he could get his next sentence out, two guards turned around the corner and started shooting at them. As the bullets flew over their heads, they ran around the corner closest to them, but not before Seth and Cypher grabbed guns too.

After shooting back at the guards a few times, Florian ran for the Capitol Office door and yelled, "What's the code?" as he dodged bullets.

After Cypher shouted out the numbers, Florian yelled for him and Seth to follow. Once inside, he closed the door and locked it. They could hear the guards shooting at the door but were relieved when they realized the walls and doors to the office were bulletproof.

They stopped to catch their breath for a second and turned around to see President Liam holding his wife and kids in his arms in the corner behind Sophia's desk. To the left was a door leading to Liam's office and to the right was a small sitting room.

"Please. Don't hurt us. I never liked this. I was trying to change it. Honestly," Liam begged nervously.

Cypher walked over to him and grabbed his arms with his family crying, refusing to let him go. "You, go in there," Cypher commanded his wife and kids, nodding to Liam's office to the left of them. "I wouldn't try to leave if I were you. It's a bloodbath out there. You're safer in the office."

Liam nodded at his wife, instructing her to go. She reluctantly led the kids into his office and Cypher closed the door behind them.

After the door was closed, Cypher turned around, only to be met by Colton's gun pointed at him from the sitting room on the other side of the office and Sophia standing behind him, using Colton as a shield. Colton took a step forward and nodded to Seth and Florian, motioning for them to stand next to Cypher. They walked forward slowly, turning to their right to face Colton and Sophia when they got there.

Once they were in sight, Sophia let out a gasp. Colton turned his head to look at her and immediately recognized the look in her eyes. A look of love and hurt at the same time, a longing that caused a weakness in her that he had never seen before. He realized at that moment that she was looking at Seth. He looked back and forth between them as they had their eyes fixed on each other.

This sparked a rage inside of Colton. Sophia broke her focus from Seth as soon as she realized that Colton had just seen that exchange between them. She tried to grab Colton's arm but he pulled away from her. She tried to reach for him again but Colton yanked his arm away violently and walked towards the door. Seth and Florian raised their guns up and yelled at him to stay back or they were going to shoot but he ignored them and kept walking.

"Get out of my way!" he yelled, still pointing his gun at them.

"Don't leave me, Colton! Don't leave me with them! They'll kill me!" Sophia yelled out.

"Not my problem anymore," he responded as he left the room with anger in his eyes.

He pressed the button to get out of the office, and as soon as he got out, he shot the guards that were trying to get in and kicked one as he stepped over him to leave. He suddenly stopped.

Cypher ran behind him and quickly pressed the button to close the door and changed the lock's combination from inside, locking Colton out.

***

Zinnia, May, and Lilly ran down the halls, still trying to find their way to the transfer pods. After what felt like an hour, they finally found the room and were excited to see TOP members there with the explosives. They looked around but couldn't find Florian anywhere.

"Where is he?" Zinnia asked frantically.

"Who are you looking for?" Casey turned around and asked.

Lilly jumped up and down. "Casey! I know Casey, guys... Well, I don't know him, know him, but Cypher introduced us before, when he showed me the drills..."

"We're looking for Florian," May blurted out, interrupting Lilly's rambling.

"I don't know. He told us to go on because he had to stop and help Luke and Toby," Casey answered.

"I saw him heading up the elevator with Seth and Cypher," another TOP member added.

"Then that means he went up to the Capitol Office with them. They're headed up to capture the presidents!" Zinnia yelled as she turned around. "Thanks guys! Oh wait, hold on!" She reached into her pockets and pulled out a few of the flower bombs and handed them to Casey.

"Thanks, but these are useless. They knocked the guards down for like five seconds," he said, trying to hand them back to her.

"You don't understand. These have mature flowers inside. They are deadly. Not like the stun bombs you brought," she insisted, not taking them back.

Casey's eyes widened. "Oh... Thank you," he said as he watched the girls run back the way they came.

Zinnia took her PED out. Somehow, she remembered the turns they had made and was able to find her way back to the bot hall they had come through. As they climbed out to the lobby, they heard a loud buzz and all the lights turned on. The electronic music resumed playing in the background and they saw the elevator doors open up. Everyone stopped what they were doing and looked around for a moment.

"What just happened?" May asked, frozen in place.

"The original electricity must have kicked on. Like a backup," Zinnia answered. "That's good, though. I was worried we would have to take the stairs up. Now we can use the elevators. Come on," she said as she ran toward them and the fighting carried on around the courtyard.

Right as they were about to enter the elevator, another symphony of screams broke out around the courtyard. They flipped around quickly to see hundreds of the colorful birds flooding the courtyard and dropping flowers on the guards, causing them to drop to the ground, shaking and frothing at the mouth. They noticed that some of the birds were now swarming around the citizens, shielding them from the flower's toxins and ushering them away from the guards. The citizens were utterly frightened and swinging their arms around, trying to get away from the birds as they screamed. The girls couldn't believe what they were seeing, but they pulled themselves away and jumped on the elevator.

As they went up, May, out of breath, turned to face Zinnia and said, "Hey, Z, you know what I just realized? You haven't panicked in a while… I mean you started to when we realized we didn't have the masks, but besides that, not since we were back in the Underground, I think."

Zinnia thought for a moment. "Huh, you're right. I haven't," she responded as she looked up at Lilly and then May. May smiled warmly at Zinnia and nodded her head, putting her hand on her shoulder.

When the elevator got to the top floor, they immediately covered their mouths and coughed as they saw the horrific bloody scene in front of them. They were frozen again.

"Well, this isn't the worst thing we've seen today," Lilly broke the silence, looking down at the bodies on the ground as they stepped out of the elevator. When they looked up, Colton was standing there, across the foyer with his gun pointed at their heads.

"Well, who are you?" he asked with a psychotic sneer. "Zinnia, May, Lilly? I was wondering if I'd ever get to meet you three."

The girls stood there shaking, not sure what to do, when Theo suddenly burst into the foyer from a different elevator. He was now frozen with them, not moving, looking back and forth between the girls and his dad.

***

Cypher grabbed Sophia's arms and held them tight as Florian grabbed her wrists to put the handcuffs around them.

"Florian, Florian, please…don't do this," she begged.

"Wait a second. How does she…how do you know my name?!" Florian demanded angrily.

"Don't do it, Sophia. I'm warning you," Seth said, glaring at her.

"Or what?" she laughed. "You'll tie me up?"

"Dad?" Florian interrupted.

"I'm your mother, Florian!" she blurted out.

Florian's face went pale. His head started spinning. He looked down at the ground, searching his brain for answers. "This whole time?" he asked, looking up into his father's eyes.

Seth had a soft, apologetic look on his face and he answered, "I'm sorry, son. I wanted to tell you, but I wanted to wait until after all of this was over. You weren't supposed to be up here. You were supposed to be down with the transfer pods."

Florian looked at his dad for a few more moments and then got even more angry. "No! You are NOT my mother! I could never have a murderer for a mother! You will never be my mother!"

"See what you did, Seth?! He hates me! He never even got to know me because you took him away from me!" she yelled out with tears forming in her eyes.

"And what should I have done? You knew the truth and you refused to leave!" Seth yelled back.

"Oh, come on… Everyone knows that human beings don't become self-aware until they go through puberty…" Sophia started making excuses but Seth cut her off.

"Those are lies! We know the truth, and you *know* that I know the truth. You told me yourself! Or have you forgotten?"

"I told you to just wait until my term was up and we could be a family and go back to normal, but you didn't listen. I should have never told you about TOP," she said, shaking her head.

"In forty years?? You wanted me to wait forty years to have my wife back?" Seth asked, baffled at what she was saying.

"You wouldn't have lost me. We would still be together. We just needed to live with the truth together for a while," she pleaded with him to see reason.

"I couldn't have lived with the truth. I couldn't believe that you could," he replied, shaking his head.

She stood there silently for a moment and then quietly added, "I'm not a murderer."

"There are millions of children who, if they were alive, would disagree with you," Seth responded, disgusted.

"Those parents made that decision, not me!" she yelled, defending herself.

"They never had a choice! The uncertainty, the question of our mortality, is what drives us to live meaningful lives. It's what makes us cherish the time we have! Not knowing if you are ever going to see your loved ones again, makes us love them until our last breath. It's what makes us fight for our children!" He paused to look at Florian. "...not kill them, or 'send them on to their new lives.'"

Sophia stayed silent. Seth continued, "I begged you to leave with me, but you wouldn't. I took Florian with me because I sure as hell wasn't going to leave him with you. You knew the truth and you stayed, Sophia. You made your choice. You chose power over your family."

***

Colton took a few steps toward the girls and they were now standing face to face with his gun pointed up at them.

"What are you doing, Dad?" Theo asked, taking deep breaths.

"Mind your own business, son. This doesn't concern you, and what are you doing up here?! You should be down in the holding cell watching Rob."

"I know damn well that you only put me down there to hold me against my will! Whatever is going on right now, I'm not going to let you hurt these girls," Theo said firmly, looking over at May. May looked nervously back at him.

"Yeah? And what are you going to do about it?" he challenged, turning his gun on him.

Theo slowly lifted the gun he had taken from the guard and aimed it at Colton's face.

"Oh, you're a tough guy now?" Colton said, laughing mockingly.

Just when tensions were highest, Zon's voice blasted over May's PED.

"May! May! I'm coming! I'm close! I got through to Casey and he said you were going up to the Presidents' office! Wait for me! Don't go up there! "

May yelled into her PED. "Zon! I'm here! We're already up here! We're outside of the office!"

Colton suddenly took a few more steps forward, grabbed May, and put his gun up against her temple.

Zinnia and Lilly screamed out, "No! May! Let her go!"

"Get out of my way, Theo!" Colton yelled as he started making his way toward the elevator Theo had come up. "You guys want to see what happened to your father? I'll show you!"

Theo, not wanting his dad to shoot May, slowly got out of his way. He'd never shot a gun before and didn't trust himself to shoot Colton without hitting May.

Colton dragged her into the elevator with him and as soon as his back was turned to Theo, Theo lunged at him but Colton pushed him away and smacked the "down" button, shooting Colton and May to the bottom level.

"We have to go after them!!" Zinnia yelled, panicking.

"Here, let's go this way!" Theo yelled as he ran toward the elevator the girls had come up. Once inside, he shot them down.

When they got to the bottom, they saw Colton dragging May into one of the transfer rooms. Theo ran out ahead of the girls and dove into the room right before Colton pressed the button to shut the door, closing all three of them inside.

Zinnia and Lilly ran up to the glass door and started banging on it, yelling and screaming.
The nearby TOP members, who had been planting the explosives, ran over to the door and started trying to get it open. The girls heard Zon on their PEDs and Zinnia yelled into it that Colton took May into the transfer room. May still had her PED in her hand and could hear Zon too.

"I can't find you! Tell me where you are!" he yelled.

May tried to yell out to him, but Colton covered her mouth with his hand, ripped her PED away from her, and threw it down to the ground. Theo ran over to Colton and knocked his gun out of his hand. Colton then punched Theo, bloodying his face and knocking him almost unconscious.

"I have a secret to tell you," Colton said, laughing. "You're getting it easier than your dad did. You get to keep your fingers."

Suddenly, May bit Colton's hand, causing him to let go. She yanked her arm out from his grip, grabbed her dog whistle from her neck, and blew into it with all of her might.

Colton ripped the whistle out of her hand and off of her neck as he shoved her into the transfer pod and closed the door. They weren't like basins at all. They were like upright coffins with glass doors. You could see the terror on her face. Theo slowly dragged himself over to the transfer room door. Right when he got to it, he stood up and yelled to his dad, "I won't let you do this!"

All of a sudden, Zon and his dogs zipped around the corner. Theo smacked the button and the door slid open quickly.

May met the panic in Theo's eyes before shifting her gaze to Zon's and then to Zinnia's. Colton swung his arm up to the button but paused for a fraction of a second so he could see the look in Zinnia's eyes. Then, as if it were in slow motion, he smacked the button, and just like that, she was gone.

Seconds after her lifeless body sucked down into a shoot, Zon's dogs bolted into the transfer room and ripped Colton to shreds, killing him, and leaving pieces of him scattered around the room.

The whole world stopped spinning. Time stood still. All that remained was a tiny breath escaping from Zinnia's chest, before being replaced with sorrow and coming out again with every piece of her heart. What was left was just a shell. The outside layer of what used to be a scared girl. One more breath and what came with it was not sadness, or pain, not sorrow, or confusion. What came with it was anger, hate, and a rage that would not stop until it got its revenge.

Zon was on the ground crying a deep soundless howl, while Lilly stood frozen, tears streaming down her face. She watched Zinnia rise to her feet, with a cold emotionless glaze over her eyes. Zinnia started walking toward the elevator.

"Zinnia, stop! Come back!" Lilly shouted, but it was too late. Zinnia was now in a full sprint and disappeared into an elevator with Lilly yelling out to her.

Cypher set up a hovering video bot and faced it toward Sophia's desk, where Seth sat and prepared for his address to the nation, his delivery of truth, his call to action. Sophia sat in the corner with Liam, both with their mouths covered and their hands cuffed behind their backs.

"There, that should work," Cypher said as he nodded in Seth's direction and pushed a button. The screen on Sophia's wall lit up and Seth could see himself. Florian opened the curtain and saw the screens lit up all over the New Life facilities, and he noticed that things seemed to have quieted down outside.

Seth dove into his speech. "Hello, Citizens of New Life. It pains me greatly to bring such a horrible truth to you today." He paused for a second. "You have been lied to your whole lives. The story that you go on to your next life through transfer pods was completely fabricated."

Zon and the South Team watched on their PEDs from the transfer rooms. Shortelle and Pacer could see Seth displayed on screens in the room where they were still helping kids get out of their restraints. Luke and Molly held Toby and watched on the large screen in the courtyard, where all of the citizens had been gathered up against the walls by the birds, guards and TOP members lying dead all over the ground.

The other members of the North Team had finally shown up and were entering the courtyard. They saw the citizens standing around scared, soaked in blood and crying, and immediately went to their aid.

"I know that what just happened was horrifying, and I know that what I'm telling you is horrifying as well, but you deserve the truth," Seth continued. "Our government, over time, provided the necessities of life, which was great…it was wonderful… When they discovered The Fountain of Youth, not only did people have what they needed to live, but they lived *longer.* They feared resources would be depleted too quickly to replenish, so they fabricated this story with the hope that people would decrease the population by their own hands…and that is exactly what happened.

"But life isn't about how long you live. It's about the life you live while you're here. We have to stop living our lives waiting for the next one. Live here and now in this one. When we choose to leave, we hurt the ones we love. Stay! Stop giving up when things get hard or when life isn't what you thought it was going to be. Just *be*… Break your bones, get sick, bleed, cry, scream, be scared, lose your mind…make mistakes. Fight with each other, lose a job, feel the sting of rejection, lose a loved one…and be thankful that you get to *feel*! Nothing's perfect and it never will be. You can't truly appreciate the good if you never feel the hurt and the pain. So, I call on you today to accept the pain…accept the pain and live!"

As Seth finished his sentence, he saw Zinnia banging on the glass door to the office. He nodded in Cypher's direction and pointed to the door behind him. Cypher turned around and opened it for her, and as soon as it was open, she ran in and scanned the room with tears in her eyes. She spotted Sophia in the corner, and as she started to go for her, Liam jumped to his feet and ran for the door to his office. Florian followed Liam with his gun and fired it, hitting him in the shoulder and knocking him to the ground. Liam screamed out in pain. Cries and gasps echoed throughout New Life as people watched this happening on the screens.

Zinnia's eyes were locked on Sophia as she reached into her pocket, grabbed one of the bombs with the mature Open Eden flowers, and threw it right at her. In less than five seconds the ball popped open, and Sophia fell back, shaking and frothing at the mouth. A few seconds after that, Sophia let out her last breath of air while everyone stood frozen around her.

Zinnia collapsed to the floor, breathing through her tears, as Florian took off his jacket and threw it over the flower bomb.

Lilly ran into the room and scooped Zinnia up, hugging her as she cried. All was silent for them in that moment. They no longer existed in the world, just in that embrace, if only for a minute…but that was all she needed. Zinnia raised to her feet, wiped the tears from her face and walked over to Seth who had his mouth open in shock. He looked into her eyes and then backed away from the camera as she stepped in front of it.

"We are not the bad guys here! They took my dad and my sister from me, just like they have taken your loved ones from you!" She got the words out painfully as she shook.

Florian, Seth, and Cypher looked at Lilly and she nodded, confirming that what Zinnia had just said was true. A tear fell down Seth's cheek as Florian punched the wall and Cypher threw his head back, clasping his hands behind his neck. Tears filled their eyes.

"This has been going on for long enough! This is war! You're either on our side or in our way. WE WILL NOT STOP UNTIL WE HAVE TAKEN EVERY LAST TRANSFER POD DOWN!"

She started crying again and Florian pulled her from the camera and hugged her tight, holding her up as her legs wobbled. Lilly grabbed her in her arms again.

Seth moved back into the view of the camera and finished his speech. "I come to you today and ask that you join us. I ask that every Life-House hear our voice, every citizen hear our cries. And to every other Underground there is, join us. They cannot outnumber us if we all band together. I know you didn't ask for this fight, and before today you didn't even know there was anything wrong. Now that you know, can you sit by and watch your loved ones die? It won't be easy, but if we do this together, we will not fail!"

Zinnia let go of Lilly and pulled out her book. "Here," she said as she opened it to page "A" for "access files" and handed it to Seth. "Don't let them take your word for it. Show them. My dad left me this. I think this code will unlock the files so everyone can see them for themselves."

Seth took the book from her in disbelief. "Cypher, come here," he said, waving him over. "Can you figure out this code?"

"Yes, I know this code. Hold on," he said as he pulled out his PED and typed a few things into it.

Suddenly, everyone's PEDs flashed and every file was displayed on their screens. Every last one of them.

There were shocked looks of disbelief and horror on everyone's faces as they scrolled through the files.

After a few minutes of looking through them, Seth stood up and said, "There's one more thing to do," and he called the South team on his PED. "It's time. Do you and your men have the explosives ready?"

They heard Casey say through his PED, "Yes. We're ready!"

"North Team, clear the courtyard," Seth instructed.

"Wait!" Lilly yelled out. "Your friend, Zinnia! The kids downstairs! They might not've gotten out yet!"

Zinnia looked at Seth. "Downstairs, we found children hooked up to machines, with tubes coming out of them. Their machines failed when we shut down the power. Some of them died. My friends Shortelle and Pacer stayed behind to help the survivors, but we don't know if there are more kids in labs in other places. I think they were experimenting on them," she said as tears started falling down her face again and she grabbed her lightbulb necklace.

"Okay, we'll send some of the North Team down to the basement to find them," Seth said. Florian got on his PED and called the North Team and sent them to help Shortelle and Pacer.

Meanwhile, Zon made his way up to meet the rest of his team in the courtyard, and they started leading the citizens out of the New Life facilities. When they got outside, he saw the birds circling around. Some of the citizens were jumping and flinching as they watched them, stepping carefully as they left the courtyard.

Not too long later, the North Team started bringing kids up from the basement one by one. There were dozens of them still hooked to tubes. Some of the New Life medical staff had run to help. Shortelle and Pacer were covered in chemicals and they were each carrying a child on their backs.

Once everyone was outside, Casey detonated the explosives and everyone fell to the ground as it rumbled and shook, sending debris everywhere. After a few seconds, the citizens stood up and dusted themselves off and looked around, still confused.

Casey got on his PED and said, "It's done."

Seth responded, "Thank you. Good work, everyone." Then he turned to look at Zinnia. He walked over to her and gave her a hug, holding her in a gentle embrace as she cried. She felt strangely the most comfort she'd felt, there in his hug, since her dad was alive. This made her hug him tighter.

"What are we going to do about him?" Florian asked, pointing to Liam.

"That is another question, isn't it?" Seth said as he let go of Zinnia and she grabbed hold of Lilly again.

"His family is in the other room," Cypher reminded them.

"Yes, well," Seth said, walking over to the door to his office and opening it. "Go ahead and go to your family for now. Someone will see to it that you get your shoulder bandaged up. Cypher, change the code on his door's lock too and keep them in there for now, until we have a plan."

Cypher walked into Liam's office and changed the lock code on his door. He stopped to look around to make sure there wasn't anything Liam could use to get out or hurt anyone with, and left, locking the door behind him.

Florian stood over his mother, looking at her body as if it was a foreign object, completely emotionally detached. He glanced up at his dad and shook his head.

"I'm sorry, Florian," Seth said, walking toward him.

Florian put up his hand. "I don't want to hear it right now," he said and walked over to Cypher to help him with his hovering video bot.

Suddenly, there was a loud humming outside. Everyone stopped what they were doing and Seth went to the window to see what it was. He saw hundreds of flybots coming in from every direction. Some had already landed.

Zon called up to them. "There are some people here who want to talk to you, Seth."

"Okay, can you bring them up?" Seth asked.

"There are too many. I'll bring a couple up for now."

Zon instructed the other TOP members to help the people out of their flybots and bring them into the courtyard. They looked completely horrified as they walked in and saw all the bodies lying around. None of them had ever seen anything like it before.

Zon entered the President's office and Seth stood up to shake the first person's hand. "I'm Seth. Hi, welcome."

"Yeah, we know who you are. You told the whole country who you are," the guy said, gruffly. He looked to be about Seth's age, only he was a bit rougher around the edges. His hair was dark brown, with a dark brown mustache and beard, and he was wearing jeans, boots, and a plaid, long sleeved shirt. "I'm Emerick. I'm here from the Montana Underground."

Seth nodded to him, "Welcome."

The next person was a rather small woman with soft blonde hair and pale skin, wearing a nice pink skirt and a white blouse. "I'm Emily. I'm from British Columbia. I'm not a Leader or anything, just a mom who would fight for her kids' lives. I always knew something was wrong. People thought I was crazy," she said with a nervous laugh.

"Welcome," Seth said, shaking her hand.

"I'm Rufus. I'm from the Life-House in California," said a tall muscular man with dark skin, wearing a nice suit. "I had my suspicions as well." He shook Seth's hand vigorously with a big smile and sigh of relief.

Last was a young, small guy with sandy brown hair and a lip ring. "Hey," he said, nodding and shaking Seth's hand. "I'm Lander. I'm from the Oregon Underground. I want you to know, I'm with you all the way. We all think you guys are heroes. You've truly inspired us. Let's do this!" he cheered, and then put his arms down when he noticed the somber looks on everyone's faces. He spotted Lilly and sent her a small wave and a smile. She sent a half smile back to him, still holding onto Zinnia.

Seth took his time meeting every person who'd arrived. Some people took a moment to give their sympathies to Zinnia. After a while, she was too exhausted to take any more condolences. She told Seth she needed to rest and he gave her one last hug. As she walked toward the door she stopped and turned around.

"Hey, Seth."

"Yes, Zinnia," he responded warmly.

"There's another page in that book. The page with the second 'S,' it says, 'save the kids.' I think it's referring to the kids we found in the basement. There must be more kids out there that this is happening to."

"Okay, well, we will figure that out together. For now, go get some rest. I think you've had about all you can handle today. How about you take her to May's apartment, Lilly?"

Lilly nodded and walked Zinnia out, holding her up as she felt the weakness in Zinnia's legs trying to buckle beneath her. She opened the door to May's apartment and led her over to her small bed, but Zinnia stopped in front of it.

"No. Not in here," she said as she turned towards May's room.

"Okay, Z," Lilly said. She helped her into May's bed and pulled the blanket over her. They both laid there quietly and Lilly kept her arm around Zinnia as she cried and held onto May's blanket as tight as she could.

The next morning, Zinnia's mom rushed to the apartment and they hugged and cried together. She was mad at her for not contacting her, but she understood. Zinnia told her all about the Underground and what they learned while they were there. She told her about Zon and how May had finally found love. This warmed her mom's heart. She only ever wanted her to be happy. She chased love so hard. In the end she got what she had been looking for.

Zinnia nuzzled into her mom's tightly curled red hair and breathed in her familiar smell. The smell of home and warm summer nights, riding tractor bots, laughing as she caught frogs with May. The smell of oil on the flybot because they always had to fix it. She remembered all the times her sister breathed with her through a panic attack, all the times she hugged her when she was upset, even if what she was upset about was totally stupid. She smiled as she remembered the time she borrowed her dress without asking and got mud on it when she wore it out in the field. She was so mad; it made her red hair look like it was on fire...literally. She remembered summer vacation with Dad. All four of them gained a few pounds eating the fish they caught. They never forgot how delicious it was compared to the rations they lived on. She thought about all of the things May didn't get to do, too. She knew she wanted to visit other countries. She was particularly fond of Australia. They still had some animals there because there were too many to get out completely. She had been hoping to see a koala bear.

"Maybe I'll go see one for you May," Zinnia said out loud.

"What next, Elise?" Lilly asked.

"You tell me. I'm not really sure what's to come of all this," she responded.

"Well, I imagine when we've had enough rest, we'll head back to Seth and he'll tell us what the next step is. We weren't supposed to be a part of this takeover, Mom. Just so you know," Zinnia said, looking up at her. "We were supposed to stay back in the Underground, but I'm glad we left. I'm glad I got to see you again." Zinnia hugged her tight. "Things aren't ever going to go back to normal."

"I know," Elise said. "But I'm here now… Whatever happens from here, I'll be by your side the whole time."

She gave Zinnia another hug and they all spent the rest of the day looking at May's family picture wallpaper.

If it weren't for the birds, they wouldn't have stood a chance. But where did these birds come from? Why did they help them? They didn't have any answers, but they were more than happy for their help and their continued assistance at that. The birds kept the guards out of New Life while barricades were set up surrounding the facilities. Cypher hacked all the bots and set them to surround the facilities too. No one was getting in unless they wanted them to.

"Let's just hope we prepare a little better going forward. We got by on sheer luck and Zinnia's book...and those birds," Seth said, shaking his head and pacing around the Capitol Office. "I've put some thought into this, and I think we will all agree that we need to continue taking down the pods as originally planned. We need to gather all of the weapons here at New Life. I want your teams trained on how to use them right away," Seth said to Casey.

Casey nodded in agreement. "No problem. Rob gathered his guys up last night and he said he knows where they keep all of the weapons. We're going to start pulling them out tomorrow."

"Yes, great," Seth responded seriously. "Has anyone heard from Zon? He never came back after we blew up the pods."

"Uh, yeah he said he just needed some time. He's not in the facilities though. He left," Casey answered reluctantly.

"What? That's not a good idea," Seth responded in shock.

"Well, you know Zon… He's a Runner. He'll be back," Casey reassured him.

***

Zon had traveled back down the ZGS track in search of his buddy, his fallen comrade. He took the dog up into the Thrill Seeker mountains and gave him a proper burial. After that, he spent a couple of nights lying out under the stars with his dogs, being careful not to be seen, and allowing himself to mourn. His heart hurt more than he ever thought possible. He cried until he couldn't see. He tried to sleep but every noise woke him up and reminded him of his pain. His dogs laid by his side and gave him as much comfort as they could. They didn't understand what was going on. They just knew he needed them.

He knew he should return and be there for his colony, but he couldn't give them his all until he found some solace, some peace. He just couldn't get the image of her life being pulled out of her to leave his mind. He felt angry every time he saw that man's evil face in his thoughts. But it was time. Time for him to return. Time for him to turn his anger into the biggest weapon ever to threaten those who caused it. He was going back and he was bringing his rage, his hurt, and everything he could do to bring them down.

***

Zinnia and Lilly had spent the last few days resting, crying, and reminiscing over their fondest memories of May, but the time had come for them to return to Seth for further instructions. Zinnia's mom tried to convince her to go back home with her but she refused. She passionately expressed her desire to rip the life out of the government like they ripped the life out of May.

It wasn't very long ago when it wasn't a big deal for someone to transfer. Maybe it was because May didn't have a choice…or maybe it was because Zinnia lost her sister and she didn't have a say in it either that angered her so much. Death looked so much different than it did before. She never liked the transfer system and she never knew why. But now that she knew the truth, it was the most horrifying thought that she may never see her again. No one ever had a choice…in any aspect of their lives. But all of that was going to change. She would not let this go, and she was not going to let them win.

When Zinnia and Lilly got back to the Capitol Office, Zon, Florian, and Seth were there planning their next moves. They had the screen lit up with a map of North America and each state's Life-House and their surroundings. One of the people in charge at the California Life-House, Rufus, came to help, which gave them an advantage since they now had top secret information available to them. They wanted to go to California next, but Lander reminded them that Oregon is on the way and should probably be dealt with first. He let them know that the Oregon Underground was ready when they were. This made everyone excited because they could gather the Oregonians to help in California, and then they'd continue on to the next state and the next and gather more people as they went.

"So, it's decided," Seth said, smiling. "Next stop is the Oregon Life-House with help from the Oregon Underground. Then after that we will head to the California Life-House. We'll decide after that where we go next."

"Seth," Zinnia interrupted.

"Yes, Zinnia, how are you doing?" he asked caringly.

"I'm okay. I'm mad...but I'm okay," she answered, tearing up. He gave her a sympathetic smile. "I just wanted to remind you about the book and the kids. I know my dad was trying to tell us something, I'm just not sure about the last page. We figured out the other pages. One was to help us get out of New Life...or *in*, in our case, one was to turn off the dome shield, one to shut down the Glass Project, one to access the files, and the last page says, 'Save the kids.' We saw all those kids downstairs. It was horrible."

Seth walked over to Zinnia and put his hands on her shoulders. "It's okay, Zinnia. If you aren't ready to deal with this, we will understand. If you want, we can take the book and work on figuring it out so you can rest."

Zinnia clutched the book tight against her chest. "No. It's okay. He left it for me. I can figure it out. He knew I could. That's why he left it for me."

Seth stepped back and gave her another warm smile. "Okay, that's fine too. Let's figure this out then."

She set it down and opened it up to the last "S" page. Everyone gathered around the desk and looked down at the book. The last "S" page didn't have any diagrams or charts but it had a picture. The picture had soft tones of yellow and orange. At the top, there were cacti and a curved structure that almost looked like a stocking cap. Below that were seven rounded cubby holes opening up at the center in a circle, filled with a bunch of heads and footprints. Below the picture were the words, "The 7 Caves of Chicomoztoc, say to be from Historia Tolteca-Chichimeca."

The 7 Caves of Chicomoztoc, say to be from Historia
Tolteca-Chichimeca.

Everyone looked down at the picture for a few moments, scanning it for any clues. After a few moments Zinnia murmured, "The word 'caves' is italicized."

Zon suddenly remembered what he found when he was making his way to New Life and he spoke up. "When I was trying to get here, I fell into a valley in the Thrill Seeker mountains and I found a cave."

Everyone stood up from where they were leaning over the book and were now looking at Zon seriously.

"When I went inside, I found beds, tables, and chairs. It looked like people had been living down there."

"That's it!" Zinnia yelled, "I just know it. He wants us to go to the cave!"

"He couldn't have known that Zon would find that, though," Florian added.

"No, you're probably right," Zinnia said, disappointed, and started scanning the book more.

Zon pointed to the cacti on the top of the caves in the picture. "There was a cactus at the top of the ladder. You see these rocks on the side here?" Zon asked, pointing to the top left side of the picture with rocks going up the side. "There are only rocks in the mountains at New Life. You would have figured that out eventually, even if I hadn't discovered the cave."

Zinnia felt a little more hopeful when Zon pointed that out. "Okay, so we need to go there," she decided.

"I'll take you back there. I think I remember where the ladder is," Zon offered.

"I'll need to stay here but Florian, why don't you go with them?" Seth suggested.

"I'll go too," Cypher added.

"Come back and let me know what you find," Seth said as he patted Florian on the shoulder.

"Hey!" said Lander, who had been helping Cypher with his camera equipment. He jogged over to them. "Can I come? The adults can handle it up here. I want to see the cave too."

"Sure," Lilly said, waving at him to follow.

"Sweet. Thanks," he said, smiling at her and nearly tripping on the way over. She giggled as she grabbed his arm and pulled him in the direction of the door.

They made their way down to the facility courtyard where there were beds filled with injured people being tended to by medical bots and doctors. There was a whole section taking care of the kids they found downstairs. Shortelle and Pacer were helping them when they looked up and spotted Zinnia walking toward the door.

"Hey, Pacer come on. There's Zinnia," Shortelle said, grabbing Pacer's arm and pulling him so they could catch up to her.

"Hey Zinnia," Shortelle said when she got to her. "How are you? I mean…stupid question. I heard about your sister. I'm sorry," she said, giving her sympathies.

"Thanks," Zinnia said. "I'm glad you were able to help those kids."

"Not all of them unfortunately," she admitted sadly. "Pacer and I were thinking, if you guys need help with anything, we'd really like to help. I mean, this was nuts, but it is what it is and we liked saving those kids. It felt good actually doing something that wasn't on a screen in a VR headset."

"Well, we're on our way to a cave Zon found. You guys can come with us if you want," Zinnia offered.

A smile spread across Shortelle's face and she nodded quickly. "Yes. Yes, absolutely."
Pacer couldn't believe what he was hearing. "Really?" he whined. "Hunny, no. I can't keep doing this with you. You are going to get us killed, girl," he said, shaking his head, throwing his hands up, and turning around. He only took a few steps away before he stopped and turned back to look at her. "Ugh, okay fine, but you're telling Theo why I'm not there to make him the chocolate mousse I promised him later."

"Oh, Theo!" Shortelle blurted out suddenly and got her PED out. Everyone standing around started getting impatient. "It's okay this will only take a second," she said, reassuring them.

Theo answered his PED and his face appeared on the screen. It was still badly bruised and it looked like his dad had broken his nose. Shortelle turned her PED so he could see Zinnia. He waved at her. "Hey Zinnia. I'm sorry about your sister. She was a wonderful person."

"Yeah, yeah. Theo listen," Shortelle cut him off rudely. "We're apparently going to find a cave. Get your butt down here and come with us."

He paused and thought for a second looking up from the screen. He looked back down and said, "Okay. Why not? I'll be right down."

Shortelle hung up the PED, clearly excited. Pacer rolled his eyes at her and shook his head as he looked off at the busy medical bots. Theo showed up after a couple of minutes.

"Okay can we go now? You good?" Florian asked, annoyed. Zinnia, Lilly, Zon, Florian, Cypher, Lander, Theo, Shortelle, and Pacer all headed for the north exit. They all had some form of a weapon. Zon had his dogs, of course. Theo, Florian, and Cypher had guns. Zinnia still had flower bombs, and everyone else was carrying wave guns. It was safe to say that they would be able to handle whatever came their way together.

Zon led them down the ZGS track to the place he had lost his dog. They all had to climb over the spheres that were still laying everywhere. Zon had to think for a few minutes. The place he had spent the last few days was not the same place he fell. Eventually he found the trail he took to get down to the ZGS station and followed it up to the top where he found the valley he had fallen down. He walked along the edge and looked around for the hidden ladder with the cactus. When he found it, they all took it down into the cave containing the beds, tables, and chairs. They looked around for a few minutes and examined the large area. They gathered in the middle of the room when they didn't find any clues or hints.

Zinnia examined the page in her book one more time. She studied the picture. She saw the caves, the cacti, the rocks, the heads and the footprints, the weird stocking cap looking thing. She tried to put them together, what they were, what they symbolized, the colors and shapes. She spelled out the words, remembering that her dad's first clues included the spelling of the word "glass." She couldn't find anything in the picture. She moved her eyes down to the words below the picture. The word "caves" was italicized and led them there. She read it quietly out loud. "The 7 caves of Chicomoztoc, say to be from Historia Tolteca-Chichimeca." She read it quietly to herself a few times. She kept getting hung up. It sounded weird. Something was off.

"Say to be from? Say? This shouldn't be 'say.' It should be 'said'! My dad would never make that error... TO BE FROM HISTORIA TOLTECA-CHICHIMECA!" she yelled suddenly. "We're supposed to say 'TO BE FROM HISTORIA TOLTECA-CHICHIMECA'!" She yelled it one more time, and suddenly kids of all ages started to come out of their hiding spots. They came out of holes in the ground under the beds and tables, as well as holes in the corners of the room. Some came from the long tunnel Zon had taken to get there before.

They all looked around the room at the kids in disbelief. There were about 15 to 20 of them. They looked dirty, but it looked like they had done that on purpose, because they matched the dirty walls and floors perfectly. One of the older kids approached Zinnia and pointed to the book. She looked at the kid whose eyes were fixed on her intently.

"You're Zinnia?" he asked. This took her breath away.

"Yes," she answered as she teared up.

"Your dad saved us. He said you would come one day. To be ready. He said you would save all of us."

A few tears fell down her cheeks. The older kid grabbed Zinnia's hand and put a chip in it. "He left this for you."

Cypher said to Zinnia, "Here. I got it." He pulled a strange cord out of his pocket, plugged it into her PED, and attached the chip to the end of the cord. After a minute, the screen lit up and her dad appeared. More tears fell as she saw his face and Lilly grabbed hold of her from the side, offering her support.

"Hey, Z. I'm so sorry I had to leave you like that. I didn't want to go, but if I hadn't turned myself in, they were going to take all of you, and I couldn't let that happen. As I'm sure you've probably figured out by now, New Life has been experimenting on the kids they take from the Little Angels program. They are trying to find an anti-Fountain of Youth. They want to change our DNA back to the way it was before, hundreds of years ago.

"They weren't just experimenting on kids. They were experimenting on animals too, specifically birds. They synthesized a highly toxic and poisonous plant that super charged them somehow. This plant serves two purposes though. When the plant is in its dormant state, it has properties that heighten memory sensors. The trick, though, is that the memories may not always be true. The power of suggestion. When New Life has you read your reincarnation letters, they have you drink a serum made from that plant. Anything you may have read would be in your mind already, which makes you believe that you are remembering your past lives. They were trying to make the birds into weapons, but they grew too intelligent for them. They tried to kill them when they realized they couldn't control them, but the birds escaped.

"North America isn't the only nation experimenting, either. The other 7 Nations are doing their own experimenting on animals and children. I realized that I could only save a few children here. I needed to do something about this but I ran out of time. So, I leave this to you, Zinnia. We may not be able to stop New Life with our own hands, but we can take down their Army.

"The guards are being controlled by chips planted in their heads. The main control center that powers them is in Australia. You will need seven keys, one from each nation, in order to shut it down. They needed a failsafe in case the guards were to turn on them like the birds did. I was able to get the first key for you. I convinced President Liam to give it to me. I promised him I'd fix this, all of it, somehow... He was waiting for this day to come, too, so go easy on him," he said, laughing lightly. This made Zinnia laugh too, as she wiped the tears from her cheeks.

"This is the code to reactivate the glass system," he said as the kid handed her the key and a card with a code written on it. "You'll need it to power on the ZGSs. I've charted your course for you. Go from here to South America. The second key is in Brazil. From there go through the underwater tunnel to Sierra Leone and travel down to South Africa for the third key. Head up to the United Kingdom for the fourth, Moscow for the fifth, then Beijing for the sixth. Your last destination will be in Sydney, Australia, where you will find the control center. Take all seven keys and shut it down." He paused and took a deep breath in. "This is where I say goodbye. I love you, Zinnia and May."

Zinnia's heart broke at the mention of her name.

He finished with his last and final instruction. "Make your dad proud. Save the kids...and the world."

Zinnia fell to the ground as her father disappeared from the screen. She cried for a few moments and then wiped her tears one last time. She rose to her feet, looked at Lilly, Florian, and the others and said, "Well, I'm going. Who's with me?"

"I'm with you all the way, Z," Lilly said, putting her hand on her shoulder.

Everyone else took their time agreeing with Lilly and devoting themselves to the quest.

After a few minutes, when the room got quiet again, Lilly said, "Uh, hey there Z, I think you just gained another spur."

Zinnia looked at her, confused. Then Lilly smiled and added, "You're a Leader now."

About the Author

Nicky Flinkfelt is a phlebotomist by day and a single mom, writer, and owner of an obnoxious terrier by night. She is the author of her debut novel Zinnia and The Original People and is currently working on the sequel to this seven-book series. Nicky's life-long desire to get lost in other worlds pulled her into a realm of imagination and brought her back out as a creative story-teller full of color and excitement. She grew up in Tacoma, Washington and was the second to the youngest child out of six kids. She's been to several countries but hasn't nearly gone to enough. Her biggest dream is to become a full-time writer while traveling to every corner of the world.

Read more at www.nickyflinkfelt.com.

CPSIA information can be obtained
at www.ICGtesting.com
Printed in the USA
LVHW050255040422
715223LV00001B/52